# TO LOVE A HIGHLAND DRAGON

## HIGHLAND FANTASY ROMANCE

### ANN GIMPEL

CONTENTS

# TO LOVE A HIGHLAND DRAGON

## DRAGON LORE, BOOK TWO

**Highland Fantasy Romance**
**By**
**Ann Gimpel**

**Tumble off reality's edge into myth, magic, and Celtic dragon shifters.**

# COPYRIGHT PAGE

# AUTHOR'S NOTE

There is a prequel to this series. *Highland Secrets* is the first Dragon Lore book.

For special offers, fun contests, and pre-release reads, sign up for Ann's newsletter at www.anngimpel.com! You'll get a free book just for signing up.

**Books in the Dragon Lore Series:**

*Highland Secrets,* Prequel and Book One
*To Love a Highland Dragon,* Book Two
*Dragon Maid,* Book Three
*Dragon's Dare,* Book Four

A dragon shifter stirs and wakens deep in the Scottish Highlands. His cave is the same and his hoard intact, yet something's badly amiss. Lachlan ventures above ground—and wishes he hadn't. His castle is gone, replaced by ungainly row houses. Men aren't wearing plaids, and women scarcely wear anything at all, particularly the woman who accosts him with unseemly banter. What manner of wench is she to dress so provocatively?

In Inverness for a year on a psychiatry fellowship, Dr. Maggie Hibbins watches an oddly dressed man pick his way out of a thicket. He looks so lost—and so unbelievably, knock-out gorgeous—she takes a chance and stands him a meal. Lachlan's shock when he picks up a local newspaper is so palpable, Maggie jumps in with both feet.

The hard-to-accept truth bashes gaping holes in her equilibrium. He looks odd, sounds odd, acts odd because he's a refugee from another era. Born of powerful witches, Maggie runs headlong into the myth and magic that are her birthright.

and endearing. I'm usually one who can see what's coming next, however Ann has really surprised me with her twists and turns. This book was pure heaven to read, had me hooked from the start.

To Love a Highland Dragon was a mix of two of my favorite fictions elements—hunky Highlanders and shapeshifters, specifically dragon shifters. I absolutely adored Lachlan, Maggie, and the dragon, Kheladin.

I'm not big on time travel books, but this one I loved. It was awesome to read about the different levels of love between the characters.

I've never read a dragon shifter book before, and didn't know if I would like it, but this is one of those stories that carries you on a wave so wonderful you just don't want to get off.

# CHAPTER 1

Kheladin listened to the rush of blood as his multi-chambered heart pumped. After eons of nothingness, the unexpected sound surprised him. A cool, sandy floor pressed against his scaled haunches. One whirling eye flickered open, followed by the other.

*Where am I?*

He peered at his surroundings and blew out a sigh, followed by steam, smoke, and fire.

*Thanks be to Dewi*—Kheladin invoked the blood-red Celtic dragon goddess—*I'm still in my cave. It smelled right, but I wasna certain.*

He rotated his serpent's head atop his long, sinuous neck. Vertebrae cracked. Kheladin lowered his head and scanned the place he and Lachlan, his human bondmate, had barricaded themselves into. It might've only been days ago, but somehow, it didn't seem like days, or even months or a few years. His body felt rusty, as if he hadn't used it in centuries.

*How long did I sleep?*

He shook his head. Copper scales flew everywhere, clanking against a pile littered around him. More than anything, the glittery heap reinforced his belief he'd been asleep for a very long time. Dragons shed their scales annually. From the amount circling his body, he'd gone through hundreds of molt cycles. But how? The last thing he remembered was retreating to his cave far beneath Lachlan's castle and working with the mage to construct strong wards.

Had the black wyvern grown powerful enough to force his magic into the very heart of Kheladin's fortress?

*If that's true—if we really were his prisoner, why'd I finally waken? Is Lachlan still within me?*

*Stop! I have to take things one at a time.*

He returned his gaze to the nooks and crannies of his spacious cave. He'd have to take inventory, but it appeared his treasure hadn't been disturbed. Kheladin blew a plume of steam upward, followed by an experimental gout of fire. The black wyvern, his sworn enemy since before the Crusades, may have bested him, but he hadn't gotten his slimy talons on any of Kheladin's gold or jewels.

He shook out his back feet and shuffled to the pool at one end of the cave where he dipped his snout and drank deeply. The water didn't taste right. It wasn't poisoned, but it held an undercurrent of metals that had never been there before. Kheladin rolled the liquid around in his mouth. He didn't recognize much of what he tasted, but he was thirsty and it seemed safe enough, so he drank some more.

*The flavors aren't familiar because I've been asleep for so long. Aye, that must be it.* Part of his mind recoiled; he suspected he was deluding himself.

"We're awake." Lachlan's voice hummed in the dragon's mind.

"Aye, that we are."

"How long did we sleep?"

"I doona know." Water streamed down the dragon's snout and neck. He knew what would come next, and he didn't have to wait long.

*"Let's shift. We think better in my body."* Lachlan urged Kheladin to cede ascendency.

*"I doona agree."* Kheladin pushed back. *"I was figuring things out afore ye woke."*

*"Aye, I'm certain ye were, but..."* But what? *"Och aye, my brain is thick and fuzzy, as if I havena used it for a verra long time."*

*"Mine feels the same."*

The bond allowed only one form at a time. Since they were in Kheladin's body, he had the upper hand. Lachlan wasn't strong enough to force a shift without his help. There'd been a time when he could have but not now.

Was it safe to venture above ground?

Kheladin recalled the last day he'd seen the sun. After a vicious battle in the great room of Lachlan's castle, they'd retreated to his cave and taken their dragon form as a final resort. Rhukon, the black wyvern, pretended he wanted peace. He'd come with an envoy that turned out to be a retinue of heavily armed men.

Both he and Lachlan expected Rhukon to follow them underground. Kheladin's last thought, before nothingness descended, was disbelief because their enemy hadn't pursued them.

*Humph. He* did *come after us but with magic. Magic strong enough to penetrate our wards.*

*"Aye, and I was thinking the same thing,"* Lachlan sniped in a vexed tone.

*"We trusted him,"* Kheladin snarled. *"More the fools we were. We should've known."* Despite drinking, his throat was still raw. He sucked more water down and fought rising anger at himself for being gullible. Even if Lachlan hadn't known better, he should've. His stomach cramped from hunger.

Kheladin debated the wisdom of making his way through the warren of tunnels leading to the surface in dragon form. There were always far more humans than dragons. Mayhap it would be wiser to accede to Lachlan's wishes before they crept from their underground lair to rejoin the world of men.

*"Grand idea."* Lachlan's response was instantaneous, as was his first stab at shifting.

It took half a dozen attempts. Kheladin was far weaker than he imagined and Lachlan so feeble he was almost an impediment. Finally, once a shower of scales cleared, Lachlan's emaciated body stood barefoot and naked in the cave.

LACKING the sharp night vision he enjoyed as a dragon, because his magic was so diminished, Lachlan kindled a mage light and glanced down at himself. Ribs pressed against his flesh, and a full beard extended halfway down his chest. Turning his head to both sides, he saw shoulder blades so sharp he was surprised they didn't puncture his skin. Tawny hair fell in tangles past his waist. The only thing he couldn't see was his eyes. Absent a glass, he was certain they were the same crystal-clear emerald color they'd always been.

He stumbled across the cave to a chest where he kept clothing. Dragons didn't need such silly accoutrements; humans did. He sucked in a harsh breath. The wooden chest was falling to ruin. He tilted the lid against a wall, but it canted to one side. Many of his clothes had moldered into unusable rags, but items toward the bottom fared better. He found a cream-colored linen shirt with long, flowing sleeves, a black and green plaid embroidered with the insignia of his house—a dragon in flight—and soft, deerskin boots that laced to his knees.

He slid the shirt over his head and wrapped the plaid around himself, taking care to wind the tartan so its telltale insignia was hidden in its folds. Who knew if the black wyvern—or his agents—lurked near the mouth of the cave? Lachlan bent to lace his boots. A crimson cloak with only a few moth holes completed his outfit. He finger-combed his hair and smoothed his unruly beard.

"Good God, but I must look a fright," he muttered. "Mayhap I can sneak into the castle and set things aright afore anyone sees me.

Surely my kinsmen will be glad the master of the house has finally returned."

Lachlan worked on bolstering a confidence he was far from feeling. He'd nearly made it to the end of the cave, where a rock-strewn path led upward, when he doubled back to get a sword and scabbard—just in case things weren't as sanguine as he hoped. He located a thigh sheath and a short dagger as well, fumbling to attach them beneath his kilt. Underway once again, he hadn't made it very far along the upward-sloping tunnel that ended at a well-hidden opening not far from the postern gate of his castle, when he ran into rocks littering the way.

He worked his way around progressively larger boulders until he came to a huge one that totally blocked the passageway. Lachlan stared at it in disbelief. When had that happened? In all the time he'd been using these paths, they'd never been blocked by rock fall. If he weren't so weak, summoning magic to shove the rock over enough to allow him to pass wouldn't be a problem. As it was, simply walking uphill proved a challenge.

He pinched the bridge of his nose between a grimy thumb and forefinger. His mage light weakened.

*If I can't even keep a light going, how in the goddess's name will I be able to move that rock?*

Lachlan hunkered next to the boulder and let his light die while he ran possibilities through his head. His stomach growled and clenched in hunger. Had he come through however much time had passed to cower like a dog in his own cave?

"No, by God." He slammed a fist against the boulder, and it went right on through. The air sizzled. Magic. The rock was illusion. Not real.

*Counter spell. I need a counter spell.*

*Mayhap not.*

He stood and took a deep breath before walking into the huge rock. The air did more than sizzle. It flamed. If he'd been human, it would've burned him to ashes, but dragons were impervious to fire, as were dragon shifters. Lachlan waltzed through the rock, cursing Rhukon as he went. Five more boulders blocked his tunnel, each more charged with magic than the last.

Finally, sweating and cursing, he rounded the last curve, and the air ahead grew brighter. He wanted to throw himself on the ground and screech his triumph.

*Not a good idea.*

*"Let me out. Ye have no idea what we'll find."*

Kheladin's voice in his mind was welcome but the idea wasn't. *"Ye're right. Because we have no idea what's out there, we stay in my skin until we're certain. We can hide in this form far more easily than we can in yours."*

*"Since when did we take to* hiding?" The dragon sounded outraged.

*"Our magic is weak."* Lachlan adopted a placating tone. *"'Tis prudent to be cautious until it fully recovers."*

*"No dragon would ever say such a thing."* Deep, fiery frustration rolled off Kheladin.

Steam belched from Lachlan's mouth. *"Stop that,"* he hissed, but his mind voice was all but obliterated by wry dragon laughter.

*"Why? I find it amusing ye think an eight foot tall dragon with elegant copper scales and handsome, green eyes would be difficult to sequester."* Kheladin paused a beat. *"And infuriating we need to conceal ourselves at all. Need I remind you we're warriors?"*

*"Of course we're warriors,"* Lachlan said affably, sidestepping the issue of hiding. He didn't want to risk being goaded into something unwise. Kheladin chuckled and pushed more steam through Lachlan's mouth, punctuated by a few flames.

Lost in a sudden rush of memories, Lachlan slowed his pace. As a mage, he would've lived hundreds of years, but bonded to a dragon, he'd live forever. In preparation, he'd studied long years with Aether, a wizard and dragon shifter himself. Along the way, Lachlan forsook much—a wife and bairns, for starters, for what woman would put up with a husband so rarely at home?—to bond with a dragon, forming their partnership. Once Lachlan's magic was finally strong enough, there'd been the niggling problem of locating that special dragon willing to join its life with his.

Because the bond conferred immortality on both the dragon and their human partner, dragons were notoriously picky. After all, dragon and mage would be welded through eternity. The magic could be undone, but the price was high. Mages were stripped of power, and their dragon mates lost much of theirs too, as the bond unraveled. Rumor suggested that mages who became dragon-less risked madness—an additional stumbling block and strong incentive to choose wisely.

Lachlan hunted for over a hundred years before finding Kheladin. The pairing was instantaneous on both sides. He'd just settled in with his dragon, and was about to chase down a wife to grace his castle, when the black wyvern attacked.

Rhukon had approached Kheladin long before Lachlan did, but the dragon rejected the bond, spawning long-standing animosity. That Rhukon finally acquired a dragon of his own hadn't lessened his ill will one whit.

*"What are ye waiting for?"* Kheladin sounded testy. *"Daydreaming is a worthless pursuit. My grandmother is two thousand years old, and she moves faster than you."*

Lachlan snorted. He didn't bother to explain there wasn't much point in jumping right into Rhukon's arms through the opening in the gorse and thistle bushes growing at the mouth of the cave. An unusual whirring filled the air, like the noisiest beehive he'd ever heard. His heart sped up, but the sound receded.

"What in the nine hells was that?" he muttered and made his way closer to the world outside Kheladin's cave.

Lachlan shoved some overgrown bushes out of the way and peered through. What he saw was so unbelievable, he squeezed his eyes shut tight before opening them and looking again. Unfortunately, nothing had changed. Worse, an ungainly, shiny cylinder roared past, making the same whirring noise he'd puzzled over moments before. He fell backward into the cave, breath harsh in his throat, and landed on his rump.

Lachlan shook his head and balled his hands into fists. Frustration and disbelief battered him, making him wonder if he'd died only to waken in Hell. Not only was the postern gate no longer there, neither was his castle. A long, unattractive row of attached structures stood in its stead.

"Holy godhead. What do we do now?"

*"Go out there and hunt down something to eat,"* the dragon growled.

Lachlan gritted his teeth until his jaw ached. Kheladin had a good point. It was hard to think on an empty stomach.

*"Here I was worried about Rhukon. At least I understood him. I fear whatever lies in wait for us will require all our skill."*

*"Ye were never a coward. 'Tis why I allowed the bond. Get moving."*

The dragon's words settled him. Ashamed of his indecisiveness, Lachlan got to his feet. He brushed dirt off his plaid and worked his way through bushes hiding the cave's entrance. As he untangled stickers from the finely spun wool of his cloak and his plaid, he gawked at a very different world from the one he'd left. There wasn't a field—or an animal—in sight. Roadways paved with something other than dirt and stones were punctuated by structures so numerous, they made him dizzy. The hideous incursion onto his lands stretched in every direction.

Lachlan curled his hands into fists again. He'd find out what had happened, by God. When he did, he'd make whoever erected all those abominations take them down.

An occasional person walked by in the distance. They shocked him even more than the buildings and roads. For starters, the males weren't wearing plaids, so there was no way to tell their clan. Females were immodestly covered. Many sported bare legs and breeks so tight he saw the separation between their ass cheeks. Lachlan's groin stirred, his cock hardening. Were the lassies no longer engaging in modesty or subterfuge and simply asking to be fucked? Or was this some new garb that befit a new era?

He detached the last thorn, finally clear of the thicket of sticker bushes. Where could he find a market with vendors? Did market day still exist in this strange environment?

"Holy crap! A kilt, and an old-fashioned one at that. Tad bit early in the day for a costume ball, isn't it?" A rich female voice laced with amusement sounded behind him.

Lachlan spun with his hands raised to call magic. He stopped dead once his gaze settled on a lass nearly as tall as himself, which meant she was close to six feet. She turned so she faced him squarely. Bare legs emerged from torn fabric that stopped just south of her female parts. Full breasts strained against scraps of material attached to strings tied around her neck and back. Her feet were encased in a few straps of leather. Long, blonde hair eddied around her, the color of sheaves of summer wheat.

His cock jumped to attention. He itched to make a grab for her breasts or her ass. She had an amazing ass: round and high and tight. What was expected of him? The lass was dressed in such a way as to invite him to simply tear what passed for breeks aside and enter her. Had the world changed so drastically that women provoked men into public sex? He glanced about, half expecting to see couples having it off with one another willy-nilly.

"Well," she urged. "Cat got your tongue?" She placed her hands on her hips. The motion stretched the tiny bits of flowered fabric that barely covered her nipples still further.

Lachlan bowed formally. He straightened and waited for her to hold out a hand for him to kiss. "I'm Lachlan Moncrieffe, Laird of Clan Moncrieffe, my lady. 'Tis a pleasure to—"

She erupted into laughter—and didn't hold out her hand. "I'm Maggie," she managed between gouts of mirth. "What are you? A throwback to medieval times? You can drop the Sir Galahad routine."

Lachlan felt his face heat. "I fear I doona understand the cause of your merriment…my lady."

Maggie rolled midnight blue eyes. "Oh, brother. Did you escape from a mental hospital? Nah, you'd be in pajamas then, not those fancy duds." She dropped her hands to her sides and started to walk past him.

"No. Wait. Please, wait." Lachlan cringed at the whining tone in his voice. The dragon was correct that the Moncrieffe was a proud house. They bowed to no one.

She eyed him askance. "What?"

"I'm a stranger in this town." He winced at the lie. Once upon a time, he'd been master of these lands. Apparently that time had long since passed. "I'm footsore and hungry. Where might I find victuals and ale?"

Her eyes widened. Finely arched blonde brows drew together over a straight nose dotted by a few freckles. "Victuals and ale," she repeated disbelievingly.

"Aye. Food and drink, in the common vernacular."

"Oh, I understood you well enough," Maggie murmured. "Your words, anyway. Your accent's a bit off."

His stomach growled again, embarrassingly loud.

"Guess you weren't kidding about being hungry." She eyed him appraisingly. "Do you have any money?"

Money. Too late he thought of the piles of gold coins and priceless gems lying on the floor of Kheladin's cave. In the world he'd left, his word was as good as his gold. He opened his mouth, but she waved him to silence. "I'll stand you for a pint and some fish and chips. You can treat me next time."

He heard her mutter, "Yeah right," under her breath as she curled a hand around his arm and tugged. "Come on. I have a couple hours, and then I've got to go to work. I'm due in at three today."

Lachlan trotted along next to her. She let go of him like he was a viper when he tried to close a hand over the one she'd laid so casually on his person. He cleared his throat and wondered what he could safely ask that wouldn't give his secrets away. He could scarcely believe this alien landscape was Scotland, but if he asked what country they were in, or what year it was, she'd think him mad.

Had the black wyvern used some diabolical dark magic to transport Kheladin's cave to another locale? Probably not. Even Rhukon wasn't that powerful.

"In here." She pointed to a door beneath a flashing sigil.

He gawked at it. One minute it was red, the next blue, the next green, illuminating the word *Open*. What manner of magic was this?

"Don't tell me you have temporal lobe epilepsy." She stared at him. "It's only a neon sign. It doesn't bite. Move through the door. There's food on the other side," she added slyly.

Feeling like a rube, Lachlan searched for a latch. When he didn't find one, he pushed his shoulder against the door. It opened, and he held it with a hand so Maggie could enter first. "After you, my lady," he murmured.

"Stop that." She directed the words toward his ear as she went past. "No more *my ladies*. Got it?"

"Aye. Got it." He followed her into a low ceilinged room lined with wooden planks. It was the first thing that looked familiar. Parts of it, anyway. Men—kilt-less men—sat at the bar, hefting glasses and chatting. The tables were empty.

"What'll it be, Mags?" a man with a towel tied around his waist called from behind the bar.

"Couple of pints and two of today's special. Come to think of it…" She eyed Lachlan so intently it made him squirm. "Make that three of the special."

"May I inquire what the special is?" Lachlan asked, thinking he might want to order something different.

Maggie waved a hand at a black board suspended over the bar. "It's right there. If you can't read it—"

"Of course, I can read." He resented the inference he might be uneducated but swallowed back harsh words.

"Excellent. Then move."

She shoved her body into his in a distressingly familiar way for such a communal location. Not that he wouldn't have enjoyed the contact if they were alone, and he were free to take advantage of it.

"All the way to the back," she hissed into his ear. "That way if you slip up, no one will hear."

He bristled. Lachlan Moncrieffe did *not* sit in the back of any establishment. He was always given a choice table near the center of things. He opened his mouth to protest but thought better of it.

She scooped an armful of flattened scrolls off the bar before following him to the back of the room. Once there, she dumped them on the table between them. He wanted to ask what they were but decided he should pretend to know. He turned the top sheaf of papers toward him and scanned the close-spaced print. Many of the words were unfamiliar, but what leapt off the page was *The Inverness Courier* and presumably the current date: June 10, 2012.

His heart thudded in his ears, deafening him with the roar of rushing blood, as he stared at the date.

It had been 1683 when Rhukon chivied him into the dragon's cave. Three hundred twenty-nine years ago, give or take a month or two. At least he was still in Inverness—for all the good it did him.

"You look as if you just saw a ghost." Maggie spoke quietly.

"Nay. I'm quite fine. Thank you for inquiring…my, er…" Lachlan shut up. Anything he said was bound to be wrong.

"Good." She nodded approvingly. "You're learning." The bartender slapped two mugs of ale on the scarred wooden table.

"On your tab, Mags?" he asked.

She nodded. "Except you owe me so much, you'll never catch up."

Still shell-shocked by the realization hundreds of years had slipped past while he and Kheladin slept, Lachlan took a sip of what turned out to be weak ale. It wasn't half bad but could've stood an infusion of bitters. Because it was easier than thinking about his problems, he puzzled over what Maggie meant about the barkeep *owing her so much he'd never catch up.* Why would the barkeep owe her? His nostrils flared. She must work for the establishment—

probably as a damsel of ill repute from the looks of her. Mayhap, she hadn't been paid her share of whatever she earned in quite some time.

Protectiveness flared deep inside him. Maggie shouldn't have to earn her way lying on her back. He'd see to it she had a more seemly position.

*Aye, once I find my way around this bizarre new world.*

Money wouldn't be a problem, but changing three-hundred-year-old gold coins into today's tender might prove challenging. Surely banks existed that could accomplish something like that.

*One thing at a time.*

"So." She skewered him with her blue gaze—Norse eyes if he'd ever seen a set—and took a sip from her mug. "What did you see in the newspaper that upset you so much?"

"Nothing." He tried for an offhand tone.

"Bullshit," she said succinctly. "I'm a doctor. A psychiatrist. I read people's faces quite well, and you look as if you're perilously close to going into shock."

# CHAPTER 2

Margaret Melissa Hibbins looked appraisingly at the man seated across the table from her. She'd hesitated before speaking to him, but he exuded such a raw sexuality, it was impossible not to say something. Once they began talking, she struggled against an inane desire to drag him behind an empty building. She wanted to wrap her legs around his waist and find out what was under that kilt of his.

Maggie put the brakes on her imagination. So what if he looked like a homeless vagabond, and she hadn't been laid in a couple years? Lachlan was a stranger, but a damned attractive one in spite of his unkempt appearance. More important, though, he needed… something. Maybe she could help.

*Back down Dr. Hibbins, champion of the underdog. Yup, give me your tired, your poor… What a load of shit. He's the best-looking man I've ever seen. Makes the altruism argument fly right out the window.*

Before she could catch herself, half a snort escaped.

Lachlan's head snapped up from where he'd been studying the daily rag, his lips moving as if reading were difficult for him.

She shook her head. "Sorry, didn't mean a thing by it. My imagination gets away from me."

He drained half the mug of ale and returned to reading the paper. She took advantage of his apparent inattention and looked at him carefully, starting with his unkempt tawny hair, rather like a lion's mane. Though his eyes were downcast, she'd seen them earlier. An unusual shade of pure, deep green, they had golden flecks circling their irises. High, sculpted cheekbones led to a strong, square jaw. What she could see of it, anyway, beneath his beard. His nose was straight, his skin a coppery gold. He hadn't smiled, but the teeth she'd seen were very straight and very white.

*Maybe he's not as destitute as I thought. He's been able to afford dental care.*

Her gaze strayed lower, to broad shoulders encased in a shirt and old-style kilt, where part of the material wrapped about his upper torso. A cape hung from his shoulders. The sword suspended from his slender waist looked chillingly real. Buff-colored, leather boots laced up the sides and disappeared beneath his kilt. She wanted to reach out and touch the fabric. It looked like an unbelievably fine wool, soft and thick, woven into a green and black plaid.

The bartender sashayed over with a tray and dropped it onto their table. "Here ya go, Mags."

She inhaled the sharp odors of vinegar-soaked fried cod topped with crisp potatoes and smiled. "Thanks."

Lachlan pushed the papers to one side and reached for one of the plates. Without bothering to pick up a fork or knife, he drew a short dagger from somewhere beneath his kilt, stabbed a piece of fish, and stuffed it into his mouth whole. He chewed and swallowed. "Are ye not planning to eat?" he asked. "I should've waited for you afore beginning. I'm most humbly sorry."

"It's all right. You go on ahead."

For the next few minutes, he shoveled fish and chips into his mouth like a starving man, only slowing after the first two plates were empty. He polished the rest of his ale. "Barkeep," he cried in a clear, ringing voice. "Another."

*It's almost as if he's used to people obeying him,* she mused. If there was one thing she was good at, it was dredging information out of the unwilling. It went with the territory. "Go ahead." She gestured toward the last plate of food. "I'm not especially hungry. There's always food at the hospital.

"You said you're a stranger. Where are you from?" She kept her tone conversational and non-threatening.

Lachlan had begun to empty the third plate the moment she indicated it was up for grabs. "Um, one of the neighboring villages, a long day's ride from here."

*Neighboring villages? Long day's ride?*

Maggie focused intently on him, trying to figure out what was wrong. He was lying, but she couldn't understand why. "I've been here for six months and haven't seen you. I'm guessing you don't visit Inverness often."

"Aye. Not often." The bartender walked to their table with Lachlan's ale, and he held out a hand for it. "Thank you, my man. Good service is its own reward."

Maggie cringed, knowing full well the bartender would much rather have had a tip. "Well," she persisted. "Which village?"

His eyes narrowed. "What's it to you, lass?"

She shrugged. "Just curious."

"Aye, and ye did a fair job looking me up and down while I perused yon pamphlet." He crumpled a piece of newsprint and wiped grease from his fingers. Then he grinned at her. "Did ye like what ye saw?"

Maggie felt her face heat. So her subtle inspection hadn't gone unnoticed. She tried a more direct approach. "You're a handsome man. Surely people have told you that before."

He narrowed his eyes. "Afore, ye said my accent was off. Yours is passing strange. Ye canna be from these parts."

"I'm from the States. Everyone who hears me talk knows right off the bat."

"States? Which states might those be?" He looked genuinely confused, his forehead crinkling as he sought to understand her.

Maggie sucked in a breath. Something was decidedly wrong here. He'd asked "which states might those be" in good faith, not realizing how odd his question was. She glanced at the empty dishes on their table and then at her watch.

*Should I?*

Maggie learned to trust her hunches long before she'd gone to medical school. She came from a prominent family of witches, starting with one who'd been hung during the trials in Salem in the sixteen hundreds. Her relatives told her she held untapped talent, should she ever choose to develop it. In truth, they'd been furious when she spurned the coven, but Maggie hadn't cared. Though magic held a certain questionable fascination, she'd relegated it to *I'll delve into it later* status so many times, she rarely thought about her gift at all anymore.

Giving in to her instincts, she pulled her iPhone from her bag and swiped a finger across its screen. She watched Lachlan out of the corners of her eyes while the message menu flared to life. Though he tried to hide his reaction, incredulity flitted across his aristocratic features. She tapped a text message, punched *Send*, and slid the phone back into her purse.

He jumped when the phone made its miniature jet airplane noise indicating her message had been sent. "What's that?" he asked, voice hoarse.

"A phone."

"That doesna help."

Maggie felt a smile tug the edges of her mouth. "No. I didn't think it would. You're done eating. How about if you come with me?"

"For what purpose?"

"Well, for starters, we need to get your hair cut and get you some clothes, so you don't stick out like a sore thumb."

His eyes widened, and he set his jaw in a hard line. "While I'm certain I could use a barber, I refuse to wear other than my plaid. It tells others I'm the head of Clan Moncrieffe."

"Look." She bent toward him and lowered her voice. "If you appear odd enough, the police will lock you up and call someone like me to come examine you."

"They wouldna dare," he thundered, half-rising to his feet. The bar had filled with patrons since they arrived. Every head in the place swiveled to stare at him. Apparently wise to the ways of crowds, Lachlan held up both hands. "Doona mind me," he murmured and sank back onto his seat.

"Need some help, Mags?" The bartender raced toward them, looking worried.

She shook her head. "No, Hank. It's fine. I've got things under control."

"Are you sure?"

"Yes, very sure." Maggie breathed a sigh of relief when Hank turned and retreated behind the bar.

"Mayhap ye're right," Lachlan said. "'Twould be prudent for us to leave this establishment afore they go for my throat, and I'm forced to defend myself." He stuffed his dagger back beneath his kilt and stood.

She smiled reassuringly and got to her feet. "There's a barbershop not a block from here. How about if we make it our first stop?" When he nodded assent, his nostrils flaring, she hooked a hand through his arm and half dragged him out of the pub. From the tension in his muscles beneath her fingertips, she could've sworn he was girding himself for combat.

*Has he had to fight his way out of places like this before?*

Maggie opened her mouth to ask but clacked it shut. They needed to talk, but the conversation she had in mind required privacy. Maybe after he'd gotten his hair trimmed, she'd come up with a secluded spot. She stole a glance at the proud set of his shoulders and his ramrod-straight posture.

*I could be wrong, but he looks like an ancient warrior.*

"Say," she ventured. "What do you want to do about your beard?"

He half-turned his head and looked at her with humor dancing in his green eyes. "Doona ye care for it?"

Maggie laughed. "I'm sure it's lovely, but you look like a reincarnation of Moses."

He snorted. "At least that name is a familiar one. Aye, lass, I plan to shave my beard. I prefer a bare face. Less problems with those wee beasties that live in human hair."

"Do you mean lice?" She untied her shirt from around her waist and slipped into it, securing the buttons. The barber was an older gentleman, and she didn't want to make him uncomfortable by exposing too much skin.

Lachlan watched her, his eyes wary. "I doona ken the term. Ye said ye were needed at your work."

"I texted them and said I wouldn't be in until tomorrow and to page me if they need me before then."

He opened his mouth as if to ask a question about what she'd just said, but closed it and shook his head. Moments later, he tried again. "Ye're a healer?" When she nodded, he went on. "Where are your healer's robes? Your staff? Your herb pouch?" He looked as if he were trying to assimilate pieces of data that simply wouldn't fit together. "The only female healers are witches, practitioners of the dark arts. Is that what ye are?"

"The barbershop is just ahead. We need to be alone, so we can talk. We can do that once we're done here."

"Ye dinna answer me."

Maggie stepped in front of him. Placing a hand on either shoulder, she gazed right into his amazing green eyes. A woman could lose herself in their depths. "The only thing you need to know right now is I would never hurt you."

He placed a finger beneath her chin, and his gaze bored into hers. Maggie felt something like an electric shock move from the top of her head to the soles of her feet, but she held herself open. Lachlan had to trust her. If she warded herself—one of the simplest magics, and practically the only spell she knew—he never would.

His expression softened. "Aye," he murmured. "A witch, but a puny one, or mayhap your magic's undeveloped."

Maggie laughed. She couldn't help herself. "Christ! You sound just like my grandmother."

A hint of a smile played around his mouth making him look hot, desirable. "She must be a wise, old crone."

"Inside." Maggie moved away from him and pushed the door to the barbershop open. "I'm going to make you earn your wages today, Fernley," she called out.

A portly, bald man wrapped in a white coat emerged from the back of the shop. Bright blue eyes twinkled behind a pair of steel-rimmed spectacles. "Maggie, my girl. What have you brought me?"

"Shave my beard and cut my hair," Lachlan ordered, the imperious tone back in his voice.

The barber raised his eyebrows. "You could do with a shot of manners, young man."

Maggie saw Lachlan's jaw tighten, but he gritted out, "Please."

"Better. Have a seat." Fernley pointed to a chair, and Lachlan settled himself. "Say, that sword looks really old. I'm fascinated by antiques. Mind if I take a closer look?" Fernly bent his head to inspect it.

Lachlan laid a hand protectively over the hilt. "Aye, that I do. No hand but mine touches this weapon."

"Humph. I see." Fernley shot Maggie a look that clearly said, *Where in God's name did you come up with this joker?* "Tilt your head back, then. We'll begin with the beard."

An hour later, much of which had been consumed getting the snarls out of Lachlan's hair prior to cutting it, Maggie withdrew her ATM card and handed it to Fernly. She felt Lachlan's eyes on her. He watched intently as the barber swiped her card through his reader, handed it back to her, and she bent to sign the small display.

He seemed either cowed or overwhelmed as they left the shop.

Maggie cast a covert glance his way. Her breath caught in her throat. If he'd been the most handsome man she'd ever seen *before* Fernley's ministrations, he was doubly or trebly so now. The beard had hidden much of his facial structure. With it gone, and his hair cut to shoulder length, he could've passed for a male model—or a movie star.

"Where to next, lassie?" He stopped a few feet from the barbershop door. She hesitated while she thought about where they could sit, safe from prying ears. Apparently, he mistook her silence for ambivalence. "Lass." His voice held a musical undercurrent. "Ye have done far more than enough for me. I can find my own way from here. If ye might tell me where I could leave some coins to repay your generosity—"

"No." She grabbed his arm and then let go, feeling she'd overstepped the boundaries of propriety. "I mean, if you'd like to leave, of course you're free to do so. But I thought if we had time alone where we could talk, it might clear up some of the questions I've seen in your eyes."

"Was talk the only thing ye had in mind, lass?" He cocked his head to one side, his gaze moving from the tip of her head to her mouth to her breasts, and then lower still.

Maggie inhaled shakily and forced herself to meet his gaze. "Like I said, you're quite the hunk, but I still think you'd be better served talking with me than fucking me."

He drew his brows together into a coppery line. "'Tisn't seemly for a lass to use such language. I doona understand how ye can be a healer yet speak like a gutter wench."

She took stock of what she knew. He wasn't mentally ill. Not any mental illness she knew about, anyway, and she was familiar with all of them. So that left out delusional, fugue state, and a fixed time or person hallucination. Besides, even undeveloped as they were, the boost from her witch senses corroborated his sanity. If he wasn't ill, there was only one explanation left. He had to be from the past.

How he'd ended up on the streets of Inverness in 2012 was beyond her, but it had happened just the same.

"Lass?" It was his turn to look appraisingly at something other than her body.

*Oh, what the hell.*

She drew him off to one side of the sidewalk. Then she moved right up next to him and stood on tiptoe, so she could talk into his ear. "Please. You were right when you intuited I have witch blood. Somehow you also knew I'd never trained my magic beyond an embarrassingly basic skill set."

He wrapped his arms around her and drew her against his body. The heat from him set her nerve endings on fire. Her nipples pebbled into peaks. Too tight shorts rubbed against suddenly swollen labia.

"Aye, lass. Now tell me something I doona know." His mouth was inches from hers. An enticing, exotic scent reminiscent of bay rum and vanilla made her want to lick him from head to toe.

Maggie fought an urge to brush her lips against his, to taste him, starting with his finely chiseled lips, but forged ahead, her mouth pressed against his ear. "You're from a different time. It's why you looked as if a demon walked over your grave when you read the newspaper. You must've seen the date."

"Aye, and what else do ye think ye know?" He ran his hands ever so slowly down her back. They left a trail of sparks before settling on her ass. He cupped it in his hands and snugged her against his unmistakable erection.

She wriggled against him, disconcertingly near coming. "I can't think when you're this close." She wrenched herself away, breathing hard.

A slow, lazy grin lit his heartbreakingly handsome face. "Aye, lass, I'll accompany you. To talk, mind ye." He winked.

For one wild, crazy moment, she thought about bringing him to her rented flat. It would certainly give them the privacy they needed. *Or I could rent us a hotel room, which would be just as chancy.* Maggie waged a brief internal war with her common sense.

*He's a stranger,* one side of her brain screamed in protest.

*So what?*

"What was it ye said about the sign over the pub door?" He asked laconically, almost as if he could read her mind. "It doesna bite. Well, neither do I."

"My car's a couple blocks from here. If I'm going to bring you home with me, we'll need to drive."

He looped an arm over her shoulders. "Lead out, lass. I understand drive, but what's a car?"

"Shh." She placed a finger over her lips and looked around them. Thank Christ no one was standing close enough to hear.

She pointed at a string of vehicles parked next to the curb and started walking. "All of them."

"Where are the horses?"

"People haven't used horses for anything other than pleasure riding for about a hundred years."

He spoke low. "What makes these car-things move?"

"Gasoline and sometimes electricity."

He chuckled and tightened his arm around her. "Aye, and this just gets deeper and deeper, doesna it?"

"I'm afraid so." Her side pressed against his body, but she blazed with need to be closer still. To clear her head, she moved from beneath his arm and trotted ahead, wishing she'd worn tennis shoes rather than sandals.

"Lass?" He chugged alongside her, easily catching her up.

"It's the red Fiat halfway down the next block." In a burst of frivolity, she added, "Bet I can beat you," and took off running.

# CHAPTER 3

*L*achlan wasn't expecting her to race away like a young child. It took him several moments to stop staring at the clean lines of ass and legs as she ran and chase after her. The lass, Maggie, was as enticing a woman as he'd ever come across. What hips she had. If ever a woman were made for childbearing…

"Caught you." He grabbed her arm and spun her to face him, before angling his mouth over hers. Half anticipating a sharp slap, he was pleasantly surprised when she opened her mouth beneath his and sparred with his tongue. She tasted sweet, like a well-aged wine. The swell of her breasts pressing against his chest nearly drove him mad.

Breaking away from a kiss that was developing a life of its own, she murmured, "We're never going to get to the car at this rate."

"Ye said red." He gazed at the row of metal things she'd indicated were cars. "I only see one red conveyance, so it must be yours."

"Very good, Einstein. Let's see if we can get there." She pulled away and started walking again. He loped to her side and took her arm.

"Einstein?"

"Never mind." She fished something black and silver from her bag and pushed a small red button that made an odd *chirrup* noise. "Go ahead, get in." She motioned to the door on the opposite side from the walkway. "I'm still not that great with this right-hand drive thing, but I promise not to kill us."

He walked into the street. An obnoxiously loud noise set his heart racing as another car sped past, scant inches from his body. *They're just like carriages,* he tried to tell himself, gulping air. *'Twas stupid of me not to look afore stepping into the roadway.*

He flattened himself against the side of Maggie's car and looked at the outline of the door. A recessed, silvery panel must be the secret to open it. He was just reaching for it when she leaned across the car, did something, and his door popped open. He folded his frame into a space that felt far too small and made certain his sword was snugged up against himself before tugging the door shut.

He gazed at dials and levers. Maggie twisted something, and the same whirring sound all these contraptions made assaulted his ears.

"Hang on," she murmured. "This will seem strange, but here we go. Whatever you do, do not open your door until the car stops—no matter how nervous this makes you."

"I'm never *nervous*." His voice wasn't as smooth and confident as he hoped it would sound. He tightened his grip on his sword hilt.

She grinned and pulled into the street. "I would be. It's nothing to be ashamed of."

"How far can one of these, er, cars travel in a day?"

She shrugged. "Depends. Three hundred miles is an easy day, but you could drive five or six hundred if you started early and drove until late. In the States, where the roads are better, I've driven as much as eight hundred, but I was pretty tired at the end of it."

He fell back against the seat cushions. Breath whooshed out of him. She couldn't have traveled such a great distance in a single day. It wasn't possible, not without a hefty magical assist. He chewed on his lower lip. Could he trust this woman? This *witch*? She could've closed her mind to him—not that it would have kept him out—but she hadn't even tried. Questions spilled through his overburdened brain.

How could he have slept so long, yet remain relatively untouched? Why had he awakened when he did? How could he locate Rhukon amid all this weirdness? For that matter, was Rhukon still after him?

Because his mind spun like an out-of-control top, he shifted to things he'd need to know so he wouldn't appear a total dolt. What did *text* mean or *page*? What was this gasoline that powered cars? How did men wage war without horses?

"Eight hundred miles in a day," he muttered. "That canna be."

"Och aye," Maggie aped a Scottish brogue, "but 'tis."

"Has everything changed so much, then?" he murmured.

"Yes, and especially since around nineteen hundred."

Lachlan shook his head. He reached inward for Kheladin, but the dragon was silent, probably as disconcerted as him. Were there dragons in this world? Or had they all died out? He was enticed with the woman, wanted her fiercely, but she'd spoken true when she said her knowledge would be more useful to him than her body.

*Well now, there's no reason why I canna have both.*

"Tell me about 2012."

"It might be better if you ask me questions." She briefly laid a hand over one of his and squeezed.

"I doona know where to begin."

"Where did you come from?"

He inhaled sharply, reluctant to disclose what might be used against him.

"Lachlan." She squeezed his hand again. "I'll never hurt you, but I need information, or I'm afraid I won't be much help."

Her words held the ring of truth when he tested them with his magic. "The place where ye found me was verra close to where my castle used to stand. I…"

"Keep going," she urged. "Just let the words come. We have a little time before we get to my flat."

He took stock of what to tell her. She didn't need to know about Kheladin or his dragon-shifter magic or the cave. If things went to hell, it was the only place he could retreat to that he could fortify with magic.

She glanced sidelong at him as if she could read his mind. Who knew with witches? They all had at least one magical strong suit. Mayhap that was hers. Lachlan shuttered his thoughts. His magic was far stronger than hers. Even a tiny trickle would be more than adequate to keep her from his mind.

"What year—?" she began

He waved her to silence. "Everything is so new..." He smiled disarmingly. "I fear 'tis a fair challenge to know just where to begin. In 1683 I had an, um, altercation with a powerful warlock. He ensorcelled me."

"Ensorcelled, as in put you to sleep?"

"Aye. I just wakened a few hours ago."

Maggie's breath whistled from between her teeth. She pulled the car into a large square area off the roadway and placed it next to another. "We're here," she said brusquely.

He grappled with the side of the car door, hunting for the trick to make it spring open. "Which little piece do I pull or press?"

"Never mind. I'll come round and let you out."

His sword clanked loudly against the car when he struggled to unfold his long legs and get out. Between making certain it didn't catch on the car's door and getting his feet under him, he longed for the simplicity of a warhorse.

"You really don't need that sword," she said.

He raised an eyebrow and shifted from foot to foot, one hand firmly planted on the hilt of his sword. "How would I defend us? Is this a world where magic is common? Ye said ye had a witchy grannie."

"Come on." She crooked a finger. "We're better off talking inside."

He followed her into a rambling grey stone building with 1846 carved over the lintel. It looked as if it had once been a manor house. Mayhap the lass had more in the way of resources than he imagined if she could afford such a place. They climbed to the second floor. It confused him. Why would she not receive him in the great room or a parlor? Maggie pulled a key from her bag and inserted it into the lockset on a peeling, oak door.

"Why do ye keep your bedchamber locked, lass, but not the house proper?"

"It's not just my bedroom. This is where I live." She pushed the door open and gestured him inside. "This was a manor house once upon a time. The family that owns it broke it up into four apartments with a common area downstairs that any of the tenants can use if they wish."

"The family must've fallen on hard times indeed to rent out their ancestral home to strangers," he said softly.

"Not necessarily. The house is quite a way out of town. The story I was told, the owners didn't want to live here anymore. They tried to sell it, didn't get any takers, and so turned it into what it is today."

Lachlan's brow creased. No matter what Maggie said, giving up one's home meant the next generation would have nowhere to live. It was a truly Draconian move, likely driven by something the lass didn't know about. He looked around, curious. Rather than a bedchamber, he saw a small, neat, sitting room with a leather couch and a puffy, soft-looking chair covered in flowered fabric. Something he couldn't identify sat on a table. It looked like a mirror, but its surface was black. Books overflowed onto every available surface. He didn't see any scrolls.

The door snicked shut behind him. He heard the *thunk* of a lock falling into place.

"There." She walked around him and headed for the far end of the room. He recognized a table and chairs in that part of her home but not much else. "Can I make you some tea?"

"Tea is a woman's drink, lass. Have ye a stiff ale, or better still, whiskey?"

Maggie spun and faced him. "I have both, but it's not evening yet."

He frowned. "What? Is that some kind of rule? No spirits except weak beer until after dark?" He chuckled at the absurdity of it.

She cocked her head to one side. "There's a saying, *It's always five o'clock somewhere.*"

"And that means?"

"People use it as an excuse to drink whenever they want, because five at night is supposedly a safe time to begin drinking."

"I doona understand. Safe for whom?"

"It doesn't matter. Sit." She waved her hands at the couch.

"Will ye be sitting next to me?" he inquired, working to keep a seductive note out of his voice. They had serious conversation ahead of them. Sex would only get in the way.

"Eventually. I'm going to make myself a cup of tea. You know..." She winked at him. "That woman's drink. And I'm going to make myself a sandwich."

"What's a sandwich?"

"Bread, meat, cheese, mayonnaise—"

"Might ye make one for me as well?"

Maggie threw back her head and laughed. "I suppose after over three hundred years asleep, you'd be hungry. Christ! You're like the male equivalent of *Sleeping Beauty.*"

"I doona understand."

"Look, if you don't want to sit, come on into the kitchen. We can chat while I make us something to eat. *Sleeping Beauty* is a children's story about a princess who was ensorcelled and slept for a hundred years."

"What wakens her?"

"A handsome prince finds her and kisses her."

"Aye. At least some things havena changed—and likely never will." He stepped to her side, watching as she drew items from a small cold box, rather like a miniature spring room. She filled a kettle and set it on the stove. Flames leapt beneath the kettle when she twisted a dial.

Lachlan nodded to himself. Life had certainly improved if you didn't have to light a fire to cook over and tend the wood, so it didn't go out or blaze so brightly the food burned. Not having to retreat outside to the spring house or the buttery for cold items was another improvement. "Where's the pump?" He tapped a silvery spigot that dripped water into the sink.

She sliced bread from a loaf and laid four pieces on the counter. "Let's see," she mused. "Where to begin. There's a city water system. Water comes to houses through underground pipes. All I have to do is turn the faucet." Her eyes sparkled. "Put your hand under this." She flipped a lever.

Though he tried for equanimity, Lachlan felt his eyes widen. "'Tis hot." He drew his hand back. "Ye doona have to heat bath water over a stove?"

Maggie shook her head and returned to the bread, spreading something on it. "Nope. Why don't you go check out the bathroom while I finish the sandwiches? I think you'll be pleasantly surprised."

Lachlan looked about. Bathroom should mean a room where a bathing tub was located. In poorer homes that was always the kitchen, usually behind a curtained alcove, yet he didn't see any hidden nooks.

"Go back to the living room and down the hall. It's the door on your right."

He was reluctant to leave her side. There was something soothing about standing next to Maggie, and exciting too. He felt he'd known her far longer than only a few hours.

Almost as if she could read his thoughts, she said, "Don't worry. I'm not going anywhere."

He bent his head and brushed his lips against her neck before following her directions toward the bathroom. It was dark in the hall, so he called his mage light.

*"What have ye gotten us into?"* Kheladin hissed deep in his mind.

*"Do ye have any better ideas? We slept for more than three hundred years. The world is vastly different. I must have information afore we can plot a course."*

*"Humph,"* the dragon snorted. Lachlan swallowed back steam that sat just at the back of his throat. *"I could overfly—"*

*"No. I doona believe there are any dragons left. I havena asked the lass about modern weaponry, but 'tis likely something exists that could blow you out of the sky. And me right along with you."*

*"What do ye mean,* no dragons left?"

Lachlan swallowed hard. There was so much about the year 2012 that troubled him, he hadn't dissected each item. And he wasn't going to now. The most important thing was seeing if Rhukon were still a threat. *"I havena seen any,"* Lachlan said cautiously. *"It may mean nothing, yet I dinna sense dragon energy anywhere."*

*"Ye must cede to my form, so we may look."* Compulsion ran strong beneath Kheladin's frantic words. *"Failing all else, I must return to Fire Mountain to see if any of my kin remain."*

Lachlan fought the dragon's magic. Fire Mountain—the dragon's home world—was the last place he wanted to go right now. No. He needed to figure out what happened to Rhukon. He clamped his jaw firmly shut. *"Soon. We need to know more—much more—afore we take unnecessary risks."* He stood in the hallway, every muscle tense, waiting. After long moments, the dragon backed down, grumbling there wasn't space for him to force a shift.

Lachlan exhaled sharply and continued down the short corridor, not wanting to think about what it meant if dragons were truly gone. He turned a doorknob and walked into a tiled room with a bathtub, a sink, and what had to be a commode, except there was no odor, and it was filled with what looked like water. Experimentally, he hiked his kilt to the side, took hold of his cock, and pissed into the basin.

Lachlan frowned and looked at the commode. A pull chain ran down from a white box mounted on the wall behind it. He pulled the chain and jumped back as water whooshed out of the commode only to be replaced with new. He grinned. Clever, but where did the piss and shit go? He'd have to ask the lass.

He stepped to the sink and turned first one tap and then the other. One discharged hot water, the other cold. *Mayhap living in this era willna be quite so bad as I feared.* Lachlan grimaced. He was focusing on small things to avoid thinking about the loss of a way of life that had been precious. Friends, family, his castle, even his servants were lost to him.

"Lachlan. Your sandwich is ready."

"Coming, lass." He turned his mind to Kheladin. *"We willna be telling her about you. Not yet, anyway, so no smoke, steam, or fire."*

*"Fine by me. Do us both a favor and bed the lass. She's nearly begging for it, and 'twill clear our heads to search for Rhukon."*

Lachlan walked slowly down the hall. He extinguished the magic powering his light before he emerged from behind the curtain that separated the hall from the front room. Maggie sat at the table. He pulled out the empty chair and joined her.

She smiled around a mouthful of sandwich. "What did you think?"

"Of the garderobe?"

She nodded. "I'd forgotten they used to be called that, but didn't those just have toilets in them?"

He took a sip of the tea she'd made for him despite his protests. It was surprisingly good, smooth and tannic-y with just the right amount of cream and sugar. "Most were as ye described. Wealthier homes had a pump for water somewhere close by. Where does the waste go?"

She set down her sandwich and took a swallow of tea. "I heard the toilet flush and thought you might be curious. There's a sewer system. Waste water flows from houses to a central processing plant where it's cleansed and recycled."

"Ye reuse shit?" He stared suspiciously at his teacup.

"Don't worry. Drinking water has to meet certain safety

standards. Without going into a whole lot of detail, there are too many people on Earth. Later, I'll bring up a globe, er, representation of Earth on my computer, so you can see all the countries." She crinkled her brow, clearly thinking. "Um, a computer is... Never mind, I'll just show you in a little bit. Anyway..." She waved a hand airily. "There's not enough water, so it's important not to squander what we have."

Lachlan returned to his sandwich. *Not enough water? The lass must be daft.* Enormous oceans covered much of Earth. Oceans so large, it took men months to cross them.

"You don't believe me, which is understandable. Let's switch gears." She must've responded to confusion on his face, because she clarified, "Topics. Let's switch topics. There's no way I'll be able to give you a primer on modern life in a few hours. At best, you need enough so you can blend in better."

"Agreed. I hate to admit it, but ye may be right about my garb. I dinna see even one other man in a plaid."

"We'll take care of that tomorrow. Have you given any thought to what you want to do now that you're here?"

"Aye. I must see if Rhukon yet lives."

"Who's that?" Maggie narrowed her eyes, almost as if she didn't trust him simply from the sound of his name.

"The warlock who ensorcelled us, er me."

"How could he possibly still be alive? You were in some sort of suspended animation. Presumably, he wasn't."

Lachlan shrugged. "Well, lass, I was trapped by his spell until a few hours ago. 'Tis a solid argument that he, too, lives. Or, mayhap, that he died and 'tis why I'm finally free."

*And wouldn't it be lovely if I knew just which of those alternatives was true.*

He smothered his frustration and took another bite of the food she'd made. It was really quite good. "Thank you." He pointed to his plate.

"You're welcome. Where would you look for this Rhukon?"

"His castle used to be in Inishowen, and he had a manor house a few leagues south of Inverness. From what I've seen, it appears unlikely either yet stands, although 'twould be a logical place to begin." An idea blossomed. "Could ye teach me to drive your car? I could hunt Rhukon while ye work."

She pushed her chair back from the table. That done, she stretched out her long, bare legs and folded her hands over her belly. "The short answer is, of course I could teach you to drive, but there's much more to it than that." She reached for her bag, lying on the floor next to her chair, and extracted a leather pouch. "Here." She handed him a card with a likeness of her face and writing on it.

"What might this be?" He flicked at the stiff card with a fingernail, wondering what the hell it was made of.

"My international driver's license. You have to have some sort of license to drive a car."

"Couldna we secure one for me?"

"You don't have any identification."

He bristled. "I have my word."

"That's not enough anymore. Besides, even if you had a birth certificate, or a family bible or something where births were written down, no one would believe you. What year were you born, anyway?"

"1316." The words slipped out before he understood he should've picked a false date, one much closer to 1683. "Sorry, what I meant was—"

She held up a hand. "No. You told me the truth. Rhukon may have bested you, but you have power. I felt it when I let you inside my head. What are you?"

"A warlock, just like you're a witch." He tried to smooth the lie over with spells, but she saw right through him.

"Try again, buddy." She sounded annoyed—and disappointed. "I may not have developed my magic, but I do recognize lies when I hear them."

# CHAPTER 4

The strains of a Braham's lullaby sounded. Maggie made another grab for her bag and pulled her phone from its pouch.

Lachlan's eyes widened. "Good God, lass. That thing makes different noises? Where in the nine hells do they originate from?"

"Ssht." She waved him to silence, tapped the *Answer* icon, and said, "Dr. Hibbins."

"It's Berta," one of the nurses who ran the mental health unit said. "Sorry to bother you, since you take so little personal time, but Chris Conley's back in here."

"What'd he do this time?" Aware of Lachlan both listening and watching her intently, Maggie kept her words neutral. Discussing patients in front of anyone but treatment staff was bad practice.

"It's not pretty," Berta went on. "He's alive but he wouldn't be if his sister hadn't found him."

Maggie glanced at the time and bit her lip. "Is he conscious?"

"Yes, and asking for you."

*Damn!*

"Okay. I'll grab my things. Be there in half an hour or less."

A weary sigh rustled through the phone. "Thanks, Doc. He's quite a handful. We need someone to write orders, so we can release him—to somewhere."

"Got it." Maggie disconnected and looked speculatively at Lachlan. "I have to go to the hospital. I could drive you back into town, or…" She inhaled sharply. "I suppose you could stay here until I get back."

"Why do ye need to leave?"

Maggie shook her head. "One of my patients needs me. I can't tell you any more than that."

"And why not?" He crossed his arms over his chest, clearly used to being obeyed without question.

"Because people are entitled to privacy regarding their medical conditions."

His forehead creased. "I'm understanding your words but not your meaning. If a man is ill, everyone in his village knows of it."

Maggie rolled her eyes. "Yes, that might've been true three hundred years ago. Not so much anymore. In any event, what do you want to do?" She got to her feet and looked at him, one brow raised in a question mark.

"How far are we from Inverness?"

"About ten miles."

"How much is that in leagues?"

"Not exactly certain, but I think there are roughly three miles to a league."

"That isna so bad. I could walk if I chose to leave here. Probably a bit chancy to rely on magic."

Maggie came to his side and laid a hand on his shoulder. "Leaving is not a good idea, until we get you different clothes. Magic's not either, but you already realized that. No one is used to it anymore. Even witches take care to shield their spells." She shook her head emphatically. "You need modern clothing if you're going to wander about. I'd planned to buy you some. Let's see, if you don't come with me..." She considered alternatives. "Aha! This could work. Get up." She clicked her tongue against her teeth and made a come along motion with two fingers.

Lachlan snorted. "I'm scarcely a horse for ye to cluck at. I will rise, but because I desire it, not because ye ordered me." He flowed to his feet and gathered her into his arms. His green gaze snared her, and the corners of his mouth twitched with amusement. "Now, lass, are ye wanting a kiss afore ye leave?"

*Of course I want kisses. Any woman would want kisses from you.*

She wriggled loose. "No, silly. I wanted to get a better look at your body. So I can bring you home some clothes. As long as I stay with something fairly loose-fitting—"

"Aye." He thrust his cloak aside. Next he unbuckled his sword belt and dropped the sword on the floor with a clatter. With the tiniest of flourishes, Lachlan began unwinding his kilt from his upper body. He was far too thin, but his body was unbelievable, simmering with barely repressed sexuality. Beautifully muscled shoulders and upper arms came into full view, along with a chest lightly sprinkled with tawny hair, as he pushed his shirt back on his shoulders.

Maggie's throat thickened. Desire shot through her so intense she wondered if her knees would buckle. She held up a hand. "Stop. That's all I need."

His eyes twinkled merrily. "And are ye quite sure, lass? I could remove my plaid and take my shirt all the way off—so ye were certain to get the sizing correct."

In spite of herself, her eyes travelled downward. The unmistakable swell of an erection belled the front of his kilt. Before she could stop herself, her hand snaked toward him. She yanked it back. "Quite certain. I—er, I have to leave. Now. If I get any closer to you, I'm not sure I'll be able to drag myself out of here."

"Really?" He cocked his head to one side and gave her the come-hitherest of looks, his expression ablaze with unmistakable hunger.

"Goddammit." She took a step backward and willed her out-of-control libido to give her a break. "You know how drop dead gorgeous you are. I'll bet those seventeenth century lassies fell all over one another to get a glimpse under your kilt."

"Aye." His voice was like liquid honey. "That they did. But I only let a few verra special ones take a peek." He unwrapped another fold of plaid. The hard, flat planes of his stomach emerged, with slabs of muscle that descended under the fabric precariously draped around his waist.

Feeling dazed, half-drunk on lust, Maggie picked up her purse, looked around for her medical bag, and then remembered it was in the trunk of her car. "I really do need to leave. Are you staying here or coming with me?"

He thought for a moment. "Staying. I believe I shall bathe and await your return."

Sudden joy bloomed inside her, so poignant it almost hurt. He'd be here when she got back. She'd been afraid he'd want to take off.

*Watch it, Maggie. Nothing can come of this—beyond maybe the greatest sex I've had in my life.*

*Why not? Talk to Grannie. See what she has to say.*

"Lass?" Lachlan looked at her with a quizzical expression, almost as if he could read her mind.

*Maybe he can. He's a centuries-old magician of some sort.* "Nothing. It's nothing. I shouldn't be gone much more than a couple hours."

"Excellent. I'll warm the bed for you, once I'm clean."

"No. You will not. This couch..." she pointed, "...makes into a bed. You'll sleep there."

A knowing smile flitted across his face. "Ye're no maid, yet ye act like one. We will discuss the topic further upon your return."

She started to ask how he could know she wasn't a virgin but clamped her teeth together to keep the words from escaping. Discussing sex with Lachlan would just make her hotter and, damn him, he probably knew it. "Look," she managed. "If you do decide to go out for a walk or something, leave me a note. Paper and pens are in the desk just over there."

He was by her side so quickly, she didn't see how he could've managed it. He closed his arms around her and slanted his mouth over hers. That delicious scent surrounded her as he plumbed her mouth with his tongue. His hands trailed down her back and cupped her ass firmly. His erect cock jumped against her belly. She'd just lifted her arms to hug him back when he let go and took a step back.

Lachlan grinned mischievously. "Aye, lass. Ye're needing to be bedded, and by a fellow who knows his way about a bedchamber. 'Tis little enough I can do to repay you for your kindnesses to me. We shall pick up where we left off once ye return."

"Oh, we shall, shall we?" she muttered, too tongue-tied to come up with a snappy rejoinder. She stumbled out the door on unsteady feet and then turned back. "Lock it after me. You turn this—"

"Things havena changed so much. I'll figure it out. Go." He made shooing motions with his tapering fingers. "The sooner ye leave, the sooner ye shall return."

"Holy shit." She glanced down at herself and clapped a hand to her forehead. "I can't go like this." She hastened back inside and loped to her bedroom. On the far side of the door, she locked herself in and shucked her cut-off shorts, shirt, and halter top, trading them for teal scrubs and a long white coat emblazoned with Margaret Hibbins, M.D. in navy blue script over the left breast pocket. She looked at her feet, decided her sandals would do, and prepared herself to run the gauntlet past Lachlan. Part of her hoped for another kiss—

*Let's get real, I'd love to rip that kilt off him and...*

*Stop it. I need to leave. He'll still be here when I get back.*

She aimed for a casual saunter down the hall and through her living room.

He eyed her appraisingly from the couch as she walked past him.

"Fascinating. Do lassies never wear skirts these days?" He laughed, the sound low and musical. "I liked your other garb far better."

She snorted. "I'll just bet you did. It was comfortable but not very professional." Not understanding what got into her, she blew him a kiss and escaped out the door.

With the taste of him still in her mouth and the scent of him in her nostrils, Maggie blundered down the steps and out of the building to her car. She wanted to rush back, make certain nothing evil befell him, but then she came to her senses. Whoever Lachlan Moncrieffe was, he'd been taking care of himself for centuries. If the evil he faced over three hundred years before was still after him, there'd be precious little she could do to fight against it.

She slid into the driver's seat and started the engine. Talking to her grandmother suddenly felt more important than just about anything else. She grappled for her cell phone, intent on activating its Bluetooth connection but then stopped. There were better ways to communicate with her grandmother. More private ones.

*"Grandma. I need you."* Maggie waited. Sometimes it took a while for telepathic communication to work, particularly with the Atlantic Ocean standing between them. If they hadn't been linked by blood, she doubted they'd be able to converse at all from so far away.

She was nearly at the hospital, when, *"Yes, child, I see some of what is troubling you,"* sounded in her mind.

*"Tell me about the man,"* Maggie demanded without preamble.

*"He is old, and his magic is strong."*

*"Do you know what kind of magician he is?"*

A hesitation and then, *"Yes."* The single word held a universe of meaning.

Maggie waited, but her paternal grandmother, Mary Elma Hibbins, remained silent. Maggie could picture the wraith-thin older woman, with her ageless face and waist-length black hair pulled into its usual braid. That hair had a few strands of silver, but not many. Right now, her grandmother's finely arched brows were probably drawn together and her dark brown eyes pinched with worry.

Maggie pulled into the hospital's lot and parked in the physicians' parking area. She started to tell her grandmother they'd have to save the rest of this conversation for another day, when Mary Elma said, *"I'll be on the first plane I can catch. I'll text you so you know when my flight arrives in Glasgow."*

*"What? Why?"*

Alarm sluiced through Maggie. It wasn't that her grandmother never traveled. Quite the contrary, but to embark on an impromptu trip that would land her by Maggie's side meant she was worried. Scratch *worried*. Her grandmother must be frantic. Maggie's heartbeat pounded loud in her ears. Something had frightened Mary Elma—badly—and her grandmother didn't scare easily.

*"I'll answer your questions once I get there, child. Don't let the man leave your side. Be extremely careful. I see darkness around him. He's in mortal peril, yet you can help. He is...one of a special breed. I'd thought them all long since dead. That he still lives is, perhaps, important in ways I have yet to discover. I must confer with the Coven Council."*

Mary Elma's voice faded. Without being told, Maggie knew her grandmother severed the connection. "What the fuck?" she muttered as she got out of her car. Going around to the trunk, she opened it and hefted her medical bag. For the first time, she wished she'd shown more interest when her grandmother and aunts tried to teach her about her witch heritage.

Her parents died when she was only six, fighting a rival coven over rights to a special, arcane magic that slowed the aging process radically. At the time, no one explained much of anything to her because she was too young to understand, which left her free to form her own conclusions—none of them good. When she began to menstruate, the coven women took her under their wing—and were shocked she had absolutely no interest in her magical heritage. The way Maggie saw things, magic killed both her parents and robbed her of being raised by them. She wanted nothing to do with such a lethal, unpredictable entity. Not now. Not ever.

Despite many lectures from various relatives, she'd never changed her mind. It wasn't accidental she chose a science-based career. At the time, she thought medicine was about as far away from witchcraft as anything could be. Maggie winced. She could still see the shrewd smile on her grandmother's face when she pointed out that some of the most famous witches of all had been healers.

Maggie punched in a code and pushed through the hospital's back door into the emergency room. A brisk head shake, and she forced herself to focus on the reason she was here, not ghosts from her distant past. The sting of antiseptic overpowered Lachlan's scent. She hadn't realized it still lingered around her. White walls and linoleum floors whizzed past as she jogged to the nurses' station.

Before she could open her mouth to say a word, Chris sidled over to her, his hospital gown flapping. "And ye finally got here, eh. What did I interrupt? Some hot little love fest?"

Maggie couldn't stop the heat that raced from her chest to her face. "Where I was is no business of yours," she said brusquely. "Why aren't you in your room?"

"Because I want to leave." His tone switched from aggressive to plaintive. "They said ye're the only one who can spring me."

"That's true."

"That's bloody unfair." He pouted. "They give shrinks too damn much power."

"That may be. How about if you lead me to your room, and you can tell me what happened."

His bright blue eyes snapped dangerously, offering glimpses of the madness behind them. He shoved a hank of red hair shot with gray out of his eyes. At over six feet, Chris's muscled frame was intimidating. As a younger man, he'd probably been attractive. At fifty, his face was deeply lined, and broken blood vessels suggested a too-intimate relationship with alcohol. "Aye, ye're wanting to follow me to my room. Sounds like sexual harassment to me."

Maggie shrugged. "If you'd be more comfortable, we can talk in the patient lounge." She glanced meaningfully at him. "You need your clothes for that."

"That's just it. They took them away."

*Of course they did.*

She altered her tone, making her words soft, non-confrontational. "It's your call, Chris. What do you want to do? The sooner we talk, the sooner I can make a decision about where you need to be right now."

He grabbed her arm. "Home," he screeched. "I need to be home, you goddamned, fucking—"

"That will be enough. Take your hand off me." Maggie squared her shoulders and met Chris's gaze. If she let him bully her, she'd be dead in the water. Out of the corners of her eyes, she saw orderlies and nurses race toward them. In moments, they had Chris well in hand.

"Are you all right, Doctor?" Berta hustled to her side, gray hair escaping its pins. Her pale green eyes were screwed into a concerned expression, and her ample curves strained against the fabric of her white uniform.

"Yes, yes. I'm fine. Let's get him back to his room. Physical restraints until I can talk with him, then chemical ones until we get him past this current break."

An hour later, Maggie rounded up her purse and medical bag. It took far longer than she anticipated to deal with Chris, who'd taken a mixture of prescription drugs, followed by a healthy jolt of whiskey, and become hostile and belligerent when his sister interrupted his drinking. Good thing she'd happened along. If Chris continued to drink, he'd probably be dead, what with all the other drugs he had on board.

Maggie sighed. She'd signed orders to keep him in-house until he stabilized. After that, he really needed a board-and-care placement to make certain he took medications for his bipolar disorder and stayed away from other mind-altering substances. She pursed her lips and strode down the corridor, heading for the parking lot. The odds of Chris being even marginally compliant with whatever she mapped out ran less than fifty-fifty. While he may have dulled his mental processes from years of boozing, he was far from stupid. The drugs she prescribed made him feel like crap, while the ones he procured on the street amped his mania.

"Why didn't I go into ophthalmology or dermatology—or even plastic surgery?" she muttered and got into her car. Maggie started for home, but then she remembered clothes for Lachlan and navigated to a shopping center where the stores stayed open late.

By the time she left a menswear shop laden with bags, she felt much better. The female shopkeeper had been a hoot as Maggie described Lachlan's build. "Och, aye, lassie," she crowed, "and 'tis a fair brawny lad ye're shopping for. With those broad shoulders and long legs, how's the rest of him equipped, eh?"

Maybe to defuse the tension from her truncated conversation with her grandmother and the drama at the hospital, Maggie laughed so hard with the shopkeeper that tears rolled down her face. She'd just dumped Lachlan's jeans, sweaters, and jacket in the backseat of her car when her phone trilled its text tone.

*Grannie!*

Maggie dug the phone out of her bag. Sure enough, it was indeed a text from Mary Elma informing her she'd be arriving day after tomorrow at six in the morning. Maggie's nostrils quivered with annoyance. Why the hell did all trans-Atlantic flights to Glasgow have to show up at some ungodly hour?

Maggie mentally rearranged her schedule as she drove, so she could meet her grandmother's flight. *Maybe I'll bring Lachlan with me. Sounds as if the two of them will be kindred spirits...* Still running on autopilot, she pulled into the parking lot adjacent to her house and glanced up at her apartment. Days were long in June, yet it seemed odd he hadn't turned on any of the lights. Her flat didn't have all that many windows and tended to feel dark and shut-in once light faded from the day.

*Perhaps he doesn't understand how the switches work.*

Balancing her purse and purchases, she locked her medical bag in her car and trudged up the steps to her flat. Maggie knocked softly, expecting Lachlan to open the door. When he didn't, her heart rocketed into an erratic rhythm, and her throat felt thick. She pushed her fragile magic outward. It didn't tell her a thing.

*Big surprise. I never embraced it, so why should it help me now?*

Maggie set the bags down in the carpeted hall and fished her key out of her purse with none-too-steady hands. She twisted it in the lock and pushed the door open. Knowledge struck her like a blow to the gut. Lachlan wasn't here. She didn't bother calling his name. Her flat felt empty without him in it. He had a vibrant energy, almost like a force field, and it was definitely absent.

*Don't panic. Maybe he left me a note like I told him.*

*Sure. That's probably it. He got restless. Went out to stretch his legs.*

*Bullshit. Who am I kidding here?*

She kicked the bags of clothes inside. Once they were out of the hall, she pulled the door shut and flipped on a light. Sure enough, a single sheet of paper sat atop her desk. She dropped her purse onto a chair and hurried over to it. In strong script, with many flourishes, he'd written an almost indecipherable note. After trying to figure out what was, in essence, an archaic form of English, she finally grabbed another piece of paper and wrote out the parts she knew. At length, she thought she had the gist of things.

He told her he was sorry, but he had to leave because danger nipped at his heels. He couldn't give her details because it might put her at risk. Lachlan went on to say he hoped they'd meet again and that she was pretty. On a separate line near the bottom, just above his signature, Lachlan Moncrieffe, Laird of Clan Moncrieffe, he told her not to trust strangers, and that he'd return if he could.

Maggie clutched the paper close. A tear snaked down one cheek. *Why am I crying? I barely knew him.*

Her attempt to reason with herself was futile. In defiance of logic, a sad, slow tide washed through her and made her heart ache. She picked up her car keys, ready to head out and look for him, but forced herself to sit. In her heart of hearts, she knew she'd never be able to find him if he didn't wish to be found.

CHAPTER 5

*L*achlan watched Maggie walk out the door. It took all his considerable self-discipline not to race after her, drag her back inside, and rip those ridiculous clothes off her. If ever there was a lass made for loving, it was her. For long moments, he visualized her without clothes. It wasn't difficult since she'd scarcely been wearing any when he first laid eyes on her.

He shook his head and rose, intent on locking the door. Careful to slide the bolt into place, he embarked on an exploration of the room. Lachlan picked up books at random and paged through a few. They looked like scientific works with full-color depictions of bits and pieces of the human body. At first, he marveled that someone had so fine a hand as to pen such drawings, but closer inspection told him the illustrations couldn't possibly be hand drawn.

He blew out a heavy breath. Mankind had obviously come a long way in three hundred years, much farther than they'd come in the previous three hundred. A stranger displaced from thirteen hundred to sixteen hundred would've noticed a few differences, but nothing like this. He polished the rest of his food and carried their plates to the kitchen, setting them on a sideboard.

"No kitchen wenches," he muttered. "Probably no more servants of any kind." He pulled open cupboards and drawers, inspecting an array of pottery and cutlery. A few items had long, black tails attached to them. Some of the tails had been cunningly shoved into holes in the wall. He flicked a silver knob, and the item in front of him buzzed loudly. Lachlan started. He returned the knob to its original position and shook his head.

*What in the hell did I turn loose?*

He stared at tiny blades, still whirling in a circle at the base of a glass cylinder, until they came to a stop. Try as he might, he couldn't fathom a use for such a thing.

Careful not to move any other knobs or buttons, he settled in front of the cold box, opening it to inspect its contents. It held an intriguing array of fruits and vegetables, cheese and meat. He tasted a few items, surprised that the things he recognized—like blackberries—were so bland.

"What are we doing here?" Kheladin's voice was annoyed, sharp, as he repeated a variant of his question from earlier.

*"Waiting for the lass to return."*

*"We canna risk remaining in one place for long, until we determine if Rhukon yet lives."*

*"We havena been here verra long. I wish to bathe. Then if the lass hasna returned, we can pick up this conversation."*

Something like a slow twisting in his midsection told Lachlan the dragon was restless and near to rebellion. *"Bedding her was a good idea when we dinna have to wait. I doona have a good feeling about remaining here. In fact..."* The dragon hesitated for emphasis. *"I sense a trap."*

*Have I grown so soft and unobservant?* Lachlan sent his mage senses spinning outward and waited for information to flow back to him. He pinched the bridge of his nose between thumb and forefinger. *"Things feel...strange to me, mayhap because everything has changed. I do not sense Rhukon's presence, though. Do ye?"*

*"Not exactly,"* Kheladin admitted grudgingly. *"But we canna be too careful."*

*"Agreed."*

Lachlan fired his mage light and walked down the hall to the bathroom. On a whim, he opened the door across the hall. Her bedchamber. The scraps of clothing she'd been wearing were tossed on the end of a rumpled bed. Maggie's scent hit him like a wall. Sensual and enticing, it stopped him in his tracks. He inhaled deeply and his cock, never far from hard since he'd met Maggie, thumped against his belly.

He tried to back out of the bedroom, but it was as if his feet had grown roots into the carpeted floor. All he could think about was sex: bouncing breasts and hot, slick cunnies. His balls ached for release. He shoved a hand beneath his kilt and wrapped it around himself. What would it take? Surely not more than a few strokes. He pumped his swollen member into his hand and groaned. The lass wakened something primal in him. He couldn't remember being this aroused—ever.

An image of her tall, well-muscled form danced before his closed lids. He imagined suckling her full breasts, with their generous nipples that had been visible beneath what passed for clothing. In his fantasy, she threw herself on the bed in front of him and opened her long legs in invitation. Before he could enter her, he exploded into his hand.

A feral shriek split the stillness of Maggie's bedroom. Lachlan almost couldn't believe the primitive sound came from him. He caught what he could of his seed in his hand and stood gasping for air, his heart hammering. Semen dripping from his fisted hand tugged him back to the present. He hastened into the bathroom and rinsed himself at the sink before bending to fill the tub.

An hour later, he emerged clean and scrubbed. Lachlan took a last look around the bathroom, marveling at its modern plumbing. He'd let the hot water run until it turned cold. What warmed it was still a mystery, but one he was sure could be easily solved once Maggie returned, and he asked her about it. He donned his shirt and wove his plaid around himself before returning to the front room.

He thought about passing more time in the lass's bedchamber, but it felt perverse to surround himself with her bedclothes and work himself until he spent, again and again.

*Nay, better to wait till I have the real thing.*

Lachlan laughed, pleased with how things were going. The lass was just as besotted with him as he was with her. He'd scented her arousal, seen heat-lust mist her eyes. His cock swelled, and he forced his mind to other things.

He'd just settled into a softly padded chair, mage light suspended off to one side and a book in his lap, when a chill marched down his spine. Lachlan straightened. He hadn't liked the feel of the stray bolt of power, almost as if someone were searching for him. He held himself very still, shrouding his energy. Ach, there it was again, a slow, cautious questing from a well-shielded source that was likely Rhukon. He strengthened his warding.

*"I told you we should've left."*

*"Quiet. The dragon energy is a dead giveaway."*

Lachlan cast a subtle *don't look here* spell, gratified when the alien tendrils withdrew. He sat dead still for long minutes to make certain whatever he'd felt was truly gone. *Did Rhukon find me?* He had no way of knowing.

Kheladin jostled him, radiating displeasure. Smoke curled from Lachlan's mouth. Talons pressed against the ends of his fingers and toes.

*"Stop that. I have to think. I already know ye want out."*

*"Ye can think once we've left this place. I have no desire to be trapped within a space that wouldna hold me if we shift."*

Lachlan gazed around Maggie's small, neat home. Kheladin had a point. The rooms were much smaller than what he was used to, sized more like a peasant's hovel than a proper house.

*Maggie.*

He blew out a sad breath, not fully understanding why the prospect of abandoning her left him so desolate. Maybe it was because she was the first person he'd met upon wakening, yet it felt much deeper than that. Almost as if they'd known one another in a previous life.

*No matter. 'Tisn't fair to remain if I bring danger into her life.* A fierce protectiveness stirred in his breast at the thought of anyone harming the lass. He'd pit himself against anything that harmed so much as an eyelash or frightened her or made her feel uneasy.

*"That's all fine and well. We must leave now, while we still can,"* Kheladin insisted.

*"I agree. I would use magic to transport us back to the cave. What think ye?"*

The dragon was silent so long, Lachlan started to ask again, but Kheladin spoke before he got the words out. *"We will know more outside these walls. The lass's scent muddles things. 'Tis much like a potion."*

Lachlan trusted the dragon's instincts. They were usually sharper than his own. He moved the books on his lap to the floor and got to his feet. Unwinding his plaid, he rearranged his tartan, securing it. That done, he picked up his sword belt and buckled it into place. Nothing more to do but leave. Why was such a simple thing so difficult? He snatched up his cloak.

A note. He owed her at least that. Lachlan strode to the desk and pulled drawers open until he found parchment, though it felt pathetically thin, and a stick he ascertained would write, once he fiddled with removing its end piece. He considered what to say. He didn't want to give her information that might compromise her safety. In the end, he merely adjured her to take care, told her she was a bonny lass, and said he hoped their paths would cross again.

He stared at the piece of paper, came close to crumpling it and starting again, but that damned alien power slammed into his ward. Not subtle this time or questing. Whatever was out there was certain they'd found him—and aimed to do something about it.

Lachlan prepared himself for battle, expecting Rhukon—or one of his minions—to break into Maggie's home at any second. He gathered power, held it balanced between his hands. It sizzled, giving the air a burnt smell. Long moments passed.

*"'Tis trying to lure me outside,"* he told Kheladin. *"'Tis a risk, but a lesser one, to conjure traveling magic."*

When the dragon didn't answer, Lachlan began to chant, warming to his spell. Like everything else, his mage skills—at least the ones demanding more than the simplest magics—were rusty. The walls of Maggie's living room wavered, solidified, and shimmered again. On his third try, Lachlan began to panic. He'd just pulled enough power to light a small town, surely alerting any enemy within a fifty league radius to his presence. If he couldn't transport himself and the dragon to the cave, he'd have to fight goddess-only-knew-who right here. Without Kheladin's help, since there wasn't space to shift.

Sweat ran down his face and sides. It stung where it ran into his eyes. In desperation, he nearly dropped his warding to pour his full power into what should've been a neophyte's spell, when he felt the tightening in his stomach that meant they were in the in-between place—the one that could open to any destination in this world or any other. He realized his eyes were screwed shut and pried them open onto blackness.

"Thank the mother goddess," he breathed, shocked at how weak his magic had become.

*"We're far from safe. Doona disperse your warding as ye were about to do."* Censure rang in the dragon's words. *"'Tis not all you,"* Kheladin continued. *"There's something amiss in this world. It fights against magic. Competes with it."*

*"Bloody good there's a reason."* Lachlan struggled to catch his breath. The darkness yielded to gray, just before the walls of Kheladin's cave materialized around him. He sank into the sand and poured handfuls through fingers that were trying to morph into claws. Lachlan didn't fight the transformation. He welcomed it, unwinding his clothing so it wouldn't end up in a heap of tatters. If wickedness followed them, they were better off in Kheladin's form.

He dropped deep inside the dragon's scaled body and gazed through his whirling green eyes.

With his wings stretched to their full span, nearly touching the sides of the cave, Kheladin trumpeted a challenge. Smoke and fire belched from his mouth. Lachlan reveled in the dragon's strength. The first time he'd experienced Kheladin's latent power, Lachlan got so drunk on it he didn't sleep for days.

*"Look sharp,"* the dragon hissed. *"Something comes. I need you present, not daydreaming."*

Lachlan stretched his senses through the dragon's. Indeed, a subliminal thrumming set his nerves on edge. Without access to Kheladin's preternatural senses, he'd never have sorted it out from stray magical impulses pinging through the ether.

He pushed farther, extending himself to the ragged edges of his ability, amplified by Kheladin's. Someone with great power drew near, yet the power didn't have a corrupt feel about it. A gout of dragon fire scored the far wall of the cave, lighting it bright as day.

*"Hold."* Lachlan made his voice stern. Kheladin ignored him. The next spray of flames shot high into the air. *"Damn ye! Hold. It may not be a foe. We willna know, if ye toast them to cinders afore they set foot on the floor of our cave."*

*"What I felt in the lass's hovel held deep evil. Ye were scarcely subtle getting us here. Your casting left a trail a league wide for them to come after us."*

Lachlan winced at the unpleasant truth. Once upon a time, he'd been a better mage than that—one of the strongest in all of England, Scotland, and the Gaelic kingdoms. He'd regain his ability, but mayhap not quickly enough to save them from ruin. He picked his words with care to secure the dragon's cooperation. *"Aye. I sensed the evil as well. Yet what I feel here is different. If ye'd stop tossing fire about like a lamplighter gone mad, ye could test it for yourself."*

Kheladin grunted. He lifted his great snout and snuffled loudly. Lachlan held his breath, waiting. Rather than speaking internally, the dragon called, "Show yourself. Now. Or I shall burn you to ashes."

Lachlan grimaced. Not the most attractive greeting, but it should do the job. If whoever lurked wasn't their enemy, they should come forth. He had to admit to curiosity. Surely other magic-wielders besides witches had survived through the years he and the dragon slumbered.

"Och aye, and ye've finally come to your senses." The voice was whispery. It echoed at the bare edges of Lachlan's dragon-enhanced hearing.

"Mayhap aye. Mayhap nay." Kheladin breathed out steam. "Show yourself. Ye are still…elsewhere."

A spot in the ether near the pool brightened, pulsated, and flashed so brilliantly, spots danced in Lachlan's vision. When the brilliance fell away, a tall, slender figure clothed in black robes stood stock still. Dark hair fell to his waist. Sharp, dark eyes narrowed. "Ye aren't exactly the last dragon this side of Fire Mountain, but there are not many left," he announced without preamble. "Gwydion and I hunted you for long years. Ye must've lain hidden behind an enchantment."

"Of course I'm not the last dragon on this side of the veil," Kheladin announced with surprising dignity. "There were many when my bondmate and I were ensorcelled. Even unbonded dragons are close to immortal, so there *must* be others." The dragon inhaled noisily and blew out steam. "If ye couldna locate us, mayhap ye couldna locate others, either." He crossed scaled forearms over his chest. "There may be more of us than ye think."

Recognition hit Lachlan between the eyes. *"Tis Arawn,"* he told the dragon. *"God of the dead. Be respectful."* He paused a beat before adding, *"I would converse with him."* Lachlan reached for ascendency, but the dragon fought him.

*"I ken well enough who 'tis. Ye can speak through me,"* Kheladin growled.

*"Not easily. First, I must send the thought to you, and then ye must give*

*voice to it. 'Tis far easier for ye to speak through me when our positions are reversed. Please."* Lachlan heard groveling in his tone but didn't care.

*"We're stronger in my body,"* the dragon insisted.

*"Of course we are, but right now we need information. Let's see what Arawn knows."*

The air next to Arawn brightened. In moments, another man, as fair as Arawn was dark, took form. Deep blue robes fluttered around him. Blond braids hung halfway down his back. Ice-blue eyes flashed in his strong-boned, ageless face. "Gwydion," he announced, bowing low. "At your service. Lachlan, if ye're in there, come forth. Now." The master enchanter brandished a richly-carved staff.

A whoosh of magic buffeted Lachlan. Not waiting for the invitation to be spelled out, he latched onto the offered power and forced a transformation. Kheladin subsided, muttering imprecations. Lachlan strode to the two Celtic gods before his human form fully settled. He bowed so low his forehead brushed his knees before straightening. "Thanks be to Danu, goddess of the Earth, that some with power still live. I havena seen much of this world, yet it seems sadly changed."

Arawn laughed, but the sound lacked mirth or warmth. "Never fear, even if ye canna recognize aught else, evil hasna gone away."

"Tell me..." Lachlan stopped midstream. He wanted to know so many things, he couldn't figure out where to begin.

Gwydion shot a meaningful glance his way. "Ye'll wish to know of the black wyvern—the one responsible for your disappearance."

"Aye, I havena forgotten his treachery." Lachlan drew his lips into a snarl.

Gwydion's features twisted as if he'd bitten into something distasteful. "We've hunted him for many a long year, but he made such a nuisance of himself recently, we upped our ante and dealt him a grievous blow."

"Aye," Arawn broke in. "It happened but a few hours ago. 'Tis likely why ye wakened."

*"If ye fought Rhukon, ye must know where he is,"* Kheladin sniped. *"Tell us, so we may finish what he began."*

"My dragon asked—"

"We can hear him." Gwydion set his jaw in a hard line. "No need to translate. If we knew where Rhukon went, we'd go after him ourselves. The black wyvern, and his crony, the red, joined forces with the Morrigan in all her forms and have been wreaking havoc this past century or two. We get close—and today we were verra near to capturing Rhukon and that dragon of his—but the Morrigan showed up and pitted her strength against us, allowing Rhukon opportunity to escape—again."

"Aye," Arawn cut in. "Today makes three times she's foiled us. That one is a scourge. Far worse than rogue dragon shifters. 'Tis why the air and oceans are poisoned. This world is dying. A few of the Celtic gods have even left. Fighting one of their own isna to their taste."

*The Morrigan in all her forms...*

Fear, an unfamiliar emotion, rocked Lachlan to his bones. One of the oldest tales predicted that when the Morrigan split into Badb, Macha, and Anann, destruction would follow in their wake. "Can aught be done?"

"We doona know." Gwydion spoke softly.

"Yet, we were unwilling to flee this world like rats deserting a foundering ship," Arawn muttered. "Some humans possess strong magic. We've watched over them. Augmented their power. Made certain they wouldna fall to the Morrigan."

"Aye, 'twasna right to toss them to Rhukon or the Morrigan—or any of the other corrupt dragon mage pairs." Gwydion drew his sharply arched brows into a thick, angry line.

"What role have Connor and his red dragon, Preki, played? They fought alongside Rhukon during the battle that ended with Kheladin and me deeply asleep."

Arawn glanced at Lachlan and shrugged. "So far, he's been more of an annoyance. His magic isna verra strong, yet he does augment

Rhukon's efforts. There are other corrupt dragon mages too, but we've only sensed their wickedness. They've escaped precise identification so far."

"Only because we havena expended sufficient energy on that front," Gwydion huffed.

Lachlan cocked his head to one side, mining for unsaid meaning beneath their words. The Celtic gods were notorious for only telling half the story. Nothing he could do at the moment about either Rhukon or Connor. Or the Morrigan.

His thoughts returned to Maggie—maybe a puzzle he could figure out—and he groped for understanding. "I met a woman," he began, seeking a link that seemed elusive. "A witch, albeit a weak one. She, that is, I—"

The Celts watched him intently. Arawn's nostrils flared. "Ye must say whatever 'tis, lad. We canna put the words in your mouth."

Lachlan drew a shaky breath. "'Twill sound as if I'm fey, but I believe this woman and I are linked in some way. 'Tis as if I know her well, despite having just met. She was there when I emerged from this cave. We'd be together still, had she not—"

"Not what?" Gwydion pressed.

Lachlan shook his head. "I doona rightly know. Some magical thing played music. She spoke into it, said she was needed at work, and fled."

Arawn snorted. "A cellular telephone." To Lachlan's confused expression, he added, "I will explain later—to the extent such things are explainable." His dark eyes gleamed hotly. "Ye were a bit of a laggard. Why did ye not bed the lass when ye had the chance?"

"I dinna say aught. How is it ye already know I dinna bed her?" Lachlan's mind raced. Something was afoot, but he had no idea quite what.

"All in good time. I asked my question first."

Lachlan's lips twitched. How like the gods to not pull any punches. "Because she had to leave. She wanted me as much as I wanted her. She said as much."

Arawn and Gwydion exchanged a significant glance.

"What?" Lachlan stared at them.

Arawn nodded half to himself before saying, "The woman comes from a long line of witches. Her father's mother is on her way here right now. She's the head of a powerful coven."

"Oh for the love of Danu, do quit nattering," Gwydion broke in. "I swear, ye'd talk a saint into their grave." He turned to Lachlan. "We've been, ahem, shadowing you ever since ye and Kheladin emerged from this cave. The woman showed up so quickly, we thought it odd and conferred with Bran, god of prophecy. He believes ye and the lass are linked in a way that amplifies all our power."

Lachlan frowned, narrowing his eyes. "Why dinna you show yourselves?"

"We were being polite, waiting until ye bedded her." Gwydion grinned lasciviously.

Lachlan rolled his eyes. "You wanted to watch."

"Aye, that too," Arawn concurred. "More important, though, the tide may have finally turned. This could be the opportunity we've been waiting for to oust Rhukon, the Morrigan, and the red wyvern —and the other corrupt dragon mages as well."

Lachlan envisioned Maggie's lush, blonde hair and dark blue eyes and smiled. "I can think of worse fates than to fuck her—for the good of the world, of course. But the lass may not see it that way. She lusts after me, yet I sense a fierce independence in her."

Arawn snorted. "Aye, 'tis no doubt why Mary Elma is on her way to Scotland."

"Is that the grandmother?" Lachlan asked.

Gwydion nodded. "A lusty wench herself, by all reports. I was thinking of offering myself—as a sacrifice of course—if she were so inclined."

"Two can play that game." Arawn chuckled. "Mayhap she's partial to tall, dark, mysterious types."

"If it wouldna be too much trouble," Lachlan interrupted. "There's much I doona know. Kheladin and I—"

*"Oh, so ye finally remembered my existence."* Sarcasm encased the dragon's words.

"He's right to censure us." Arawn inclined his head. "Apologies, dragon. Let us sit. We shall conjure food and wine and answer all your questions."

"Tell me more about the woman, about Maggie," Lachlan blurted. That he asked about her first surprised him. There was so much he needed to know to survive in a world turned upside down, yet the woman was foremost in his mind and heart. He walked to his shirt, kilt, and boots. Lachlan dressed before following the Celts to a corner of the cave near his clothing chest. He settled with his back against it and waited.

"Bran's prophesy is that your love will save the world," Gwydion said. "I understand it sounds far-fetched, but hear me out."

Lachlan resisted rolling his eyes. Not only did it did sound far-fetched, but highly improbable. How could love possibly do anything to fix the brokenness he'd sensed in his brief sojourn into the year 2012?

# CHAPTER 6

Maggie tossed and turned on sheets damp with sweat. She'd tried to reach her grandmother over and over again, but Mary Elma hadn't answered her voice mails, texts, or pages. During the brief stints when Maggie slept, vivid, disturbing dreams wakened her. She opened her eyes and looked at the window, trying to judge the time by the amount of light creeping around its shades.

"Five a.m.," she muttered. "May as well get up." She yanked her clammy sleep shirt over her head and draped it over a chair back to dry. Feeling dazed, like a sleepwalker, she plodded out of her room and across the hall. She was just bending over to start water for a shower when one of the images from her dreams darkened her vision. It was so real—and so chilling—her heart slammed against her chest.

Fighting vertigo and a roiling stomach, she straightened and grabbed her robe from a hook behind the door. Maggie snugged it around her waist and marched to the living room. She debated making coffee. The caffeine-lift would be welcome, but she was afraid she'd puke it back up.

*It's only another excuse to put off writing last night's dreams down. I need to do that now. While they're fresh.*

Maggie squeezed her tired eyes shut for a moment. She'd taken advantage of the psychoanalytic track in her residency program. Even though very few patients were interested in plumbing their unconscious, Maggie had never been sorry she spent those months studying Jung and the more modern practitioners like Hillman, Woodman, and Von Franz, who'd come after him. She'd kept a dream journal religiously—until she moved to Scotland six months ago. Something always got in the way here in Inverness. Not only did she not know what, she'd never put much effort into trying to figure it out.

She forced her weary mind into action and didn't like the obvious answer that rose to the surface. Something in Scotland blocked her access to her unconscious mind. Well, maybe not totally blocked it. Whatever stood between her and her dreams had done a hell of a job creating enough subtle interference that she hadn't realized it was a problem—until right now. An uneasy breath whooshed out of her. Even though she'd been raised around metaphysical events, this felt too woo-woo for words.

*Why target me? And my dreams?*

Maggie recognized her mental machinations for what they were: just one more excuse to put off analyzing last night's dreams. She sat in her cane-backed desk chair and booted up her computer. As the Microsoft logo flared across the screen, she puzzled further over why she'd stopped writing her dreams down. "It doesn't matter." She spoke aloud to steady herself. Fingers poised over the keyboard, she typed *Dream 1* and then stopped.

*Maybe I could skip that one.*

Heat rose to her face. Her first dream—and the only pleasant one of the night—had been of Lachlan. They were in a medieval stone castle, and she lay on a bower of sweet-smelling flowers. He'd made love to her over and over again with his mouth, knowing fingers, and incredible cock. Though far from a virgin, her dream interlude with Lachlan had been more tangible—and far more intense—than any of her real life experiences.

She frowned. Her fingers moved over the keys with practiced ease as she transcribed how that dream ended. Its bizarre conclusion had jolted her from sleep. She'd been wrapped in Lachlan's arms. He'd been kissing her and telling her he'd loved her throughout time. That he'd been born loving her and would die loving her. A sudden shadow had fallen over them. Faster than she would've thought possible, Lachlan leapt to his feet and spun to face something. She couldn't see because first his human body, and then something else, blocked her view.

Her typing slowed. Maggie clamped her jaws together to stop her teeth from chattering. As often happened once she tapped into psyche—home of dreams—memories swamped her, drawing her deep into their dark maw. Though it had to be some impossible trick of the dream world—a symbolic representation of something she had yet to figure out—Lachlan had turned into an immense dragon with copper scales right before her eyes. The transformation hadn't taken more than a moment. She'd wakened when the dragon opened its mouth and spewed blindingly bright fire at the thing she couldn't see.

Once sleep claimed her again, the next dream was full of foreboding and fear. Lachlan was nowhere to be found. A tall, heavily-muscled man with shoddy good looks, dark brown eyes, and midnight dark locks curling about his shoulders sat next to her. Though he smiled prettily, he exuded evil. She drew away when he reached to stroke her arm. He told her his name was Rhukon, and that he was just like Lachlan. Through a leering grin he added, "If ye like Lachlan, ye'll adore me."

Maggie tried to scramble to her feet but couldn't move. Rhukon enclosed her in arms that felt like steel bands and then closed his mouth over hers. She writhed in desperation. He tightened his arms around her. She bit his tongue and scratched her fingernails down his face and neck as hard as she could. Through it all, she fought the impression that she was living far more than a dream. Things became even more surreal after he drew back and slapped her.

"Holy shit," she muttered. "Right after that, he turned into a fucking dragon too. A black one. What is it with dragons and last night?"

Had he really slapped her? Her hand flew to her cheek, and Maggie jumped up so abruptly her chair toppled to the floor with a crash. She ran to the mirror mounted on the living room wall. Eyes wide, she stared at her face, but it was too dark to see much, so she snapped on a nearby light. Her mouth fell open, and her gut seized. She barely made it to the kitchen sink before her empty stomach spewed bile.

Maggie ran water into the sink and splashed it on her face. She cupped her hands and swished some around in her mouth, spitting out the taste of sickness.

*Impossible. It's impossible.*

Still bent over the sink, she ran a hand along the right side of her face. She'd seen a bruise there. One that would no doubt darken with time. The mark was congruent with the flat of Rhukon's palm and his splayed fingers.

*I was right. That was no dream. I got dragged into some sort of parallel universe.*

Her sense of helplessness was so overwhelming, Maggie could scarcely bear the feel of her own skin. If something was so powerful it could march into her dreams and commandeer her body... She tried desperately to remember what happened after he turned into a dragon but couldn't.

Her phone trilled its text tone. Maggie sprinted for the bedroom and scooped it up. So shaky her breath came in little, panting gasps, she stared at the display. Air swooshed from her lungs when she saw a text from her grandmother. Maggie's eyes filled with tears of relief, but the respite from terror was short-lived. The words were gibberish. She sank onto the bed and stared at them. Had Mary Elma gone mad?

*Shit! For the first time in my life I need my witch heritage, and Grannie's checked out.*

Maggie tossed the phone down. She felt like throwing it against the wall but understood her own vulnerability had mind-tripped her. Fear was a funny thing. Once it got its claws into you, you were screwed.

"Maybe it's not me. Maybe it's something darker. That...thing. The man who wants me would probably really like it if I couldn't communicate with the outside world," she muttered through clenched teeth. Maggie curled into a ball on the middle of her bed and forced herself to take nice, deep breaths, making sure to blow the last one out completely.

It took a few minutes, but she did feel calmer. Calm enough to think. Something nagged at her. She snapped up the iPhone and stared at the text message, mentally rearranging its letters. When she was very young, just learning to read, she and her grandmother played a game where they transposed the alphabet. Sort of like a sophisticated version of Pig Latin.

*Maybe.*

Afraid to let herself hope, Maggie repositioned herself and grabbed her sadly neglected dream journal and a pen from the bedside table. She plumped up a few pillows and propped herself against the headboard. Reasonably comfortable, she went to work on the few words in the text. Once she began, it didn't take long before the strange game she'd played with Mary Elma came crashing back. Maggie stared at what emerged from her grandmother's message.

*You face grave danger. Do the unexpected. The man could help, but he's gone to ground. Until you meet my plane, do not contact me. It compromises us both.*

The tears that had welled earlier overflowed, but she brushed them aside. No matter how bad things were, soon she'd have help from her grandmother, someone who knew how to deal with things when Jung's shadow world came alive. When the bogeyman moseyed from under the bed and stuck out his tongue—or slapped you. She winced and reread the text. *Do the unexpected.*

"Guess that means I'm not going to work today." Her gaze flitted about her familiar bedroom. Shadows menaced from its corners, and she shivered. Never one to wallow—in anything—she got to her feet and started for the bathroom for a second time that morning.

What drew her back this time was her transliteration. She ripped the page neatly from her dream journal, crumpled it, and stared hard at it, willing it to burn.

"Yes!" she crowed as it began to smolder. Maggie dropped it into a ceramic dish and focused harder. The sense of power she felt when the scrap incinerated was heady.

*Heh. Maybe I have more aptitude for this than I thought.*

Once she was certain the paper wouldn't set anything else on fire, she tromped into the bathroom and got under the shower. As she soaped herself and washed her hair, she thought about all the hours her grandmother and aunts had spent trying to interest her in magic. Though she'd cast a few small spells, she never developed her talents—because she hadn't wanted to. Scenes from her childhood bombarded her.

*Damn, I was a stubborn child.*

*Yes, but I had good reasons. I built a wall around my heart after Mom and Dad were killed. I've never really taken it down.*

The warm water cooled perceptibly. She didn't realized how long she'd stood beneath its spray until then. Maggie shut off the jets and dragged a towel off the rack. She buried her nose in it to dry her face, and Lachlan's scent filled her nostrils. Desire knifed through her, so fierce and primal it was all she could do not to scream.

Fear for his safety gnawed at her. *If I'm in danger, it must be because of him. The man who came to me in my dreams obviously knows Lachlan—and hates him.*

"That's it." She stepped from the tub and snapped damp fingers. "That's how I'll spend today. I'll look for him. A good place to start would probably be that sticker bush he was picking his way through when I first saw him."

Maggie clapped a hand over her mouth and looked around her small bathroom. It didn't feel benign anymore. Nowhere in her apartment did. For all she knew, this Rhukon person was hiding behind some sort of psychic veil spying on her. If he could enter her dreams, he could probably invade her living space as well. She did her best to drape a shield around her mental processes—and her body.

*Why the hell isn't any of this witchcraft stuff written down? It would be helpful to have a handbook right about now.*

*Yeah, then I could look up wards. Something stronger than the primitive one I already know.*

Maggie rolled her eyes. Even if such a grimoire existed—and she was practically certain it didn't—she likely lacked some major ingredient, like eye of newt or blood from a freshly-slaughtered goat essential to a successful casting.

She finished drying herself and brushed out her hair, braiding it wet to get it out of the way. It took half an hour to blow-dry, and she didn't think she'd have that kind of time. As she worked, a plan formed in her mind. She'd dress, pack a small bag, and drive to one of the car parks in town. From there, she'd walk to a car rental agency, secure a different car to stymie Rhukon, and see if she could find Lachlan. For a moment she felt like an idiot. As if swapping wheels would thwart a powerful magician.

*It might not slow him down, but it'll make me feel better.*

*Wonder if he knows any more about modern times than Lachlan. If not, I might have more latitude than I think.*

So long as she was en route for Glasgow by midnight, she'd arrive at the airport in plenty of time to collect her grandmother. It was only a hundred seventy miles or so. For a moment, she wondered about the advisability of spending any more time than she absolutely had to in Inverness but shook her head. Lachlan was in trouble. He had to be. If she could do something—anything—to help, there wasn't any choice in the matter.

Not really.

What was that he'd said in her dream? *I was born loving you, and I shall die loving you.* Yes, that was it. A reluctant smile tugged the corners of her mouth. Hell, even Rhukon knew she'd met up with Lachlan—and seemed oddly threatened by it.

*Maybe that's why I never married. I've been saving myself for Prince Charming. If I'd just tuned into my psychic side, I'd have known he'd be along sooner or later.*

*Oh for Christ's sake, give it a break, Hibbins.*

Give it a break indeed. The probable truth of why she'd been blocked from her dreams roared home and left her reeling. Maybe if she'd had access to her psychic side, she'd have found Lachlan long before she stumbled onto him yesterday.

*Too many maybes. I sure hope Grannie can figure this out.*

The older woman started to tell her something the day Maggie mentioned she'd accepted a fellowship in Inverness. In the end, her grandmother shook her head and muttered, "Best not." Despite Maggie's questions, Mary Elma remained close-mouthed.

Maggie shimmied into jeans and a T-shirt. She looked at her sandals and discarded them as impractical. Instead, she fished tennis shoes out from under the bed and put them on over a pair of socks before tightening the laces. Planning settled her nerves. It always had. She'd never been a seat-of-the-pants sort. She didn't like surprises. A snort escaped.

*For someone who's fond of predictability, I've had more than my share of bombshells since I met Lachlan.*

Maggie grabbed a gym bag from behind the door and stuffed a jacket, a sweater, and fresh underwear into it. She stopped by the bathroom and tossed in her brush. It was amazing how little she actually needed.

*Work. What will I do about the hospital? Can I risk calling them on my cell phone?*

She creased her forehead in concentration and chewed on a torn fingernail. It was apparent her grandmother saw any sort of electronic communication as risky, so that left e-mail out of the equation as well.

She walked down the hall and looked in the refrigerator. Because it was fast, easy, and would probably stay down, she made four peanut butter and honey sandwiches, snapped up her bottled tea, and set everything on the table with her gym bag.

What else?

She strode to her computer. Though in sleep mode, it was still on. She didn't save her unfinished dream document and shut the machine down. It was password protected, which might—or might not—keep someone out of it. A shiver tracked down her back. Maggie squared her shoulders against the sudden sensation she was being watched.

Her cell phone trilled. Not the text tone this time. Realizing she'd left it lying on her rumpled covers, she raced down the hall. It took a few moments to find but was still ringing when she stared hard at the caller ID. The hospital.

*Thank Christ! Maybe I can kill two birds with one stone.* "Dr. Hibbins."

"Ach, Doc," Berta said, "'twas afraid I was you wouldn't pick up."

Maggie's stomach tightened. Well-honed instincts told her whatever Berta had to say wouldn't be good. "Whatever it is, just tell me." She infused a calm she didn't feel into her tone.

"Chris tried to hang himself." A muffled sob followed the words.

*Aw, shit.* "Is he in ICU? Did the attending let the family know?"

"Aye to both. Will you be in soon?"

Maggie closed her eyes. Hope of hiding her movements if anyone was keeping tabs on her from behind a psychic veil went up in smoke. The hospital hadn't been in her plans, but she didn't see how she could say no. "I'm not feeling very well this morning. Think I got a mild case of food poisoning, but I'll be in soon. I may not stay long, though."

"Ach. If you're ill, maybe you ought to remain abed—"

"I'm not that sick." Guilt over her lie nipped at Maggie. "I'll be there soon. Make certain someone is with Chris at all times."

"He's sedated."

"I don't care. I want twenty-four hour surveillance until he leaves our care." Maggie grimaced. Her tone was sharper than she meant it to be.

She opened her mouth to apologize when Berta said, "Yes, Doctor," and disconnected.

Maggie stared at the phone. *Christ!* What else could possibly go wrong? She gathered her purse and her gym bag and returned to the living room. After eyeing the sandwiches and tea, she decided it would be best to make more than one trip to her car. On a whim, she plucked her laptop from its spot leaning next to her desk and slid the strap from its case over one shoulder. Feeling like a sneak thief, she unlocked her front door and opened it a crack, craning her neck to peer up and down the empty hallway.

With a small, uncomfortable laugh, she tugged the door shut behind her and chugged down the stairs. No reason to be particularly quiet. If what was after her was some sort of supernatural being, he'd have ears like a lynx. If he even relied on something as prosaic as his five senses.

Keyed up, nerves jangling unpleasantly, Maggie locked what she had in her arms in her trunk and went back into the old manor house. She'd no sooner gotten inside when the heavy front door slammed shut behind her. A cold like nothing she'd ever felt before surrounded her. Frost formed on her eyelashes, her lungs burned, and the small hairs inside her nose felt frozen solid. Rooted in place by panic, she reached for her ward, only to understand she'd loosed it somewhere between her apartment and car.

Maggie tried to resurrect protection around herself, but her teeth chattered so hard, it was impossible to concentrate. *It's illusion,* she told herself, fighting a sick desperation. *Has to be. No way it suddenly plummeted to below zero in here.*

She wrapped her arms around herself, seeking solace in the meager warmth of her body, and visualized heat, lots of it. A whole blast furnace full.

Maggie concentrated. She gave it all she had. Whatever had her trapped in its icy maw receded but then roared back with a vengeance. She bit her lip until she tasted blood.

*I have to try harder. If I don't, I'll die.* She'd no sooner thought the words than she understood the truth in them.

"Goddamn you." She spat, but her phlegm froze before it hit the floor. "Whoever the fuck you are. Leave me alone." Maggie squared her shoulders. To hell with the cold. She drew her lips back from her teeth in a sneer. "You can't bully me with your sick machinations." The words helped. She wasn't any warmer, but strength poured into her from some quarter. "Go. Back. To. The. Hell. You. Came. From." She spaced the words, breathing after each one. Each breath felt warmer. Her lungs began to thaw.

Because she was tuned into her psychic side, she felt something shift just before she heard the words, "Lass, thanks be to all the gods I havena come too late." Out of nowhere, Lachlan swept to her side, and then pushed her gently behind him. He chanted in Gaelic. Moments later, the room's temperature normalized. "Och aye, and he's gone—for now. He willna want to fight the two of us. Not by himself, anyway."

Lachlan turned to her and pulled her against his body. "Ye were brave, lass. No warrior could've been more courageous. Are ye unharmed?" He drew back enough to look her up and down before he bent his head and kissed her.

His mouth on hers was warm, imbued with the life she'd come so close to losing, but she pushed him away. "I need answers more than kisses," she sputtered, reluctant to let go of him. "Who's Rhukon, and why is he after you? While you're at it, what do dragons have to do with all this?"

Lachlan opened his mouth, but Maggie shook her head and laid a finger over his lips. "I'm not thinking. We need to get a couple more things from my apartment. Then we need to leave. There's been a bit of an emergency. We can talk on the way to the hospital."

He followed her up the stairs and through the door of her apartment. The heat of him behind her was full of passion and promise. She wanted to turn around and pull him against her, but there wasn't time. Her gaze fell on the bags of clothing she'd bought for him the night before. "Quick." She thrust them into his arms. "Change into these. You'll be driving into Inverness with me, and it's better if you look normal."

A wicked grin lit his face, melting her heart. God, but he was beautiful with those emerald eyes twinkling. "Aye, lassie. Ye just want to see me buck naked."

"That, too. But this time, I'm not looking. I'm due at the hospital as soon as I can get there."

# CHAPTER 7

*L*achlan gritted his teeth. Far from his absence keeping the lass safe, it actually left her vulnerable to attack. His conversation with the Celtic gods came to an abrupt halt when Gwydion bolted to his feet, face like a thundercloud, screeching, "That bastard. Who would've guessed Rhukon could move so quickly?"

Lachlan didn't waste time asking questions. He'd pulled magic as fast and hard as he could—gratified his power was recovering—and hastened to Maggie's side.

Intensely relieved he'd appeared soon enough to thwart his adversary, Lachlan pulled garments from flimsy bags made of some slick, alien substance. "What is this?" He pinched a bag disdainfully before tossing in onto the floor.

"Plastic. A relatively new invention. Come on, Lachlan, I really do need you to hurry."

He ran his hands over breeks made of a stiff, blue fabric, a softer shirt and another, thicker shirt, and then held up what had to be smallclothes. "Aye, I think I understand just what goes where." Never taking his gaze from her, he laid the new clothes over the arm of a puffy chair and unbuckled his sword belt. Next he unwound his plaid from his upper body and removed his shirt.

By the time his chest was bare, spots of color bloomed on Maggie's cheeks, and he could smell the heat of her arousal from ten paces. She gave a muffled squawk and turned away from him.

"Am I so unattractive ye canna bear to gaze upon me?" The folds of the plaid fell from his body. He folded it carefully, laying it aside, and unbuckled his thigh sheath before working his way into the far less comfortable attire.

"You know damn well that's not it. It's taking every shred of self-discipline I have to stay on this side of the room." Breath rattled against her teeth as she exhaled. "I shouldn't tell you this, but one of my patients tried to kill himself last night. The nursing staff is upset. They need me. I won't stay at the hospital very long, but I have to stop in, check on my patient, and sign orders for his care. It doesn't look good when suicides happen on my watch. People aren't lawsuit-happy here like they are in the States, but that's no excuse not to provide the best care I can."

"I doona quite catch some of your meaning." Lachlan slid into the shorts and T-shirt. He pulled a top made of some soft material that wasn't wool, but felt like it, over his torso and stared at the breeks. They looked as if they'd be uncomfortable as all get-out. He shoved a leg into one side, then the other, and pulled them into place. Because his cock was erect, it didn't want to be stuffed into the confining space behind a row of metal buttons.

"Are you dressed?"

"Mostly. Ye're fairly safe if ye turn about. This fellow ye're caring for, he must be old and sick, eh? When people decide they've had enough of life, 'tis their choice to go far from their loved ones and meet the goddess. I doona understand why ye feel the need to prolong his life beyond—"

She turned slowly and let her gaze sweep over him from head to toe. "Customs have changed dramatically since you were here last."

She waved a hand dismissively. "How society views suicide isn't important right now. Ready?"

He grinned sheepishly. "Not quite. I canna get the breeks buttoned."

Maggie's cheeks turned crimson, and her intense blue eyes zeroed in on his groin. "That's because your, er, uh… Oh, for Christ's sake, I'm an M.D., not a bumbling schoolgirl. Your erection is in the way," she finished. "Push it to the side, and the buttons should go. I'd help…" She quirked a brow. "But I won't make the problem any better."

He half-turned from her and fumbled with his crotch. The buttons finally slipped into their fasteners, but his cock was wretchedly uncomfortable, trapped between his stomach and the rough fabric. Without the smallclothes providing a bit of shielding, the sensation would've been unbearable. "I doona see why a man would choose something like this over a plaid."

If Maggie had an answer for him, she didn't offer it. She handed him the other, thicker shirt and gathered food items from her table. "Let's go."

"Just a minute." Lachlan picked up his thigh sheath and started to fasten it around his upper leg."

Maggie shook her head. "You won't need that, and it defeats the whole purpose of having you in modern garb."

He eyed his sword. "I suppose next ye're going to tell me to leave that behind as well." She nodded. He chafed against leaving his weapons, but in truth, magic trumped steel every time. Lachlan gathered sword and dagger. He placed them against a wall and turned to face Maggie.

"Here." He took a large bottle of amber liquid from her, hoping it was mead, and held the door open. She locked it behind them and vaulted down the stairs. By the time he got to her car, she had the back part open. He put the shirt and bottle inside and got into the car.

She settled behind the wheel and made a few adjustments. The metal monster on wheels rolled toward the street. "I was thinking, while you dressed. The first thing I need to know is who Rhukon is."

"Did he reveal himself to you, then?"

Her lips pursed. "Of course he did. How else would I know about him? He showed up in my dream. See this bruise?" She held her braid back and pointed. "He slapped me, and it left a mark. That's how I knew it wasn't a dream. My grandmother is on her way here to help, but we can talk about that later. Who's Rhukon?"

"The black wyvern."

Maggie blew out a tense-sounding breath. "Okay. So he's a black dragonesque creature. That tells me less than nothing. Why is he after you—and now me?"

"'Tis a long story, lass."

"Give me the short version. I don't have to understand everything, just the essentials."

"Out of all the dragons, a few from each clan are overly attracted to power. The Dragon Council in Fire Mountain tries to corral them, but 'tisn't easy since Fire Mountain is far away, and dragons can live wherever they choose." Lachlan collected his thoughts, wanting to highlight the important bits. "So far, the Dragon Council has either imprisoned miscreant dragons or barred them from returning to Fire Mountain. Dragons value family, so being forbidden contact with other dragonkind is serious punishment."

"How many dragon clans are there?" she cut in. "And what is Fire Mountain?"

"If ye interrupt every other word, I willna be able to tell you aught."

She rolled her eyes. "Sorry, bad habit. I'm used to asking questions. Lots of them. I'll shut up and listen. Promise."

He inhaled, considering how to attack reams of information and distill it into something Maggie could understand. "Dragon clans are based on color. There are several. Red, green, gold, copper, and black. Fire Mountain is the dragons' eternal home. 'Tis where their life was forged in volcanic craters, and where they return to die. It exists on the other side of time. Many dragons chose to live out their years there when things became difficult for them here." He caught her gaze and held it. "'Tis why ye've probably never seen dragons in your lifetime. A few remain, but not many, and they know how to shield themselves from mortal eyes."

"No *probably* about it. I haven't."

Lachlan nodded before continuing. "Danu promised dragons immortality if they bonded with a human mage. The mage becomes immortal through that process as well. Dragons are extremely picky, though, and long-lived enough even without Danu's boon, so they only bond with the strongest magicians. Many doona choose to bond at all."

"Awk! Jesus Christ! You're bonded to a dragon. That's why you turned into one in my dream." Maggie clamped her jaws shut with an audible clack. Spots of color bloomed on her high cheekbones. "Sorry. I really will try to keep my mouth shut."

Lachlan snorted. Maggie being quiet was starting to seem like an oxymoron. He loved her forthright nature, though. "I studied for hundreds of years to strengthen my magic enough to attract a dragon. Not long after I bonded with Kheladin, the black wyvern laid siege to my person and my lands. It never occurred to me he was doing aught but making mischief. Certain dragons always have misbehaved, and rather badly. 'Tis only occasionally been so serious, the Dragon Council told them they couldna return to Fire Mountain.

"With Rhukon, I chalked his meddling up to a particular dragon —my dragon—rejecting him when he attempted to bond with it."

A muscle twitched beneath one of his eyes. It was hard to admit serious miscalculation. By all the gods, he was a warrior. He didn't want the woman sitting a hand span away to see him as weak. His stomach muscles tightened. "There were many things I dinna know back then—"

"Like what?"

"Goddesses' tits, lass, but ye're determined." He pressed his tongue against his teeth, thinking. "I dinna know Rhukon had cast strong magics with the intent of annihilating me. Perhaps 'twas arrogance on my part, but it never occurred to me he'd do such a thing."

"Are any other dragons mixed up in this mess on Rhukon's side?"

"'Tis prescient ye are." He shot her a wry smile. "Malik is Rhukon's dragon. The mage he's closest to is named Connor, and his dragon is a red named Preki." Lachlan waited for Maggie to break in with another question, but she remained silent, so he continued. "Before I returned to your home, I met with Gwydion and Arawn—"

"The Celtic gods, Gwydion and Arawn?" Breath whooshed out of her, making a hissing noise. The car swerved, narrowly missing colliding with another one, and a hellacious blatting filled the air.

Her next words sounded thin, strained. "Surely you must be talking about men like yourself. Others who were trapped in the same time warp that snared you. You couldn't mean the warrior magician and god of the dead."

"What the hell was that hideous noise?" Lachlan stared out the car's windows.

"Just the other guy's horn. I pissed him off, and he honked at us. It's nothing. Go on."

"Aye, I did mean the Celtic gods, but Gwydion is better known as a master enchanter. In any event, Rhukon and Connor—and their dragons—joined forces with the Morrigan. Do ye know who she is, lass?"

Maggie nodded. "The Battle Crow. She's like a goddess of war or something."

Lachlan took a measured breath. "The Morrigan feeds off energy from the dead and dying. She wanted more battles. Bloodier ones. Rhukon and Connor simply wished to rule the world. To do that, they've made things so unpleasant for other dragons that many retreated to Fire Mountain."

Maggie swallowed, the muscles beneath her jaw working. "You

said this Fire Mountain place is somewhere outside of time, so I guess it's not on Earth."

"Nay, lass, 'tisn't."

She cleared her throat. "Recapping here. There's a black dragon, and a red one—both shifters—and the Celtic Battle Crow?"

He nodded. "Arawn and Gwydion intimated there might be other dragon shifter-mage partnerships that have shaded into darkness."

"Oh."

Lachlan kept his gaze on Maggie. The lass looked battle-shocked. "Was aught I said unclear?" he asked softly.

She shook her head. "I feel like I fell asleep and woke up in a fairy tale—and not a very nice one. We're nearly at the hospital. Maybe you should come in with me. You could wait in the lounge. We have a security team in house."

"I'll be better off out of doors, lass. I can make myself invisible."

"You can?" Her voice cracked. "Sorry. That shouldn't surprise me. Not really. Hell, Grannie can do that." She maneuvered the car beneath a sign that said *Physician's Parking*. "I won't be long."

Lachlan wrapped a hand around her wrist. He reached across her body with his other hand and turned her head so she had to look at him. "I know 'tisn't easy, but doona be afraid, lass. There hasna been a chance to speak of this, but we, ye and I, hold a power betwixt us strong enough to unravel the Morrigan's plans."

She gazed at him out of her beautiful, blue eyes, looking troubled. "I had more-or-less figured that out on my own. Something cut me off from my dreams from the time I came to Scotland—"

"Why *did* ye come here, lass?"

"I—" She captured her lower lip between her teeth and shut her eyes. When she opened them, she met his gaze evenly. "I don't have a good answer for you. Something—God only knows what— compelled me to apply for the rural psychiatry fellowship advertised at the hospital here. Even at the time, I knew it was a bad career move. I was done with residency and had received several attractive job offers, offers that wouldn't still be there a year later, once I was done with the fellowship."

"Yet ye came anyway."

Maggie nodded. "It was what I had to do. I tried to explain what I was feeling to my grandmother. She started to tell me something but never did."

Understanding raced through him like a lightning bolt. "Aye. Ye came here to find me. Somehow your grandmother must've realized that." Two white-coated physicians waltzed past. Both stared frankly into the car. Lachlan glared back. "I could show them a thing or two about manners. Young pups without even so much as a ribbon to denote their clan."

"Not a good idea. It'll draw attention you don't want." She pulled away from him. "Look, I really do have to check on my patient. Don't do anything foolish. I need you to be here when I get back."

"Doona worry, lass. I willna stray far from your side again. Ever."

Maggie got out of the car. Rather than his spoken words, the ones she'd heard him say in her dream rang in her mind. *I was born loving you, and I will die loving you.* Before she shut the door, she bent her head and said, "I don't know what this thing between us is, but I want to live long enough to find out."

"That makes two of us." He smiled softly. "Go. The sooner ye go, the sooner we can move on to what we must do next."

"Good that he seems to know what that is," she muttered half to herself as she strode toward the hospital door. She keyed in the code and pushed her way inside. Maggie jogged down the hall, anxious to discharge her duty to her patient and do what she could to soothe Berta and the other nursing staff. It seemed odd they'd be so upset about a suicide attempt. After all, they worked in a mental health unit.

*Maybe it's not like it is in the States. Perhaps suicide's not quite so commonplace here.*

Maggie thought about it. Inverness was fairly rural. While the big, urban areas, like Glasgow and Edinburgh, likely saw their share of suicides, there were probably fewer of them here.

She took a hard left into the ICU. It was a small unit, and she located Chris immediately. Maggie picked up his chart—this hospital was years from an electronic records conversion—and glanced at his vitals. She blew out a tense breath she didn't realize she'd been holding. He was stable and improving. From the looks of things, if they withdrew the IV sedative, he'd regain consciousness.

Maggie pulled up a chair and took Chris's hand. She bent her head and spoke low near his ear. "I'm not certain if you can hear me, but maybe you'll be able to. What you did upset the nurses. They care about you. So do I. We'll be discontinuing the drug keeping you asleep. When you come around, we'll get your family in here, and we'll all put our heads together and decide what will work best. I promise you that you'll have a say in things."

"Now why would you tell him that?" a male voice said.

Maggie whipped her head around. She got to her feet and turned to face Dr. Frank MacDuff, chief of the psychiatry service. In his late fifties, he had a full head of steel-gray hair, sharp blue eyes, and a rangy build. Like most native Scotsmen, he had well-defined cheekbones and an angular jaw. Though he usually preferred dress shirts and slacks, today he wore green scrubs and a white lab coat with the hospital's insignia on its collar.

"Let's talk in the lounge," she suggested.

"No need for that. He's the only patient here, and he's unconscious."

Maggie latched a hand through the other doctor's arm and pulled him away from Chris's bed. "Research suggests patients can hear when they're comatose," she hissed into Dr. MacDuff's ear.

"Aye, I read that paper, too. Never put much stock in it."

"Humor me." She tried a fetching smile and didn't point out that it had been far more than a single paper promulgating that finding. "Come on." She tugged again.

"For a bonny lass, anything."

Maggie would've rolled her eyes, but things were going well, and she didn't want to rock the boat. As they walked to the physicians' lounge, she asked, "What's your suicide rate here?"

"Very few. Less than half a dozen each year."

"No wonder Berta was so upset." Maggie went through the door into the lounge and straight to the teapot. She poured herself a cup. "Would you like one?"

He nodded. They took their tea and settled across from one another in the rather spartan lounge. Medical reference books lined one wall. The floor was linoleum and the walls an industrial green. The ever-present scent of antiseptic was just as strong in here as it was in the wards.

"Were you the one on duty last night when he was found?" Maggie asked.

"Aye, and I've talked with his two sisters. They can't handle him at home. Oh, they say he's fine enough if he's sober. Problem is he's rarely that way anymore."

"I see." Maggie sensed a *fait accompli* and trod lightly. "What did you work out with them?"

"There's an establishment not far from their community in Fort William that caters to men with bipolar disorder and drinking problems. Everyone is in agreement—"

"Except me. I'm his attending, and I didn't know." Maggie couldn't help herself. Outrage flooded her.

"Dr. Hibbins."

*Oh-oh.* Maggie recognized that tone. It was the *I've-been-a-doctor-for-longer-than-you've-been-alive one.* "Yes, sir." She looked away, so she wouldn't seem too argumentative.

"Better," he snapped. "You might want to take a few days off. I'm certain you'll be feeling more…rational once you've had a chance to rest up. I took a look at your timesheets. You haven't taken as much as a long weekend off since you came to work for us."

"Really? I wasn't aware of that. It's just there's so much to learn and I—"

"Americans," he cut in, his tone making it clear just what he thought of people from the States. "Always so driven. You need perspective, Dr. Hibbins."

"Maybe you're right," she murmured. "I'll just check in with the nurses because I promised, and then I'll take the rest of the week off."

"Perfect." He beamed, ill-humor apparently forgotten. "I knew you'd come to your senses. You're just tired. It's why you're wound so tight. My dear." He leaned forward and laid a hand on her knee. "I know just the antidote to physician burnout. Have dinner with me tonight."

*Crap! Just what I need, a middle-aged lothario. But I can't piss him off, either.*

"Thanks for caring about me, Doctor—" She moved his hand off her leg.

"Frank, call me Frank."

Maggie dredged a smile from somewhere. "Sure, Frank. I think I caught a bit of food poisoning yesterday. I was up most of the night, and I'm still feeling a bit under the weather. I'd planned to stop by here, catch a few hours' sleep, and then drive to Glasgow. My grandmother is arriving on an early morning flight."

"Excellent. You have family coming to visit. Another perfectly despicable American trait—estrangement from blood kin. Maybe once you bring her to Inverness, you could be my guests for supper."

"Let's give her a chance to get over jet lag, first." Maggie stood. "If there's nothing else, I'd like to stop by and see the nurses."

"Go on, Maggie. Enjoy your time away."

"Thank you, sir, er, Frank." She scuttled out of the doctors' lounge, so anxious to get away from Frank MacDuff, she could almost taste the relief once she escaped. She'd thought he had designs on her, but thank Christ he kept them under wraps.

Until now.

*Look,* she spoke sternly to herself as she walked briskly toward the psychiatric unit, *whether I complete this fellowship isn't even marginally important. I can always show up from my few days' vacation, give them thirty days' notice, and quit.*

# CHAPTER 8

*L*achlan sank back against the cramped seats in Maggie's car. At first he warded himself, and then he extended his enchantment to include the car, casting a *don't look here* spell. He'd have to keep an eye out for Maggie's return. If he didn't loosen his spell, she might think her car had been nabbed.

*"We must speak with other dragons who returned to Fire Mountain,"* Kheladin said, his voice a quiet rumble in Lachlan's mind. *"The ones here on Earth and on other worlds as well."*

*"I agree. Other tasks take precedence, though. Ye heard the discussion with Gwydion and Arawn."*

*"Aye, but I dinna agree with much of it."*

Lachlan shook his head. The dragon was willful and headstrong, yet he had a pure heart and a generous soul. *"If we canna get this problem with Rhukon, the Morrigan, and the red wyvern—Connor—well in hand, 'twould be an excellent time to call on your kin for assistance."*

*"We could live in Fire Mountain. Gwydion told us other dragon shifters went there with their dragons."*

Lachlan's eyes widened. That option hadn't even occurred to him, though he'd certainly heard what Gwydion said. While Lachlan had traveled outside the British Isles, so far as he was concerned the

Scottish Highlands were his home. Despite their current level of contamination with modernity, he had no desire to leave. Because he didn't want to hurt Kheladin's feelings, he said, *"Aye, 'tis a possibility. At the verra least, we could plan a visit."*

A long silence ensued. Lachlan gave the dragon space. When he finally spoke, he said. *"I'd like that. Ye willna forget?"* Kheladin's fretful tone didn't sound at all like him.

*"Nay. I promise. If there's a way for us to visit Fire Mountain, I shall do everything in my power to make certain it happens. In the meantime, surely we can locate dragons who havena been tainted by evil on this side of the time veil."*

*"If they're here, they're well hidden,"* Kheladin groused.

Lachlan inhaled through his mouth, tasting the air. It held a metallic undercurrent that stung his nose and dried his throat. Without fully understanding the why of things, he thought about what Gwydion and Arawn had shared. The conversation was brief, but they'd hit a few salient points. Water was fast disappearing from many places on Earth, and species were dying every day. Manmade chemicals were well on their way to poisoning the oceans and the air. Brighid, Danu, and Ceridwen, most powerful of the Celtic goddesses, were so furious, they'd washed their hands of humans.

Lachlan shook his head. How could things have gone to hell in so little time? Humans had been around for thousands of years. According to Gwydion, it took less than a hundred to wreak the current disaster.

*'Twas the Morrigan's prodding. She thrives on chaos. Rhukon and Connor are merely bit players she snared to move her scheme forward.*

Lachlan ground his teeth together. He could just see Rhukon and the Morrigan chortling with delight over the disaster they'd created, with Connor cheering from the sidelines.

According to Arawn, humans had welcomed one convenience after another into their lives, apparently not paying one whit of attention that all their labor-saving amenities were destroying Earth. Lachlan felt infuriated and incredulous by turns. Had men turned into such stupid fools they'd sully the very ether that sustained them? His hands were fisted so tightly they ached. He stretched out his fingers to get circulation back into them and thought about the rest of what the Celts told him.

With Rhukon and Connor by her side, the Morrigan was in her element during various wars riddling Europe, Asia, the States, and the Middle East. Flitting from battle to battle in her crow form, she'd positively glowed as blood dripped from her beak and feathers.

Long ago, Arawn and she had an alliance. It was a logical coalition since she chose who was to die in battle, and he was god of the dead. Lachlan asked Arawn about it, but the god waved him to silence, saying, "The partnership has eroded beyond hope of repair."

Lachlan took stock. The world was in serious trouble. In a large part, it was a result of Rhukon, Connor, and the Morrigan. For some curious reason, no one opposed their efforts to sow disorder. He asked the Celts why the gods hadn't stepped in. Gwydion raised a bushy brow and reminded him, "We doona trouble ourselves with mortal concerns."

"Even if the world is at stake?" Lachlan asked, finding it hard to believe they'd turn a cold eye in the face of such a major disaster.

"Even if," Arawn concurred. "We can always retreat to the *Dreaming*. Some Celts already have."

Probably egged on by the Morrigan—or maybe because he was feeling invincible—Rhukon finally made a significant error. In dragon form, he'd rained fire on a gathering of the Celtic Gods. They fought back, driving both black wyvern and red from the skies, but they hadn't been able to capture them once the Morrigan flapped her way into the melee.

*Aye, 'twas only then, when Rhukon was hard pressed, that he withdrew power from the magic keeping Kheladin and me ensorcelled.*

Lachlan knit his brows together. He'd give a lot to know which god or goddess was behind making certain Maggie got to Scotland. *Mayhap not a god. Perhaps 'twas that witchy ancestry of hers. Magic-*

wielding humans all had agendas, and their magic had a mind of its own. Sometimes everything meshed. More frequently, the witches, druids, and human magicians ended up at cross purposes.

He rolled first one shoulder and then the other. The car was deucedly uncomfortable, and it was becoming unpleasantly warm from sun reflecting off its glass. He craned his neck and looked out all the windows. The parking area appeared empty. He spoke a word to sever his spell, making certain no one saw Maggie's car appear where nothing had been seconds before. Manipulating the door handle, he got out and stretched to his full height. Even if the air stung his lungs, it was still better than being folded like a child's doll in a metal box.

A few trees grew next to the building Maggie had disappeared into. He walked over to them and laid his hand on a large ash's trunk. The tree sang into his mind, grateful for the touch of one with earth magic. Lachlan let his thoughts drift to Maggie. Heat flared in his loins, mingled with tenderness and a savage protectiveness. He'd never met a lass such as her. Women from his own time were more...submissive to men's suggestions.

The way Maggie gazed right at him—and broke in whenever she wanted to say something—made him proud of her mettle. The lass must be made of steel to survive a dream visitation from Rhukon. Doubtless, the black wyvern had planned to enter her dream and shanghai her.

*What happened? How did she fight him off?*

"Hey!" Maggie's voice trilled from behind him. "I thought you were going to wait in the car. I nearly had a heart attack when I got there, and you weren't in it."

Lachlan spun and opened his arms. She shook her head. "Not here. It's best if we leave before anyone sees you."

He cocked a brow. "Really? But I'm dressed as ye wanted."

"That's not it. I just don't want anyone asking questions. The Scots think I'm odd enough as it is."

He snorted. "Aye, and I can see how they might." He followed her back to her vehicle and got in. "Can we park this somewhere near where ye found me yesterday?"

"Sure." She started the noisy thing that made the car go and spun its wheel. The metal monster obligingly headed out of the parking area.

"How did ye defeat Rhukon in your dream?"

"Huh?" She glanced at him.

"Your dream. How did ye get away from Rhukon once he hit you?"

"I don't know. He turned into a black dragon. After that things just disintegrated. I fought him, did my damnedest to hurt him before he morphed into a dragon—and then I woke up."

"Humph." Lachlan thought about what she'd just said. "It sounds as if something moved his attention away from you."

She bit her lip. "Do you know what he planned to do with me?"

"Not entirely, but he will want to keep you and me away from one another."

"Why? You never explained anything about that part."

"Nay, I dinna. And I willna now. Bear with me, lass. I'll take you to a place where we may speak freely. I control its magic, now that I've rid it of Rhukon's taint and built stronger wards with the help of the Celts."

She pulled up near the side of the roadway. "Okay. I'm game. We have to be on the road to Glasgow, but not until midnight."

"But it takes days to get to Glasgow—without magic," he protested.

Maggie smiled with full, sensual lips. "We don't need magic." Her expression intensified the classic bone structure in her face, bringing her cheekbones into stark relief. Her beauty took his breath away. "We have a gasoline-powered engine. Shouldn't take us more than three-and-a-half hours. There won't be any traffic in the middle of the night."

Lachlan nodded slowly. "Doona mind me. I can see where this

contraption," he tapped the car's door, "wouldna take all that long to transport us sixty leagues."

A musical laugh filled his ears. "Wait until you see airplanes." Apparently responding to something she saw in his face, she elaborated. "They're long, silvery metal tubes that fly through the air at six hundred miles an hour—carrying several hundred people. That's how Grannie's getting here. If it were a shorter distance—without an ocean to cross—she'd probably have just channeled coven magic."

Trying to picture what Maggie described felt impossible. His mind balked at the visual. He got out of the car and waited for her. "Come stand by my side, lass."

"Sure. Which way are we going?" She moved next to him, all vibrant warmth and soft curves. She carried a leather bag over one shoulder and had a dark gray sweater tied around her waist. Lachlan wanted to pull her into his arms but resisted the temptation. Once he laid hands on her, he'd never be able to let go. Besides, there'd be time to hold her and explore her lush woman's parts in Kheladin's cave.

He glanced around. People were everywhere. Casting a spell was risky where someone might see them disappear. He looked toward the clumps of gorse and thistle that hid the entrance to his cave. A dense grove of beech and ash grew off to one side. Lachlan pointed at them. "Over there."

Maggie took his arm. He leaned toward her and breathed in the mingled scents of hair and skin. His groin stirred immediately, but his cock was cramped inside the stiff fabric of the breeks. It had taken forever for him to soften once he'd donned the strange trousers. He had no wish to repeat the experience, but his cock swelled anyway.

Lachlan drew Maggie close. Together, they strode into the circle of trees. Once within the protective ring of boughs, Lachlan realized it was the sacred band of beeches alternating with ash that he'd planted in front of his castle. Moving from one tree to the next, he laid a hand on each of their trunks. They trilled and cooed their pleasure.

"You act like you know these trees." Maggie pitched her voice low.

"Aye, I planted them. They sat just within my courtyard." He melted deeper into the grove and beckoned to her. "What this means is we'll be safe from prying eyes. The trees shall see to it. I'll draw magic to move us from this place. Ye must come into my arms. 'Twill feel strange—not my embrace but my magic. Doona fear. The world will dissolve and reform, but the whole of it will happen verra quickly." He opened his arms.

She came into them, and joy sluiced through him, mixed with intense sexual heat. "Hurry." Her voice was thick. Lachlan wasn't certain if she were afraid or as anxious as he to get to more private surroundings.

He thanked the trees for remembering him and asked for their protection. That done, he cast the spell to transport them from the grove to Kheladin's cave. He tightened his arms around Maggie. She was trembling. He gazed down at her, ready to mouth calming words until he saw the determined set of her jaw and the fire in her smoky blue eyes.

Lachlan smiled and kissed her forehead. He'd found a modern warrior, akin to the Valkyries of old. He snorted, amused by the comparison.

"What?" She stared at him boldly.

"Ye're beautiful. Take a deep breath, and doona fight the casting."

THE BOTTOM DROPPED out of Maggie's stomach, rather like a carnival ride, and the day darkened. Moments later, a very different scene rose before her. Being encased in Lachlan's magic felt soothing, not nearly as frightening as she'd feared. Her feet touched something solid. "Is it safe to move?"

"Aye, lass. Welcome to Kheladin's cave. 'Twas our prison for many a long year." A warm, blue globe materialized next to his head.

Maggie flicked at it, not surprised to find its surface cool. "Grannie makes light like this. I need to learn. Did you excavate the cave or was it natural?"

"Kheladin and I built it after we first bonded. There was already a natural cavern here, but we enlarged it. He needed a place for his hoard and a retreat when life in the castle felt too busy and overwhelming."

"Is that your dragon's name?"

"Aye, 'tis."

"I'll bet neither of you imagined how *busy* or *overwhelming* life could get." She walked briskly away from him, looking at things as she went. He followed her so she'd have access to his light. "Oh my God," she exclaimed and hunkered next to a pile of gold coins. She picked one up and examined it. "There must be a small fortune in here." Straightening, she held the doubloon next to his mage light. "Fifteen eighty-three, with a likeness of the King of Spain."

"Why did ye never develop your magic?" He closed a hand over the one holding the gold coin and held her gaze with his.

"Magic killed both my parents. They were fighting a rival coven and ended up as collateral damage. I had a much older brother—never knew him very well—who lost his life in the same fight. I was only a little girl, but I developed an antipathy for something that could rob me of my family in the blink of an eye." Maggie stopped to breathe. Even now, decades later, talking about it still hurt. "When my periods started, and the women wanted to indoctrinate me, I fought them."

Lachlan nodded. "I'm hoping ye can lay your qualms aside. Ye'll need every shred of power ye can lay hands on afore this is over." He let go of her. "Go ahead, lass. Look about. Ye needn't be shy. Put the coin back, though. 'Tis best if ye doona rearrange Kheladin's treasure overmuch." He bent, tugged his pants legs up, and proceeded to unlace first one boot, and then the other, while she gawked at the underground cavern.

Maggie replaced the doubloon before she half-turned toward him. "Why are you taking off your boots?"

He winked at her. "I wish to feel sand beneath my toes. It reestablishes my connection to Danu and the Earth. Go." He made shooing motions with both hands. "Wander about."

Maggie fought a sense of unreality as she gazed at the space where Lachlan had slept the last three hundred plus years away. It was warmish underground, and she heard water running in the distance. The cave was large, maybe a hundred feet by a hundred-fifty. When she looked up, she couldn't see its roof. The air above her darkened, retreating into infinity. Maggie continued her transit of the cave. In addition to gold, jewels littered its floor and were placed in alcoves. Many were huge, fist-sized gems in a rainbow of colors.

"Ye asked about how we're bound." Lachlan's voice rumbled, echoing slightly off the cave's walls.

"Yes, I'd like to know that." Maggie walked to his side and laid a hand on his arm.

"I never married. At first, I was too busy doing what young men do." He grinned rakishly. "And then I focused all my energy honing my mage skills so a dragon would accept me as a bondmate. From my earliest rememberings, though, I dreamed of a lass such as you."

Maggie cocked her head. "Why didn't you look for me, er her?"

"I dinna believe she was real. I thought 'twas my guilt over not taking a wife and doing my part to produce bairns so Clan Moncrieffe wouldna die out."

"Dreams are subject to many alternate interpretations." She started to tell him a little about her training but decided it wasn't important.

"Aye, true enough." He inhaled sharply. "This next may be difficult for ye to ken, but Gwydion drew magic and looked within me. He believes the dream was a call to action, that ye are my soul mate, and we have been bound through many lives. If that weren't enough, Arawn not only concurred, but said if I hadna been so stubborn in my pursuit of the arcane arts, I would've heeded my dreams, sought ye out long since, and wedded you."

Maggie tried to quiet her racing mind. Though it wasn't much more than sixty degrees in the underground cavern, a fever raged through her. "How would finding me three hundred plus years ago have made any difference?" She chewed on her lip. Who the hell had she been in 1683? She'd avoided past life regressions the same way she avoided witchcraft.

"We form powerful magic between us, once we've mated, that is" He shut his eyes for a moment. When he opened them, they gleamed fiercely. "Enough to right many of the wrongs in this world."

*Could that possibly be true?*

"It feels like I tumbled down the rabbit hole into Wonderland." She swallowed hard.

"Lass?" Lachlan sounded confused, as well he would, since Lewis Carroll had lived and died while he slumbered. Though he wasn't touching her, she felt an electric heat from his presence. The air between them was thick with both it and with his heady scent. Exotic and intoxicating, it pushed the danger they faced away from center stage.

"It doesn't matter." She wound her arms around him and tilted her head back. Maybe this respite would be all she'd ever have with him. She'd be a fool to let it slip through her fingers. Her nipples hardened against his chest, and her throat was dry. Desire so sharp it had form and substance balled in her belly.

He gazed down at her, his green eyes on fire with something she didn't have a name for. Lust blazed in their depths. Behind the sexual heat, a ferocious strength glowed, brighter than diamonds. *Am I seeing his dragon nature?* The thought thrilled her. She ran her tongue over dry lips. "Aren't you going to kiss me?"

Lachlan laughed. The sound was rich and warm. "Aye, lass.

Kissing and far more, I hope." He ran his hands down her arms, touching her as if she might break.

She tightened her grip on his shoulders and moved her hands down his back. With a throaty moan, he crushed her against him and lowered his mouth over hers.

# CHAPTER 9

*L*achlan tasted her witch's blood in the kiss, and he felt magic running through her veins like quicksilver. *Such power,* he marveled. *How could she turn her back on it?* His tongue tangled with hers, and the scent of her intensified, rising around them. She smelled of wildflowers and mead. Of honey and springtime. Her nipples pressed against his chest, hard as agates. She reached higher and twisted her hands in his hair. The combined rasp of their breathing was loud in his ears, louder than the pounding of his blood, more urgent than the fire thrumming a tattoo in his loins.

He slid his hands lower and cupped the curves of her ass. Where most lassies were soft, Maggie was hard, tight with muscle. She hooked a leg around one of his, and he felt the heat of her center as she pushed herself against his leg, moaning softly. Lachlan broke their kiss. "Lass. 'Tis been long since ye've lain with a man. I see it in your mind. Why? Do men from your time not appreciate your beauty?"

"I don't want to talk. Not now." Her words sounded garbled, as if she were underwater. She thrust herself against his leg.

If he were any judge of things, she was on the edge of spending.

Her head fell back on her long stalk of a neck. Her marvelous blue eyes fluttered shut, and crimson markings splotched both cheeks. He ran his mouth down the side of her face with gentle, nibbling kisses to get himself under control. If he didn't rein his lust in, he'd shove her to the cave floor and have done with things. That wasn't the way he wanted their first time to be. Nay, he wanted flowers and a bower lit with hundreds of candles. He wanted the Celtic marriage ceremony to bless their joining.

"Maggie." He unwound her leg from around his thigh and laid a hand on each of her hips. "Lass." The word stuck in his throat. What could he say that wouldn't make him seem less than a man? "I want this to be special for us. When we join our bodies, 'twill also join our hearts and souls. For that we need someone to bless our union."

"What?" Her eyes were glazed with yearning. "You want to find a priest? Didn't you Celts shun organized religions?" She made a grab for the front of his breeks. Her hand closed around his erection. "You want me. I want you. What could be simpler?" Her fingers worked the breek's buttons and pushed inside the confining material. She extracted his cock from its trouser-created hell.

Her hand felt exquisite on him. He pushed into her fingers, and all his carefully crafted resolve blew away like so much chaff. "If 'tis so simple, why have ye kept to yourself for so long?"

"I was busy." She bent toward him and licked his neck, while knowing fingers milked his shaft. Somewhere along the way, she pushed the breeks down his legs, and he stepped out of them.

Lachlan's balls tightened. He laid a hand over hers and pried her fingers off his cock. "I'll spend if ye keep that up."

She eyed him. "Yes, that's the general idea. I'm so hot, I can't think. We need to do this, you and I, so we can keep moving forward." Maggie grasped his face between her hands and forced him to look at her. "I know you want me. Why are you suddenly acting like a nervous bridegroom?"

Heat moved from his belly up his chest and neck. "I would see us wed, lass. To start our life together properly."

She knit her brows together, frowning. "We barely know one another. You believe in some ancient prophecy that says we belong together. I'm still trying to absorb all this. At least in my time, the custom is for a man and woman to spend time talking, getting to know one another, having sex together. Then, if all that feels right, they seal the deal."

"Seal the deal? Ye make it sound like buying a flock of sheep from the neighboring estate."

She snorted and then laughed. "See. Perhaps that's why I haven't had any lovers for a couple years. I'm too matter-of-fact for romance." She shrugged and had the grace to look embarrassed. "Maybe that's something you need to know about me before you tether your star to mine."

Maggie took a step back. Her eyes lit with mischief and frank, sexual need. Reflected by his mage light, they glowed like exotic blue gemstones. In one fluid motion, she took hold of the bottom of her shirt and yanked it over her head. Before he could stop her, she undid the scraps of cloth holding her breasts and dropped them atop her shirt. With an expression worthy of Aphrodite, Maggie raised her hands over her head, and thrust her chest toward him.

Lachlan's throat thickened. It was almost impossible to breathe around the thrum of blood racing through his body. "Ye are truly bonny," he managed, though his tongue felt clumsy and stupid. He couldn't tear his gaze from her breasts. They rode high on a sculpted ribcage. Red-brown nipples puckered, begging for the touch of his lips.

She ran her tongue over her lips and circled one peaked nipple with her own fingers. "It would feel ever so much better," she said around quick inhalations, "if your hands were touching me. I know what mine feel like." She rubbed one foot against the other and toed off her shoes.

His cock felt like an iron bar curved against his stomach. If he did nothing, he'd spend anyway. His balls were too full to be denied. He took a step toward her and then another. "Do you have a bed in here?" She moved her other hand between her legs. "Because if you don't, the floor will work just fine."

Lachlan's control snapped when she touched her core. He surged forward and latched his mouth over one of her breasts. He licked and suckled until she squealed with delight, and then he moved to the other. He lost count of how many times he switched sides. Her hands found his cock again. This time, she closed both of them about him. His lust was like a knife on a grindstone, honed to the sharpest edge.

He raised his head and claimed her mouth again. Tongue buried in her mouth, all he could think about was sinking another part of him deep in her body. He reached between her legs. The heat of her center was like an electric shock. With shaking hands, he fumbled with the unfamiliar fastenings of her pants. And then she was helping, and the soft fabric slithered down her hips. He pushed a hand between her legs again and rubbed her sensitive nub, slick with her arousal. His fingers slid deeper, entering her body. He was about to pull back and push inside her again when her muscles clenched around his fingers and clenched again.

She was coming, and he rubbed the seat of her woman's pleasure with the other hand to intensify her sensation. When her body quieted, he pulled his fingers from her and sucked her sweetness from them. She sank to her knees before him, twitched his smallclothes out of the way, and took him into her mouth.

Lachlan groaned and buried his hands in her hair. Her mouth felt silky, scorching as she suckled his ridged flesh. He showed her the motion he needed. It didn't take long, maybe half a dozen strokes in and out of her mouth, and his balls snugged against his body. She must've known how close he was, because she upped the pressure and grazed the delicate skin around the head of his cock with her teeth. Control fled and pleasure spewed out of him in hot, burning jets of ecstasy. Maybe he should've spilled his seed on the cave's floor, but she didn't give him any choice, holding him closer once the first spurts flooded her mouth.

He joined her on the floor and pulled her body full length against his, murmuring brokenly in Gaelic. He kissed her and tasted the sharp flavor of his semen. His cock, which had barely deflated, sprang to attention instantly. He strung kisses lower until his mouth hovered over the junction between her neck and shoulder. Lachlan sank his teeth into sensitive flesh until he tasted blood. He drew back and licked the wound clean, sealing it with magic.

"What are you doing? I've heard of love bites, but—"

"Ssht, lass." He rolled onto his side and smoothed wild locks that had escaped from her braid away from her face. "Ye know I'm a dragon shifter. Kheladin reminded me of his part in the mating ritual."

"But we haven't actually had sex yet. Although," she moved a hand between them and curved it around him again, "it looks like we could. You've got plenty left where the last climax came from." She smiled devilishly at him and pushed her hips against his body suggestively.

"Gwydion could marry us."

"I'm sure he could, but he's not here now, and we are." She turned her blue gaze on him. "From what you said earlier, the sooner we make love, the sooner that powerful magic will start brewing."

Lachlan started. What she said was true, so why was he staving off such an important joining?

Knowledge hit him like a runaway carriage. Somehow, against hope and reason, Rhukon was still within these walls. Maybe not all of him but enough to subvert the magic that would eventually be his undoing. For some unknown reason, Maggie was immune to the black wyvern's magic. *Thank the goddess for small favors.* Even Kheladin was doing his part by forcing the mating bite.

Lachlan fanned magic around them, creating a double warding. If he was correct, Rhukon would intensify his efforts the moment Lachlan sank himself into Maggie's willing body.

"Well?" She gazed at him through eyes that looked ancient beyond measure.

He didn't answer with words, just pulled her close. He rolled her body atop his and guided himself home inside her. When the heat and warmth of her body closed around him, it was all he could do not to shriek his joy. The sensation was so intense, he rushed toward a precipice. There'd be no control, no gradually bringing the lass to peak after peak while he controlled his lust.

"Ride me," he gasped through gritted teeth. "Take your pleasure. I willna last. Not this time."

She sat over him, ribcage arched like a bow. Her head fell back, showing the cords in her neck. Blonde curls cascaded around her body as her braid disintegrated. She twirled her nipples with both hands and pushed her nubbin against his pubic bone.

Dark magic battered Lachlan's ward with a fury, but Rhukon wasn't strong enough to break through. And then nothing mattered but Maggie, the heat of her, the musk of her arousal, her hands that had moved to grip his shoulders. His cock bucked and shook as he came again. Maggie screamed when she peaked, the sound deep and primal with need. Her muscles milked him, intensifying his climax tenfold.

She collapsed atop him, breathing hard. Lachlan closed his arms around her and held her tight, his shuddering cock still buried in her body. The deed was done. She was his.

Maggie turned her head to one side and said, "I felt something… evil trying to get us."

"Aye, lass. But he dinna topple my wards." Lachlan repositioned them so they were lying on their sides with him still inside her. He stroked her cheek with one hand. "It took me a while, but I finally realized part of my reluctance was Rhukon's intervention."

She crinkled her nose and laughed. "Oh ho! Now you've had me, you're not so certain about that marriage proposal."

"Nay, lass, not at all—" he began, before he understood she was teasing.

"Good. Because now I've had a taste of you," she contracted her cunny muscles around him, "I'm probably spoiled for any other man, ever."

"Only *probably*? Ye'll never have another man—"

"Pfft. Stop. Don't go all Neanderthal on me. If I could go years without fucking anyone, I don't think it's a big risk that I'll suddenly turn into a hoyden and screw everything that moves. Besides." She laid a hand over his on her cheek. "I like you. A lot. And I trust you, which is more important than almost anything."

Lachlan's head spun. He needed a dictionary to translate some of what Maggie said. "Aye, lass. Trust is important. So is this." He flexed his shaft and was rewarded with a squeeze from her.

"Ah, whoops." She bit her lower lip. "We should've used something. I'm not taking birth control anymore. Why would I be, since I didn't plan to break my sex fast with anyone?"

"I only understood part of that. If ye're worried about bairns, I control when my seed creates life. 'Tis one of the lesser magics and easily mastered."

"Okay." She nodded. "That's one less worry, but they had sexual diseases back in the sixteen hundreds. You may have called it some sort of pox."

Lachlan drew back, struggling with righteous indignation. *She canna know I'm immune to such things,* he reassured himself. He clamped his jaws and made an effort to speak calmly. "The same magic that allows me to determine when I create new life also tells me if a woman is infected with disease. I would never—"

"Never mind." She patted his hand. "I should've known." The corners of her mouth twitched into a smile. "I was too swept away by your considerable charm to bother to check. Witches have a similar radar. We're good at avoiding anyone with communicable diseases. And at protecting ourselves if we have to have contact. It's one of the few magics I cultivated."

"Why would ye pick that one?" He shifted to a more comfortable position, and his cock slipped from her body.

She rolled to a cross-legged sit. "It will take a while for you to learn about all the ways the world changed while you slept. I told you I'm a doctor. We spend most of our time with sick people. While I was in medical school, and my first year of training after that, I spent a lot of time in hospitals. It was convenient not to fall prey to staph, strep, and other bacterial infections when they ran rampant."

"Bacterial infections?"

Maggie grinned at him. "Aye, wee beasties that get inside your body and make you sick."

Lachlan chuckled. It morphed into a full-blown laugh. "Now ye stop that. I'll admit ye can do a credible Highland accent, but I prefer it when ye sound like yourself." She shivered. "Ye're cold."

"Yes, and hungry, too. Do you have food down here?"

"There's cold, pure water from a spring, but for food, we shall need to return to the world above."

She looked around her, shuddered again, and reached for her discarded clothing. "I still feel it."

"Feel what, lass?"

"It's hard to describe, but it's like a dark shadow scrabbling at the edges of something you have draped around us."

"*The lass is perceptive,*" Kheladin said.

"What was that?" Half into her top, Maggie whipped her head around.

"Kheladin."

"Oh right. Your dragon."

Lachlan thought about it and murmured, "I think he would say I'm his human."

"Regardless." She flowed to her feet in one easy motion and reached for her pants. "Why can I hear him?"

"Because ye're bonded to the both of us."

She gifted him with a curious grin. "Hmm…sounds kind of kinky." Apparently reading his confusion, she clarified, "It means sexually deviant."

*"I resent that."* The dragon stirred within him. Lachlan fought back steam and smoke that threatened to pour from his mouth.

He got to his feet. *"'Tis just that she doesna understand. Times have changed since ye and I walked the Earth."*

"I don't know if *I can manage telepathic speech.*" A broad grin wreathed her face. *"Hey! I'm doing it. Anyway."* She bowed slightly. *"I meant no offense. I was being a smartass, er, sarcastic. I was being sarcastic. It was uncalled for, and I'm sorry."*

"Apology accepted," Kheladin said. *"Ye carry my mating bite. Ye belong to us now. Both of us."*

*"I'll do my best to be worthy of the honor."* She swiped at cheeks damp with sudden tears. *"Sorry. Guess my emotions are pretty close to the surface. When do I get to see you?"*

*"If I had my way—"*

"Soon," Lachlan broke in. *"Verra soon."*

She cocked her head to one side. *"Witches live for a long time—often hundreds of years—but certainly not forever. Are you certain you both want me in your lives? Maybe an immortal woman might—"*

Lachlan was by her side in an instant. The lass was skittish as an unbroken colt. He wrapped his arms around her and stilled the rest of her words with a kiss he hoped would put an end to *that* line of thought.

Maggie gathered the rest of her clothes, shrugged into her jacket, and bent to push her feet back into her shoes. Lachlan picked up his breeks. He considered chucking them and getting another plaid from his clothing chest, but the lass thought it important for him to blend in.

"Do ye suppose we might purchase something that isna quite so tight?" He grinned sheepishly. "If I dinna have a constant cockstand around you, 'twouldn't be such a problem."

"Sure." She grinned back. "I had no idea how big your, um equipment was when I went shopping for you—or that it would be hard all the time. Although I must admit the shop girl and I had the most delightful conversation imagining what you might look like."

Maggie lowered her voice. "I promised her I'd report in if—" A low rumble filled the air, dust rose around them. Her eyes narrowed. "Rhukon?"

"Aye. I fear he's doing a better job blocking the tunnel than he did last time."

"That won't be a problem, will it?"

Lachlan drew the breeks up his legs and fastened them. Then he pulled Maggie against him. The lass was trying to sound brave, but he heard a tremor in her voice. "Nay, lass. I can use magic to move us out of here. Gather your things."

She ducked from under his embrace and picked up her bag and sweater, tying it around her waist. "I have everything."

Exhorting the dragon to lend his power, Lachlan wove complicated magic. Their underground location meant he couldn't simply blast Rhukon to the ninth circle of Hell without compromising the integrity of the cave's structure. Though he'd told Maggie about the red wyvern and the Morrigan, he didn't mention them now. No reason to alarm her since he didn't know if they were a part of Rhukon's current maneuvering.

In truth, he was absolutely certain he didn't command enough power to subvert the red and black wyverns and the Morrigan. If he and Kheladin couldn't spring them from the cave, he'd have to find a way to reach Gwydion and Arawn.

Because it couldn't hurt, and the lass needed to develop her power, he bent close. "I know ye're green as the grasses that dot the moors, but look through your third eye, and add your power to mine when I ask for it."

# CHAPTER 10

$\mathcal{M}$aggie balled her hands into fists so hard her nails cut into her palms. It didn't take magic, or her well-honed intuition, to tell her Lachlan was holding something back. For him to ask for an infusion of power from her must mean things were far more desperate than he was letting on. She stared at him. His hands interlaced in intricate patterns, and the air around him fairly buzzed with power. If she looked through her third eye as instructed, she thought she could see a huge, dragonesque form hover around him. Coppery light arced between them.

*Kheladin?*

The harder she stared, the more indistinct the dragon essence became, almost as if he didn't want to be identified.

Maggie fought against helplessness. She'd never cared for the sensation of being mired in a tar pit. Adrenaline soured her stomach and set her nerves jangling. Knowing it was her fight-or-flight response, and that her current level of discomfort was because both avenues were unavailable, didn't help her control her body's autonomic nervous system.

She opened her mouth to talk with Lachlan and then clacked it shut. He appeared to be concentrating—intensely. She didn't want to sabotage their chance of escape by diverting his attention. Rocks showered down from above. A sensation of drowning, of being buried beneath tons of earth, nearly undid her.

So she wouldn't start screaming, Maggie forced herself to breathe. One steadying breath in, followed by an equally deep exhale. As she repeated the cycle, she took stock of her body. Aware of every synapse, every nerve ending, Maggie felt intensely, vibrantly alive. She swallowed hard, choking on realization. The life she'd been living was a mere parody of what being alive could mean. She'd emerged from a long sleep into bright, searing daylight. Her body thrummed with dazzling energy, but lust for the man standing a foot away with magic churning around him trumped everything.

Though far from a virgin, she'd never felt such an intense physical connection with her other lovers. In fact, sex had been so blasé, it hadn't felt like a sacrifice to do without it. The men who'd wandered through her life never truly interested her. There'd been points when she'd wondered if she was gay, but women didn't ring her chimes either. In her worst moments, she'd seen herself as asexual.

Mid-breath, she bit back a chortle. If today were any marker, asexual wasn't anywhere on the table. Despite danger blossoming about them, if Lachlan dragged her to the cave's sandy floor and pressed his glorious cock against her pussy lips, she'd welcome him back inside. Desire knifed through her at the thought of him. He had a physical magnetism that literally stole her breath. Was that what had been wrong with her twenty-first century lovers? Had they been too...domesticated? Too tame?

*Maybe I was waiting all my life for him and just didn't know it.*

*Grannie knew.*

Maggie considered that. Her grandmother had known... something. When Maggie walked away from the coven and their training, she'd walled herself off from magics that were only taught to acolytes who signed the coven's pact with their blood.

"Lass."

Though she'd never taken her gaze from him, Lachlan's voice startled her. "Yes?"

"Take my hand. Gather what power ye have and imagine it streaming into me." His voice held a desperate edge.

Maggie closed the short distance between them and grasped his outstretched hand. Contact with him jolted her like an electric charge and reinforced her earlier impression that her other life held all the allure of a photographic negative. She imagined her essence flowing into him.

"Aye, beloved," he murmured. "Give it all to me. Imagine our bodies joined and send the energy into me. All of it."

She tried hard to do what he asked. Once she touched him, her consciousness of the doom surrounding them escalated dramatically, as did her sense of the dragon's burning core. Kheladin was furious they were under attack. He wanted to lay waste to the world with fire, but Lachlan held him back.

The peril they faced came into sharp focus and scared the living shit out of her. Her gut tightened. She wanted to shriek her fury and her fear, to rake her nails down Rhukon's tawdry beauty and mar him for life. Her gaze swept the cave. Her eyes said they were alone, but her other senses, the more arcane ones, told her otherwise.

"Ye're not concentrating." Lachlan closed his other hand over hers, sandwiching it. Thunderous booming sounded above them. More dirt drifted down, mingled with thick, choking dust and small rocks.

Truth rammed home. Maggie's teeth chattered. Talking took gargantuan effort, as if by giving voice to her terror, it might be one step closer to coming true. "Rhukon's trying to bury us alive."

"If ye help me, he willna succeed. Ye've power within you. Throw the floodgates open. Doona worry, I can channel all ye have."

A chant from her childhood rose from some forgotten pit in her psyche. Maggie mouthed the words and felt power coil upward from the base of her spine.

"Aye, lass. There's my bonny lass. Keep it coming. Goddess's tits, but ye're strong. I knew it." Exultant laughter rose from him as smoke and fire spewed from his mouth.

Maggie sensed Kheladin's magic. It was deep, eldritch, and different from Lachlan's. She opened her mind to their three powers. It was like watching three waterfalls, pouring multi-hued water down a rocky cliff. The water braided together. Once joined, it exploded, showering everything in its path with destructive force. No stranger to focusing the power of her mind on outcomes, she imagined Rhukon *dead*. Dead, goddammit.

*Hell, I'll take dismantled, disemboweled, imprisoned by the Celts. Anything.*

She dug deeper within herself. The cave walls flickered and dimmed, then reformed. Understanding at an instinctual level that they'd nearly escaped, she dragged every last ounce of strength from her soul.

This time, they fairly shot from the cave. When the world stopped spinning, they lay on the ground in the circle of beech and ash where they'd started. Maggie's gut seized. She flipped over onto her belly in time to vomit what little was in her stomach into the dirt. Dry heaves shook her, but she couldn't stop them.

Strong hands rubbed her back and shoulders. "Naught to be ashamed of, lass. 'Tis the magic. It always exerts a price, but 'tis higher when ye're untrained."

"I-I'm all right," she managed through chattering teeth. "Adrenaline overload." She pushed herself away from where she'd been sick and managed a cross-legged sit. Maggie dragged her sleeve across her mouth. She squeezed her eyes shut, then opened them, gratified the bower of trees was still there. "We got out." Tears pricked behind her lids. "Christ! I wouldn't let myself think about it, but I was afraid I was going to die down there, crushed under tons of rocks."

"Aye, lass." He gathered her shaking body against him. "'Twas your magic made the difference. Ye should be proud." He hesitated, and then added, "Your grandmother will most certainly be. I've never seen such an impressive display of power from one so untrained as ye are."

She pulled away and sat straight. "Grandma. Shit! What time is it?" Maggie scrabbled through her bag, which she'd miraculously held onto, and got her iPhone. She blew out a breath. "Only eleven-thirty. Thank God. We still have plenty of time."

"Are ye sound enough to drive that contraption ye call a car?"

Maggie snorted. "I like being taken care of, but if the options are me driving or you, I'll take me any day."

"I could learn."

"Yes, but not between now and when we need to be in Glasgow." A soft smile curved the ends of her mouth. "Help me up. I hate to admit it, but I still feel like I got run down by a train."

He pushed to his feet and held out his hands to help her. "I'm not familiar with the word, but I assume 'tis equivalent of being tied to four horses and having them all run in different directions."

"Maybe not quite so bad as being drawn and quartered," she murmured and let herself be coaxed back into his arms. His voice and hands held a soothing quality that steadied her nerves.

He laughed quietly. "Aye, and ye're familiar with the concept."

She nodded. "I have an advantage. I studied history. While I don't know everything about the time you lived in, I know far more about it than you know about the world I come from. Walk with me." She headed for her car. "I'd like to rinse my mouth out with some of the tea in my trunk and maybe eat the sandwiches I made."

Maggie led the way across the deserted street. It seemed like another lifetime when she'd made those sandwiches in her kitchen. Maybe they could find a pub somewhere off the highway and get something more substantial. Her belly felt hollow. She had the shaky feeling she got when she overdid it exercising, and her blood sugar dropped too low.

～

THERE WAS INDEED a pub on their way out of Inverness. Because they'd inhaled the peanut butter sandwiches and were still half-starved, Maggie ran in and talked the bartender into making them ham sandwiches with all the trimmings to go. They ate as they drove, with Lachlan breaking off small bites and handing them to her. They had plenty of time, so she stopped frequently, even pulled off onto a back road to give Lachlan a chance to see what it felt like behind the wheel. As she expected, his first few attempts to coordinate the gas and clutch were laughable, but by the end of forty minutes, she was confident he could drive in a pinch—if he had to. At least he'd be able to move the vehicle in a straight line and turn it. Traffic signs, and understanding how to operate in an environment with other cars was a whole different story.

*Mmph. If it comes down to him having to drive, I'll just hope he gets us to where we need to be before the cops pull him over and haul him off to jail.*

Questions swirled through her mind, but she forced herself to sit on all of them, at least until they were done eating. She needed energy and didn't want information that would twist her stomach into burning knots of tension. The darkened highway stretched before them. At a hundred kilometers an hour, her Fiat ate the distance as if it wasn't there.

"Do ye wish for any more?"

Maggie shook her head and then said. "I've had enough. You can finish whatever's left."

"How did ye guess I was still hungry?"

"You're a man, aren't you?"

He laughed long and hard. The rough edges of his mirth warmed her heart. "Aye, if ye doona watch us, we'll eat whatever's not tacked down."

Maggie stared at stars visible through the windshield. A quarter moon sat low on the horizon. The countryside smelled damp and green through the window she'd cracked to get a bit of fresh air into the car. She considered how to organize the questions she had for

Lachlan, but her mind recoiled. The knowledge she craved would change her irrevocably. She'd never again be able to walk away from the power simmering inside her.

*What the hell? I can't do that* now.

Years ago she'd established what felt like détente with her latent abilities. Sort of an I'll-leave-you-alone-if-you-don't-nag-me agreement. *Humph. Blew the lid right off that arrangement, didn't I?* She girded herself. There really were things she had to know—before Rhukon struck again.

"My stomach's full. The next thing I need is a few answers." Maggie listened to the words as they rolled out of her mouth and sat between them in the darkened car. If she didn't know better, she could've sworn they were written against the gray of the console, glittering a challenge.

"Aye, I figured ye'd get around to asking a question or two. I'd have volunteered information but thought it best if ye came to wanting it on your own." He crumpled the paper the sandwiches had been wrapped in and shoved it back into the paper sack. Lachlan fingered the bag. "In my day, all such things were woven from cloth."

"Probably better. Less waste." She licked her lips and took a slug of tea from the bottle balanced in the car's console. "Ecology's the last thing on my mind right now. My mind's still jumbled, but could you tell me what happened in your cave? Just hit the major points, and keep it simple."

"What do ye think happened?" His voice was soft, soothing. She could almost feel him infuse a calming spell into his words.

"Rhukon attacked us and tried to trap us. Damn near succeeded from what I could tell."

"'Twasn't just Rhukon. I could've managed him, even without Kheladin's help."

The short sentences settled in her stomach like a lead weight. For a moment, she fought nausea, but then her head cleared and her gut quieted, likely a result of Lachlan's spell. "So it was those other ones you told me about? The battle crow, uh, Morrigan, and the other bad dragon?" Maggie held her breath, not really wanting him to answer, but needing to hear the truth.

"Aye, but Connor would laugh himself sick to be called a bad dragon, right afore he ripped the eyes from your skull. 'Tisn't a game we play, Maggie. This is deadly serious."

Anger raced through her, bright, brittle, and hot as dragon's fire. She signaled and pulled to the side of the expressway, before bringing the car to a stop in a flurry of squealing brakes. She gripped the wheel hard and twisted to face Lachlan. "Don't you dare patronize me. As if I need reminding. I lost my parents to magic. I know how quickly—and irrevocably—it can destroy everything." To her horror, a great, choking sob escaped, followed by another. She shook her head hard, and tears flew from her eyes.

"Lass. 'Tis sorry I am. I had no mind to be upsetting you."

"Never mind. It's me. I'm on edge and kicking myself for not learning about magic when the coven offered me a chance. Tell me what happened in the cave. I'll try not to take your head off." With a glance in both mirrors, she ferried the car back onto the highway and brought it up to cruising speed.

"I doona know for certain, lass, but my best guess is Rhukon, Connor, and the Morrigan presumed I'd brought you to Kheladin's lair to consummate our relationship. The first thing they did was try to convince me, and with such a degree of subtlety I dinna recognize it for sorcery, that we needed to be married afore we bedded one another."

"Yes. I got that part. Kheladin and I disabused you of that notion."

"Aye, and I must admit I'm anxious for a repeat performance, but that's off the topic to hand."

Her left hand snaked across the console. He tucked it between one of his and the warmth of his body. "Thanks. Making love with you was so unlike anything else I've done, it should have a different name. I'm up for more of the same just as soon as we find a wall I can lean up against and—"

"Och, lass, we've barely begun in that department, but I get your drift." He chuckled. "Doona say aught more. When I get hard in these breeks, it pains me something fierce."

"The airport has lots of shops. I'm sure we can find you a pair of sweatpants." Reassured by the warmth of him and his solid energy radiating confidence, she prodded. "Is there more I need to know about the attack?"

"Ye've figured out they were trying to kill us. I'm immortal, but they can spin webs to immobilize me for long years. Rather like the net I just escaped from."

Maggie tightened her hand on the steering wheel again. What he hadn't said was she was far from immortal. A major cave-in, with its concomitant loss of oxygen, would've killed her. "Since they couldn't stop us from fucking, is doing away with me the next thing they'll try?"

"Smart lass. I've been thinking along much the same lines. Ye need a crash course in controlling your magic. I'm hoping your kin will help with that. I'm not as familiar with witch magic as I am with my own."

"*I can help,*" Kheladin said. "*We must teach her to ride me. An aerial position is a defensible one.*"

"*I heard that,*" Maggie murmured. "*Thank you for the offer.*"

"Och aye," Lachlan cut in. "'Tis much more than an offer. 'Tis a concession. No one has ever ridden Kheladin. Of course, I'm within him when he takes to the skies, but I'm not astride his back." He squeezed her hand. "The dragon likes you."

"*How could I not? She is ours.*" Kheladin reiterated his earlier statement.

Warmth simmered in her heart and created a comforting shroud. Within its layers, she found acceptance and approval. Maggie tried to send reciprocating energy back to Kheladin. It was hard to tell if she succeeded at first, but then she was certain the dragon recognized her offering. "He has ways to talk that transcend words," she murmured.

"That he does," Lachlan concurred. "How much farther to Glasgow?"

Maggie glanced at a passing road sign. "Maybe another hour. Despite how late it is, we'll run into traffic when we get closer to the metropolitan area. Fortunately, the airport is a few miles out of town. I've only driven in the downtown area once, and it was hideous. I got caught in a traffic jam that lasted so long, I was afraid I'd run out of fuel."

"A traffic jam being many cars stuck together somehow?"

"You have the general idea. There's usually an accident, where one car's run into another. Sometimes there are even multi-car pileups. Anyway, they block lanes so the other cars can't move."

He chuckled. "I should be talking with you of love and a bright future together, not metal tubes with no life in them that run into one another."

Something deep inside her grew warm and fluttery. It felt right and good, but she pushed it aside. "If we make it through this in one piece, you can sing me all the love songs you want."

"A practical lass."

"No. A lass who's scared half to death. I'm afraid if I let my guard down for even a moment or two, I'll miss something and end up dead."

"A wise lass."

"I don't know what I am. Would you mind if I turned on the radio for a few minutes? It's closing on four-thirty, and I'd like to hear the news."

"I doona mind, though I have no idea what ye're talking about."

Maggie fiddled with the dial until she got a news station. She listened to the weather forecast. The broadcast crackled. "This just in," the DJ said, his voice shifting from jovial to worried. "An inbound flight from Chicago to Glasgow disappeared off air traffic control's radar half an hour ago. All inquiries should be routed to the carrier, Air Blue Sky. I repeat. Call the airlines at…" He rattled off a number. "If you had friends or family arriving on Flight 427, Air Blue Sky will have up-to-the-minute information." A breathy sigh came through the car's speakers. "May God protect those three hundred passengers. I hope to hell He and all His saints take good care of them."

Maggie felt as if she was about to pass out. She didn't remember pulling the car off the highway to the shoulder. She didn't hear Lachlan until his anxious voice finally penetrated the fog around her brain.

"Lass, lass." He shook her arm. "Whatever is the matter? Was that your grandmother's airplane the fellow was nattering on about?"

She dropped her forehead onto her hands clutching the top of the steering wheel. "Yes," she managed, just before anger so violent she wanted to kill whatever crossed her path ripped through her. "Mary Elma is on that plane."

# CHAPTER 11

"Can you do anything?" Her voice held anguish.

Lachlan gathered her as close as he could, given the small shelf sitting between them in the car. "I doona know, lass. Ye hold an imprint of your grandmother's energy. If any one of us could reach her, 'twould be you. I will lend my magic to whatever ye wish to try."

"All those years I spent moldering away in college, medical school, and residency were nothing but a colossal waste." She raised her head and banged a fist down on a ridge that ran across the front of the car behind its steering wheel.

Lachlan chose his words with care. Since the Celts knew about Mary Elma, it was a good bet Rhukon and the Morrigan did as well. "Gwydion and Arawn were aware of your grandmother—"

Maggie jumped on his line of thought before he finished getting the words out. "Of course they know about her. My grannie is one of the most powerful witches alive today. Whatever happened to her plane was no accident." She pounded her fist against the car's steering wheel, winced in pain, and flexed her knuckles. "When Rhukon and them couldn't kill us, they switched gears to easier prey."

"Explain radar to me, lass?"

She exhaled raggedly. The sound broke his heart. The lass was in pain, suffering terribly, and there was nothing he could do to ease her anguish. "Radar is an invisible electronic beam that tracks airplanes—and other things. If the plane had crashed into the Atlantic Ocean, radar would've followed its trajectory down."

"But the fellow said the plane disappeared, which means it dinna crash."

"Exactly." Maggie bit off the word. "Those bastards did something." She shook her head, and he heard her teeth grind against one another. "I wish I knew more about magic."

"Are we anywhere near to Loch Lomond?"

"Not far. Maybe fifteen minutes. Why?"

"Do ye know Castle Balloch?"

"I've seen it. Never took the tour, though."

He blew out a breath. *Tour? Whatever did she mean by that?* "Thank the gods the castle still stands. There doesna appear to be any sense in going to Glasgow. Take us to Castle Balloch."

"Why?" she asked again.

"Magic is strong there. Once upon a time, a series of magical nodes extended betwixt the castle and the far side of the loch. 'Tis a strong possibility I can secure help from there."

"How?"

"I canna explain the whole of it, but the location will intensify my abilities. Yours, too." He paused, wondering whether to give voice to his next thought. In the end, he did, to underscore the urgency of their predicament. "Even with Kheladin's strength at my disposal, I couldna have freed us from the cave without your help."

"And you're hoping for a much stronger infusion of power from these nodes? For both of us."

"Aye, lass."

"All right. I don't have any better suggestions. To tell you the truth, I feel woefully out of my league." Her phone trilled. Maggie made a grab for it, peered at its illuminated display, and said, "Aunt Chloe."

Lachlan watched Maggie as she spoke with her kinswoman. Her features were carved into bas relief by pale moonlight. Mayhap it was a trick of Artemis's moon, but Maggie had an ethereal beauty that glowed, illuminating her from within.

Thick, golden curls fell around facial bone structure that would have done a goddess proud. His groin stirred. He wanted her, plain and simple, but now wasn't the time. The small taste of her hot, slick core, when he'd been crazed with lust and hadn't lasted five minutes, had been the merest of appetizers. He shifted in his seat and tried to move his more-than-hard cock to a comfortable position. He caught himself gazing longingly at the full curves of her breasts and the enticing swell of her rump where it rested against the seat. His heart beat faster. Lachlan forced himself to look out the window before he threw prudence to the four winds and ravished her in the dirt next to the car.

While he heard her side of the conversation, he couldn't make out the rest, despite using Kheladin's acute senses.

*Aye, and the aunt must be shielding things with magic.*

"Here." Maggie thrust the phone at him. "She wants to talk with you. I'll get us moving toward Castle Balloch and the loch."

Lachlan took the phone. Feeling odd, like he was trespassing on someone else's magic, he held it to his ear as he'd seen Maggie do and said, "Aye?"

"My name is Chloe," a strident female voice said without preamble. "Margaret is my niece. You will help her find out what happened to my mother."

"Aye. She is my mate. Of course I'll help." Because Chloe seemed overwrought, Lachlan experimented with a calming spell.

"Don't waste your magic on me, dragon shifter. Save it for what's important."

"Certainly. Of course." Apparently, the witch knew far more about him than he did about her. Lachlan stilled his racing mind and focused on what he saw as paramount. "'Tis as I told Maggie, I'm not familiar with your mother's energy. 'Twould be best if one or more of you could travel here."

"Not likely any of us would trust the airlines after tonight." A hesitation, then a sly note crept into Chloe's voice. "You're connected to the Celtic deities."

"Ye dinna ask a question, but aye, that I am."

"Could you rustle one of them up to help?"

Lachlan hesitated. "Is it possible for someone to overhear our conversation?"

"Not from my end, dragon shifter. I have no idea what magics you're conjuring on yours."

"Lass." He aimed for a placating tone since his magic appeared to upset her. "I have been ensorcelled—asleep, if ye will—for hundreds of years. The world I woke to is still passing strange to me."

"Excuses!" she snapped. "They're an indulgence. Get over it."

Lachlan couldn't help himself. A laugh rumbled up from his belly. "'Tis a feisty one ye are. In my day, a woman wouldna speak so to a man."

"What a good thing customs have changed," she retorted dryly. "Now, what are you going to do to retrieve my mother?"

"Do ye ken where she is?"

"Not exactly, but she's still alive. I'd know if she were dead."

"Excellent news. 'Tis what I meant by her blood kin having a feel for her energy. I'm not hedging, but I'm reluctant to disclose my thoughts since I have no idea how to shield this type of conversation from those who seek to harm us."

"You will do something to retrieve my mother. The state the world is in, we need Mary Elma. Her loss would be a grievous blow."

"Aye. I willna abandon Maggie. She needs my help." Lachlan considered trying to talk around the ancient prophecy regarding himself and Maggie.

He'd just opened his mouth when Chloe said, "I already know

about it. Our entire coven does, so I assume our enemies do as well. Margaret tried to escape her destiny, but that never works." A brittle laugh. "In any event, you aren't the only one with foes who'd just as soon see you out of the way. Give the phone back to my niece."

Lachlan complied. Apparently niceties such as greetings and farewells had gone the way of prehistoric beasts. Moments later, after a flurry of *I know* and *I understand* and *Yes, Auntie*, Maggie slid the phone back into her bag.

"Sorry about that," she murmured. "My aunts can be intense, even when things are going well, and Chloe is the worst of the bunch."

Lachlan chuckled. "She was a wee bit overbearing, but she has a right to be since circumstances are skidding toward Hell."

"You're being kind. Chloe was a bitch on wheels, but she's worried sick about Grandma. For that fact, so am I." A sign for Loch Lomond flashed past, and Maggie pulled off the main road onto a smaller one where the cars didn't travel as fast. "What do you want me to do once I get to the loch? As I recall, we'll reach it before we get to the castle."

"Is there a deserted area where ye could leave this beast, and it wouldna be disturbed?"

She cocked her head to one side. "It's still very early in the morning, so all the parking lots should be pretty much empty. Do you want to be closer to the loch or the castle, or does it matter?"

"It doesna matter. We can walk to where we need to be." Lachlan turned his thoughts inward. *"Do ye have any ideas?"* he asked the dragon.

After a silence so long, Lachlan figured Kheladin was annoyed about something, the dragon finally said, *"The world is vastly different. Were this a more familiar time, I would say we should shift, and I could talk with the creatures in the loch. Sea creatures are full of information."*

*"We doona even know if the loch has life in it."*

Sounding uncertain, Maggie broke in. *"Since I can hear you, I thought I'd shed what light I could. Pollution has been a problem here, just like everywhere. There are fish in the loch, but they're planted by the government."*

"Planted?" Lachlan spoke aloud. "Whatever do ye mean?"

"Fishing is a sport. People don't have to fish to eat, at least not most people. So the government grows fish in hatcheries, and when they get old enough, they move them into the lake, er loch. I'm not certain how they do it here. Back in the States, they often drop them from airplanes."

*"Forget I suggested it."* Kheladin sounded shocked and disgusted. *"Such creatures surely have no ancestral memories left."*

"He can hear us if we don't use mind speech?" Maggie asked.

"Aye, if he chooses to listen. The best way to get his attention, though, is silent speech."

Maggie turned into a large gravel area. She pulled the car to its far end and turned it off. Lachlan reveled in silence. He didn't fully appreciate how annoying the car's motor was, always nagging at the edges of his hearing, until it wasn't there anymore. He got out and sent his mage senses spinning outward. No point in walking into a trap in case Rhukon—or the Morrigan, who was much smarter than the black wyvern—anticipated his next move.

"What's next?" Maggie made her way to his side while he was hunting for danger.

"Grand news, lass. We're alone."

"Of course we are," she began and then nodded. "I understand. You were looking for something…invisible."

"Aye. Ye never know which ears might overhear." He gazed about them. Loch Lomond was about fifty paces away, water lapping gently against its rocky shore. The castle sat on the far side of the loch, maybe an hour's walk. It was lit up like a holiday festival tree. "So people yet live in the castle?"

"Not nobility or anything like that." Maggie gazed at the lights. "If anything, there might be a staff of caretakers."

"Do ye think it would be hard to get inside?"

She snorted. "Oh my, yes. I'm sure it's alarmed from here to Sunday."

"Which means?"

"There are electronic beams that set off alarms if anyone tries to break in. The alarms might be silent here, but you can bet they'd alert someone at the police station in town."

"Once we are not sore pressed, I want you to explain these electronic beams to me. Ye canna see them, yet they seem immensely powerful."

"Sure." She stood, hands on her hips, gazing at the loch. With her blonde tresses and ramrod straight stance, she might've been a Viking maid. Because he couldn't help himself, he bent toward her and brushed his lips over hers. She wound her arms around his neck and kissed him back. Their breathing escalated as their bodies strained toward one another. Her nipples pressed against his chest, and the scent of her arousal was thick in his nostrils. His cock, desperate for release, rubbed against the rough fabric of his breeks.

*Much more of this and I'll spend without her laying a hand on me.*

With a great deal of effort, Lachlan broke away from their kiss. "I want you more than is good for me, lass."

"I know. Me, too."

She stepped back, but he felt the heat of her even across the distance between them. In a rush of chivalry, he grabbed her hand and pressed his lips to its back.

Lachlan forced his mind away from his swollen member. Being lost in lust wasn't conducive to clear-minded thought. Since the castle was occupied and guarded by something he couldn't see, it would be a last resort. Even if he could work his way into its lower levels, where earth magic was strongest, it would still take time to cast a spell and hold it long enough for it to yield information. He shut his eyes and reconstructed the location of the nodes ancients had used to concentrate their magic. One was quite close. He opened himself to sense its pull. "This way."

"Where are we going?"

He drew a hand through her arm and propelled her forward. Even so small a touch was like an aphrodisiac. He wanted to crush her to him, lower his mouth to hers, and sink onto the mother goddess earth to take his pleasure. "'Tisn't easy to explain, lass, but there are places magic congregates."

"I know about them," she cut in. "We call them power points, and magic is easier to access there because of harmonics."

"I doona understand harmonics, but I know what I feel and how power flows through me. Into this grove now. Careful, someone's erected a fence."

He helped her over wooden rails. Once on the other side, they moved deeper into thick undergrowth, among friendly trees. Thank the goddess, even today's version of humans had left the sacred grove intact.

"Is this what I think it is?" She kept her voice low.

"Aye. See the stones." He pointed. "And the trees. Come stand in their center."

Lachlan laid a hand on a standing stone and mouthed a prayer. The strength with which the goddess, Ceridwen, rushed into his mind surprised him. Like everything else he'd seen in modern times, he'd expected earth magic to be faded and weak.

Numinous light rose from the standing stones and hovered. "Gwydion and Arawn told me ye were near." Ceridwen's voice held a multi-tonal aspect, as if two women spoke simultaneously.

"Blessings, lady, on you and your grove." Lachlan bowed. "I would introduce my mate."

"Aye, and well I knew her mother and grandmother. Stand tall within my grove, Margaret Hibbins."

Maggie squared her shoulders, her eyes round as small moons. She groped for Lachlan's hand. "Which of the goddesses are you?"

"In olden times, ye would not have lived to mouth the last words of that thought."

"Forgive me." Maggie bowed low. "I can't see you, only light."

"Use your third eye," Lachlan murmured.

"Even if I saw her face, I wouldn't recognize her."

"Child." Ceridwen's voice was sharp. "Why have ye abandoned the power within you?"

Maggie cleared her throat. "Because I was stubborn, willful, and grieving."

"And are ye still?"

Maggie shook her head. "I'm feeling humble and stupid right about now. Whichever goddess you are, if you knew my mother, you'll understand why I grieved her loss as a child. If you know my grandmother, could you help us find her please?"

Lachlan draped an arm around Maggie and pulled her against his body. "Forgive her, Ceridwen. She's of the modern world and doesna understand one doesna ask boons of the gods."

Tinkling laughter trilled. Lachlan relaxed his hold on Maggie. He'd been afraid the goddess would strike her dead for impertinence.

"Lady. May I speak?" Kheladin forced Lachlan's vocal chords to his bidding, something he'd only done a time or two before.

"Dragon." Ceridwen inclined her head.

"Do my kin yet live anywhere near here?"

The numinous light pulsed and took form. A tall, robust woman with long, black hair mingled with gray, and piercing dark eyes stood before them. She was clothed in flowing white robes and carried a carved staff. Gold rings circled most of her fingers. A heavy golden torc curved around her neck, and strings of pearls wound through her hair. "Aye, dragon. Would ye have them make themselves known?"

"Of course. I'm lonely. I slept for long years and wakened to find no one to fly with."

"Lachlan?"

He recovered his voice with effort. "Aye, my lady."

"I will aid all of you, but first I require a sacrifice. The earth is parched, hungry for the essence of life. Humans no longer pay homage to me. No one has prayed in this grove for many a long year."

"Of course."

"No." Maggie twisted in his arms. "No sacrifices. I can't believe you're even considering such a thing. We aren't going to harm—"

"Sssh. She dinna mean what ye think. She wants us to make love here in her sacred grove and let the juices from our bodies soak into the earth."

The sky was lightening in the east. In its glow, Maggie's eyes widened. "In front of her?"

Ribald laughter crashed around them. Ceridwen laughed so hard her eyes streamed tears. When she could talk again, she said, "Humans have turned into a horde of withered prudes. Yes, daughter. In front of me. Ye asked a boon of me. 'Tis a small enough price to pay."

An idea bloomed around Lachlan's rising urgency to plumb Maggie's lush body. They had the goddess' blessing, after all. He risked meeting Ceridwen's dark gaze. "Would ye consent to wed us?"

Maggie, who'd been half-leaning against him, wrenched herself out of his arms. "Too soon. This is all happening too fast. Sleeping with you is one thing. Tying my life to yours forever is quite another. My God, I barely know you."

Shocked, Lachlan stared hard at her. After what they'd shared in Kheladin's cave, it wasn't possible the lass could wish for another. Or was it? Heart aching, he tamped down the magic that would force her to his will. Prophecy or no, she had to come to him freely —or not at all.

## CHAPTER 12

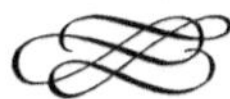

nfamiliar emotions buffeted her. Lachlan was all the things she thought she wanted and needed in a man, so why was she on the verge of spinning and running down the lakeshore path for all she was worth? She tried balancing pros against cons.

*Tall, tawny, to-die-for body, amazing eyes, good mind, compassionate, cares about me...*

*Yes, but what happens to my* life? *He won't fit into any of it. Do I just walk away from practicing medicine forever? After all the years it took me to finish my training?*

Maggie nodded to herself. There it was in a nutshell. If she stayed with Lachlan, her life would never be the same. *Am I ready for that?*

Ceridwen stared right through her, as if she saw down to her soul. "Well, witch. What shall it be? The safe and known, or throwing caution to the four winds? I've spent many a decade watching humankind erode. Will ye rise to your witch heritage or sink to the level of yesterday's gruel?"

"I-I'm not sure. He and I barely know one another," she stammered repeating her earlier words.

131

"Ye'd never want for aught." Lachlan moved back to her side but didn't try to touch her.

"That's not it." Maggie pressed her tongue against her teeth. "I've never been enamored with money or things. I guess I'm having a hard time seeing how we'll spend a lifetime together. We're just so different." The moment the words were out, it felt as if someone shoved a burning blade into her solar plexus. Even though she didn't know him well, and her life would change forever, she understood she'd rather risk that than face the long years to come without his solid, alluring energy by her side.

He gazed at her, pleading in his eyes, but pride too. He wouldn't beg. She had to choose him of her own free will. Not because of the strength in their combined magic. Not to defeat Rhukon and the Morrigan. Not because he'd help her find her grandmother, and she didn't have any other options.

"Aye, lass," he said, obviously reading her mind. "I wish to be wanted for myself. What man wouldna?"

Ceridwen cocked her head to one side. Maggie was grateful the goddess wasn't pushing her. If it had been her Aunt Chloe, she was certain she'd have made a dive for her throat just to shut her up. Ceridwen chuckled. "Och aye, and I know that blood kin of yours too. A prickly one she is. 'Twould do her good to take a man between her legs. Might improve her disposition."

Maggie didn't mention that Chloe hadn't shown any predilection toward either sex—ever. "What happens if we just make love and leave the wedding part open?"

"Tch. Lack of commitment. Another human weakness that has expanded by leaps and bounds. What is it, witch? Are ye stuck in the modern concept that ye must know and love a man afore ye bind yourself to him?"

"Yes. I suppose that's part of it."

"Far more marriages fail today than they did a century ago—or five centuries. The term divorce has been around forever, but it was rarely exercised so enthusiastically until recently."

"I know all that," Maggie sputtered. "But we're talking about a whole lot more than marriage here. My entire life, the career I spent twelve years training for, will all go up in smoke."

"I dinna ask you to quit being a healer," Lachlan broke in.

"Okay," Maggie amended. "It might go up in smoke."

Ceridwen leaned close. "Aye, ye've hit the nail on its head. Can ye be who ye are and wife to this man all at the same time? Beyond whatever ye do to earn your bread, beneath it all, ye're still a woman."

"Honest answer?"

"Of course, witch."

"I don't know." Maggie sucked air to the very bottom of her lungs. The careful planning that had been a hallmark of her life to date blew away in a whoosh of unexpected audacity. "But I'd like to find out."

"Ye're hedging," Ceridwen's dark eyes flashed.

*Oh, what the hell.*

"Yes," Maggie said, surprised to find tears in her eyes. "My answer is yes."

Lachlan closed his arms around her. He rained kisses on her hair, her face, her neck. "Ye willna be sorry, lass. I will care for you, protect you." More kisses. "We'll find your grandmother, defeat Rhukon."

*"Carve a return path for the dragons who chose leave to Earth,"* Kheladin said. *"Doona forget that part."*

*"We shan't,"* Ceridwen replied.

Something about the exchange got Maggie's attention. She ducked from beneath Lachlan's embrace and faced Ceridwen. "Why is repopulating the Earth with dragons important?"

The goddess gave her an appraising look and swept her long hair over her shoulders. "Dragons come from the first world—Fire Mountain—and hold ancient magic. They're linked to the ebb and flow of life on Earth."

Maggie narrowed her eyes. "So not having them here disturbs

some sort of cosmic balance point?"

"More or less—" Ceridwen began.

She was almost immediately drowned out by Kheladin trumpeting telepathically. Maggie pressed her hands over her ears and then understood it wouldn't do a shred of good since the dragon was inside her head. She quirked a brow at Lachlan.

He took her hands. "Kheladin's unhappy—lonely for his own kind. I told him we'd see about solving the dragon problem, but only after we had everything else well in hand. I doona think he liked my answer."

Lachlan pulled her into his arms. She heard the thud of his heartbeat beneath her ear. The sky had turned a pearlescent pink in the east with streaks of violet and teal, almost as if it were blessing their union. She turned her face up, and he closed his mouth over hers. His lips were firm and insistent as he licked at hers. She opened her mouth, and he sank his tongue inside, tasting fragrant as fresh-cut hay.

"Do ye, Lachlan, take this lass, Margaret Hibbins, to be your wife and mate?"

He raised his mouth from hers and twisted them so they faced the goddess. "Aye."

"With full knowledge she is witch born, and ye have no idea the extent of her ability."

"Aye."

"To cherish and protect and feed and clothe?"

"Now just a minute." Maggie wriggled in his arms, but he held fast. "I can feed and clothe myself."

"No more interruptions." The goddess sounded stern. She held up an index finger. "Your answers from this point on are aye or nay."

"Aye," Lachlan said, the corners of his mouth twitching.

Ceridwen nodded approval. "Now, lass, do ye take this man, Lachlan Moncrieffe, Laird of Clan Moncrieffe, to be your husband and mate?"

*Well, do I?*

It felt as if she'd pole-vaulted into fairyland when Maggie heard herself say, "Yes."

"With full knowledge he is bonded to a dragon."

Maggie's second *yes* came easier.

"There now." Ceridwen clucked. "That wasna so hard. "Will ye honor and obey him in all things without question?"

Something snapped. "Why does he get to cherish and protect me, and I have to obey him?"

"Tch, tch." Ceridwen waggled her index finger right under Maggie's nose. "And would ye be questioning the words to a ceremony far more ancient than yourself?"

"Not the words, the concepts," Maggie muttered. She drew away from Lachlan, faced him and the goddess, and squared her shoulders. "What I will do is my best to love you, to treat you as my friend. I will be faithful. I will stand by your side. We will hold our arguments in private. I will make all major decisions with you."

Maggie placed her hands on her hips. She felt shaky inside but tipped her chin up. "Those things will have to do. I obey no one."

A look passed from Lachlan to Ceridwen. The goddess' face softened. She'd looked so threatening, Maggie wondered if the next thing would be a lightning bolt channeled straight into her heart.

"'Tisn't wise to pit yourself against the gods, lass." Ceridwen spaced out her words. "In this particular instance, ye've won, but I doona recommend ye do it again. Most of my kin are not as... tolerant as me. Now, for the love of Dewi, who is also involved since Lachlan is a dragon shifter, stand next to one another again."

Maggie stepped to Lachlan's side. He gripped her hand. Ceridwen lapsed into Gaelic. Lachlan placed his mouth right next to Maggie's ear. "She invokes the Celtic dragon god."

Maggie almost hissed back, *What if Dewi doesn't approve?* but kept her mouth shut. She'd taken enough of a stand. No point in making Ceridwen so angry the goddess refused to help find Mary Elma.

Heat rose around them, so intense beads of sweat broke out on

Maggie's forehead. She held her breath and waited. The heat rose and fell basting them in steam. A sudden, searing pain shot through her arm. Maggie yelped and tried to clap a hand over it, but Lachlan held her still.

*"'Twill pass."* He spoke soothingly into her mind. *"Dewi sensed the ritual mating mark on your neck, and now he has marked you too. I have such a mark on my upper arm."*

"Lachlan." Ceridwen's voice held a warning note. "Dewi is female."

"Apologies." Lachlan inclined his head. "I had no idea."

*"I was just about to correct you,"* Kheladin said. The dragon lapsed into Gaelic, and the intense heat around them subsided.

*What the hell did Dewi do to me? It hurts like a bitch.*

Maggie breathed in and out through tightly clenched teeth, determined not to make a bigger fool out of herself than she already had. True to Lachlan's prediction, the pain did recede and far more quickly than she anticipated.

As if from a great distance, she heard Ceridwen say, "And 'tis nearly done. Give me your right hands." More pain. Blood welled from cuts in the meaty part of her thumb and Lachlan's. He rubbed his cut over hers, mingling the thick, sticky fluid.

A satisfied smile spread over Ceridwen's face. No longer formidable, the goddess looked like an indulgent grandmother, but her change of expression didn't fool Maggie. In a flash of wry humor, she thought about asking where the goddess had hidden her cauldron.

Ceridwen met Maggie's gaze and shook her head slightly before turning to Lachlan. "Ye are mated, Laird, in both your forms, to this lass."

Maggie opened her mouth to ask, *What about me?* but changed her mind. The cut in her thumb not only stopped stinging, it healed before her eyes turning into smooth, unbroken skin.

Ceridwen snorted. "Ye're learning, lass. Once we find your grandmother, the first order of business must be creating stronger links betwixt you and your magic. Had ye taken to it at a more tender age, ye'd not be so testy and resistant now."

Since her Aunt Chloe could be a poster-witch for *testy* and *resistant*, Maggie wasn't so certain Ceridwen was correct.

"Even that one knows how to follow orders when given," Ceridwen pointed out.

Maggie rolled her eyes. "I guess I'll never have another private thought."

"Pfft." Ceridwen huffed.

Lachlan murmured, "Of course ye will," so comfortingly she suspected a spell, just before he turned her in his arms and kissed her. The touch of his mouth made everything else flee. Little, nibbling kisses warmed her to her toes. Maggie wound her arms around his neck and kissed him back.

*I did it. I'm married. Christ, but I hope I don't live to regret this.*

He lifted his mouth from hers. "Not while there's breath in my body, lass." He kissed her again. His hands roamed down her shoulders and back and settled over the curve of her buttocks, drawing her against his erection. A protest about him still living in her head and sharing all her thoughts died unspoken.

Sexual need roared out of nowhere, igniting all her nerve endings. When she lived in her head—in her worries—it was as if she existed from the neck up, but when Lachlan's mouth trailed down her face, and his hands settled on her body, the anxious part of her quieted.

He pushed his hands beneath her top and raised it, bending his head to suckle a breast. Liquid heat raced from her nipple and set the rest of her on fire. Her pussy was awash in fluid. Her clit throbbed with need. Somehow, her hands found the fastenings on the pants he'd complained about. She understood the problem when it was almost impossible to undo the buttons because of tension from his cock pressing against them.

He untied her sweater from around her waist and pulled her top over her head. When he fumbled with the clasp on her bra, she helped him. Anything to give his mouth and hands better access to her breasts. He filled his hands with them and then bent his head to tongue and lave them again. Pressure built deep in her belly. If he kept sucking her nipples, she'd come just from that. But her pussy felt hollow. She needed him. Needed him now. Maggie tried to tell him, but her throat was so thick with desire, all she could do was moan.

She tugged the denim pants down his legs, and then thought about his shoes. He still probably had the lace-up leather boots on. Maybe the pants would just slide off over them. Maggie curved her hands around his cock. It was even more substantial than she remembered, so thick she couldn't reach all the way around it with one hand. Lachlan groaned and pushed his ridged flesh into her touch.

"I miss my plaid and women's skirts." His breath came fast, blurring the words. "'Twas so much easier."

He fumbled at the waist of her pants. She toed off her shoes and helped him slide her pants down her legs, so she could step out of them. Somehow they ended up on the ground, in a tangle of arms and legs. He kissed her again, hard and demanding, breath rasping against her mouth. "I have to be inside you. Now. Help me with these infernal breeks. I canna move with them twisted about my legs."

She lifted a pant leg and examined the complex lacing system that held his boots together. "Did you take the boots off to get the pants on?"

"Nay."

Maggie was so hot, even simple thought was a challenge, but logic dictated the pants should slide off the same way they went on. She got hold of a cuff and pulled. Lachlan pushed. Between them, they freed one leg. "'Tis all I need, lass." He dove atop her, his weight pinning her to the ground. Rather than cold and lumpy, the earth felt warm, welcoming.

The world turned into a kaleidoscope when his cockhead

pressed against her entrance. *It's like Wonderland, where nothing is as it seems* was her last conscious thought. She reached between them and guided him inside. Maggie wound her legs around his waist and gripped his upper arms with both hands. She felt her body stretch to accommodate his length and girth.

Rather than withdrawing and driving himself into her, Lachlan twitched tiny muscles, making his cock jump inside her. He did it again and again. She squeezed back. Maggie pressed her clit against the base of his cock and rotated her hips. Coiled deep in her belly, the climax that wanted out—needed out—spiraled to life. Surges of heat pounded her, and her body convulsed around him.

"Aye, lass. Sweet, Maggie. Come for me." He balanced on his arms and watched her, a feral gleam deep in his green eyes.

"What about you?" She tried thrusting her hips but couldn't move more than half an inch or so.

"'Tis my task to give you pleasure. Men always spend."

Her gaze roved over his body, and her mouth curved into a smile. His tawny skin was flushed a rosy gold. His nipples were taut. "Looks like this man is damned close, if I'm any judge."

"Close, but I can bring you there again. Let me."

Maggie dropped her head back and closed her eyes. Lachlan pulled almost all the way out and moved his cock in small, lazy circles around her entrance before pressing slowly inside again. After about ten of those long, slow strokes, his control crumpled, and he drove himself home, fast and hard. Lost in the wonder of his body, sucked in by his lust, tinder to her own, Maggie met every stroke.

Her pussy tightened, signaling she was almost there. Maggie moved her hands to his hips and pulled him against her. She ground her clit against him and shot over the edge, screaming her delight as wave after wave of ecstasy tore through her. In the midst of her climax, she felt him release. His spasms fed hers, and another climax crowded on the heels of the one she wasn't quite done with.

They lay trembling and panting in one another's arms for long moments. When she could talk again, she said, "Wow! Amazing. You can do that again anytime you want."

He rolled off her onto his side and propped his head on an upraised hand. "What? No undying words of love and devotion from my new mate?"

Maggie bit her lower lip. "If I said I loved you, it wouldn't be the truth. Not quite. I like you, and God knows you're the hottest thing with a dick that's wandered into my life—ever."

He shook his head slightly, and she stopped talking. "I'm falling in love with you, lass. What man could resist the wonders of your body or the blue of your eyes? Did ye know they darken to midnight when ye're about to spend?"

The sound of hands smacking together reminded Maggie they were far from alone. Ceridwen had been there the whole time, right along with Kheladin. Maggie rolled her eyes, amazed she'd totally forgotten about them.

"Perfect," Ceridwen crowed. "Simply perfect. The grove is delighted and the earth too. Get dressed, children. We have work to do."

Maggie twisted so she could look in the direction of the goddess' voice and gasped. Much as she'd imagined Ceridwen should look, the goddess sat naked on the ground behind a huge copper kettle, stirring it with her staff.

"Pull your eyes back into your head, lass. No boiled babies today." Ceridwen laughed then, a sound so full of life and promise, Maggie couldn't help herself. Joy rolled through her, and she laughed too.

# CHAPTER 13

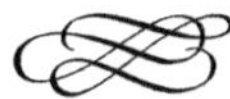

*L*achlan kissed Maggie's forehead tenderly once she was through chortling with the goddess. Ceridwen was like that. She could deal death with the best of them, yet she had a vibrant liveliness that was contagious. He bit down on a sigh, muffling it in his clothing. He'd hoped the dragon mate bond would spin its magic, and the lass would fall head over heels in love with him, but it hadn't happened yet.

*Och aye. She did wed me. Mayhap 'tis greedy to ask for more just now.*

He pushed to a sitting position and gathered more clothes. Loathing filled him when he picked up the breeks. He wished to hell he'd had the presence of mind to bring a plaid along. His cock was still half hard, and the thought of forcing it back behind the metal buttons was deucedly unpleasant.

Maggie had just shrugged back into the binding about her breasts and her shirt when music trilled. He started and then remembered it was the thing she called a phone. She grabbed her bag and fished the little noisemaker out of it.

*Worse than a hungry bairn,* he thought.

Maggie blew out an exasperated breath. "Shit. It's Chloe again."

She swiped a finger over the device. It silenced immediately, and she spoke into it. "Yes?"

Lachlan tried to eavesdrop, but the witch guarded her communications closely. After long silences when Maggie was obviously listening, and a few times when she clucked nonsensical, soothing sounds into the phone, Ceridwen snapped, "Oh for the love of Andraste, give that bloody thing to me."

"Hang on Chloe," Maggie said. "Someone here wants to talk with you."

"Well, if it's that fucking dragon shifter who's wasting time on sex—"

"It's not." Maggie handed the phone to Ceridwen and started to get into her trousers.

"Odd," Lachlan said. "I heard your aunt's last comment but not the ones before."

Maggie snorted. "Not odd at all. Chloe was in rare form. When she gets really angry, it's hard for her to hang onto her spells. She's always had that problem."

He watched the goddess out of the corners of his eyes. It was apparent Ceridwen had some level of comfort with modern devices, like Maggie's phone.

*If she could learn, so can I.*

"Either ye come here and help us, or doona meddle." Ceridwen wasn't exactly shouting, but she wasn't far from it. Her voice held an undercurrent of cold steel.

"Wish I felt comfortable telling my aunt to go pound sand." Maggie finished dressing and grimaced. "I've always placated her. The other women gradually accepted that I wasn't interested in being part of the coven and their magic, but Chloe always gave me grief." She leveled her intense, blue gaze at Lachlan. "What happens next?"

"I doona know, lass, but I have a feeling the goddess has something in mind. 'Tis why she conjured her cauldron—to concentrate her power."

"I thought we did that when we made love."

He smiled. "Aye, I could feel the verra earth move."

"Och, you Scots." She aped his brogue and punched his arm. Her brow furrowed, and she undid enough clothing to peer at her upper arm. "I didn't look when I was getting my clothes on. Is that what I think it is? It's hard to tell from this angle and without a mirror."

"What do ye think it is?"

"A dragon tattoo."

Lachlan nodded. "Without even looking, I'm certain 'tis twin to the one I bear."

"I understand the reason you're marked, but why me?" She captured her lower lip between her teeth, no doubt considering her own question.

Lachlan drank her in. No matter what her expression, Maggie was the most entrancing woman he'd ever laid eyes on. He could've watched her forever.

"Hey." She poked his side. "You're staring at me like a lovesick teenager. I asked you a question."

"The simplest answer is because I'm bonded to Kheladin. As my mate, ye're bonded to the both of us." He hesitated. "Ye're so bonny, lass. I love looking at you—"

"Here." Ceridwen waved the phone at Maggie. "Take this infernal piece of modern life back."

Maggie strolled over to her. "Thanks for not dropping it into your cauldron."

"Please. Even if I did, it wouldna harm it." Ceridwen spat into the cauldron before shrugging back into her robe. "That aunt of yours is the most annoying woman. 'Tis amazing she's still alive."

"Is she coming here?"

"What do ye think?" Ceridwen speared Maggie with her inky gaze.

"Well, she's a bully, but she's also a coward, so my first guess would be no."

"Ye'd be correct. Lachlan, get over here. I developed a plan while the two of you blessed my grove."

He trotted to Maggie's side and linked arms with her. The cauldron bubbled like an angry mud pot. Questions circulated in his mind, but he wanted to hear what Ceridwen had come up with first. In truth, he didn't understand enough about a world where people took to the skies in motor-driven tubes to be of much use.

"Come stand on my side of the kettle, children. I shall turn it to a scrying pool. Lass, no matter what ye see or how ye feel about it, doona touch the surface of the liquid. Keep quiet as well. Once we have seen the lay of things, we shall act."

Lachlan led Maggie next to Ceridwen. He flanked the goddess on her other side. "Do ye wish us to touch you?"

"Aye. A hand from each of you on my shoulders, touching flesh. Doona move or break contact, no matter what." Ceridwen pushed her robe back, baring porcelain skin dusted with gold.

Maggie dropped a hand on the goddess' shoulder and sucked in a breath. The heat radiating from Ceridwen's body must've surprised her, but she kept quiet as instructed. Lachlan nodded to himself. 'Twas good the lass wasn't always oppositional, and she could do as she was bid if it was important enough.

He stared at the glassy surface of the cauldron and felt the goddess' magic rise and swirl around them. In moments, the liquid formed a picture, followed by others in rapid succession. He recognized Rhukon, Connor, and the Morrigan. All sat watch over a complex piece of magic that formed an opaque wall. Something silvery gleamed behind it.

Ceridwen, who'd been chanting softly, cut the flow of her magic. The cauldron turned into a bubbling mass once again. "You may speak. No need to keep touching me."

Maggie pulled her hand away and gazed at her palm. "Not exactly first degree burns," she muttered, "but close." She narrowed her eyes in speculation. "Your body temperature must push a hundred fifteen degrees or better."

"I'm not human. What did ye expect? Nay, lass." She held up a hand. "Doona answer. What I want to know is what ye saw in the pool."

"The airplane is trapped behind some sort of shielding. I recognized Rhukon, because I've seen him. I assume the huge crow was the Morrigan, and the other man was the red wyvern."

"Excellent powers of observation." The goddess' sharp gaze settled on Lachlan. "Do ye have aught to add?"

"Nay. The binding is extraordinarily complex. I was trying to trace it when ye cut the sending."

"May I ask a question?"

The goddess traded him for Maggie in her gun sights. "If 'tis relevant."

"Is the plane still in the air somewhere? And if it is, will it crash once it runs out of fuel?"

Lachlan shrugged helplessly and turned to Ceridwen. "I'm out of my depth here."

"I doona know for certain," Ceridwen replied. "What I think is this. The airship is so large and heavy and alien, Rhukon and the others were unable to move it out of this world. 'Twas likely their original plan, because it would've lured us away from Earth to a less favorable environment."

Understanding dawned, and Lachlan murmured, "Since they couldna do that, they erected a barrier and are waiting us out. They will engage us in battle if we come to them, but the odds on our side are not good. First, we would need to defeat all three, and then there would still be the problem of neutralizing their casting."

"In the meantime, Gran's plane will crash if we do nothing." Maggie blew out a defeated-sounding breath. "It might crash anyway. All those things you outlined will take time—too much time."

"Aye, lass, 'tis about the size of things," Ceridwen concurred. "We need assistance."

"Could Gwydion and Arawn help?" Lachlan asked, still working on integrating what he knew about the modern world and magic to address their current problem.

"I already summoned them."

The air on the far side of the kettle took on a numinous glow. The Celts emerged as the glimmering faded. Arawn's dark hair hung loose. He wore old-fashioned battle leathers that clung to his broad-shouldered form like a second skin. Gwydion's blond hair was braided in many small rows. Mage robes, deep blue, belted with cream, flapped around him.

"Thank you for extending aid to myself and my mate." Lachlan inclined his head formally. No matter Gwydion and Arawn felt like old friends, they were still gods and worthy of deep and abiding respect.

"Och aye, and when ye described the lass, ye dinna do her justice." Gwydion winked broadly and loped to Maggie's side where he balanced his staff against his body. Laying his hands on her shoulders, he stared at her. "What a beauty ye are."

Lachlan snorted. Apparently the Celt wasn't going to mention spying on them. "Och, so my description was lacking, eh?"

Gwydion waved him to silence and kissed Maggie on both cheeks. "Blessings on your nuptials, witch. May ye live long and produce many bairns."

"I second those wishes." Arawn tossed his unbound hair back from his face and leapt nimbly to Maggie, pushing Gwydion aside. He took one of her hands and kissed it.

"Thank you. Both of you." Maggie's voice sounded strained. Lachlan imagined it was shock at coming face-to-face with mythical figures she'd probably read about but never guessed were real.

"Enough of this." Ceridwen's voice rang out. "Lachlan, we need Kheladin. He is better able to maneuver in the air than any of us. Plus, as a dragon, he's more likely to recognize the casting we must defeat."

Lachlan felt his bondmate stir. The dragon was more than ready to come out. He'd been close to the surface since their narrow escape from his cave. "Before I loose him, what's our plan?"

A savage smile split Gwydion's face and was mirrored on Arawn's and Ceridwen's. In that moment, they looked like the three ancients they were. It didn't take much of an imagination to see blood dripping from their mouths and fingers. Rhukon's blood.

"Simple," Ceridwen said. "We draw magic, travel to the psychic barrier, defeat it, and free the airplane."

"All right. Who will do what? And why do ye need Kheladin?" The dragon gave a great, rolling heave inside him. Smoke poured from Lachlan's mouth. The dragon didn't give a good goddamn why he was needed, he wanted out. Now.

"Beast getting away from you, lad?" Arawn inquired archly. Lachlan didn't answer. It took all his concentration to remain in human form.

"The weave of the barrier is dragon magic," Gwydion inserted smoothly. "Kheladin will recognize it and understand how it can be offset."

"How do you know it's not the Morrigan's work?" Maggie asked.

"It dinna have the stench of Celtic magic," Ceridwen replied. "If it had, I could likely have nullified it from here."

"Kheladin will be—" Lachlan stumbled over the word *helpless*, knowing the dragon would react badly. "Uh, unguarded while he works out the barrier's mysteries."

"We will be there," Arawn said.

"Aye." Ceridwen chuckled. "What's that modern saying? We shall have your back."

"What about me?" Maggie's voice shook a little.

"Good question." Gwydion turned his intense blue gaze to stare at her. "Ye could remain here next to the loch."

"Probably the best plan," Lachlan concurred. "By far the safest." He moved to her side and bent to kiss her, but she sidestepped him.

"What if I don't want to stay here?" she demanded. "After all, it's my grandmother. Maybe she'd be able to help us, if she knew we were there, and we needed some extra magic or something."

"Not wise, lass." Lachlan infused the subtlest spell at his disposal into his words, hoping like hell she wouldn't notice.

"Stop it." She tossed her head like a restless mare and walked a few feet away, keeping a wary eye on Lachlan. "Why couldn't all of you," she spread her arms, "just sort of encase me in a spell and bring me with you?"

"Because then we'd have to watch over you, and it would take our attention away from...other things." Gwydion sucked in a breath, his nostrils flaring. "We shall be under attack. Ye'd be helpless."

Maggie looked from one to the other of them. "There's something you're not telling me."

"Witch blood runs strong in that one," Arawn commented.

"Aye, pity she never developed her magic," Gwydion concurred.

"Oh, for Christ's sake, stop it. I agree with you. I was a fool to walk away from what the coven offered, but I didn't have a crystal ball when I made that decision."

Lachlan hurried to her side and pulled her against him. "Doona speak thus to them—" he began.

"Why not? It isn't as if I cursed them or anything."

"Because they truly are gods. They only look human."

"So?" She pulled away from him and tossed her hands in the air. "They've presumably been here all those years you were asleep, which means they're used to humans being outspoken, and they won't take offense."

Gwydion's mouth twitched. "Wonder what all that fire looks like when she's on her back with her legs spread?"

"Aye, or on top with her breasts bouncing and her hair cascading about her," Arawn added and winked.

"Men!" Ceridwen rolled her eyes. "Put your cocks back under your clothes. What they're not telling you, lass," she turned to

Maggie, "is the only way ye could come is if ye ride Kheladin. The dragon's magic would protect you."

"Excuse me?" Maggie cleared her throat and dissolved into a coughing fit. Gasping and spitting, she straightened. "People only ride dragons in children's stories."

"The topic's been broached afore," Lachlan reminded her.

"Yeah, but it was conceptual then. I need some time to get used to the idea."

Lachlan considered telling her time had just run out, but it sounded harsh, so he held his peace while he fought a pitched battle with Kheladin. He glanced at his hands, saw they'd turned to talons, and knew he'd lost. *"Wait,"* he begged. *"Let me get my clothes off."*

"What the hell?" Maggie switched her gaze from the goddess to Lachlan as he hurriedly stripped off his shirt and shinnied his breeks down his legs.

He knelt to unlace his boots and finished sliding his breeks off. "'Tis the dragon," he spoke around a mouth that was rapidly changing shape. "He likes the idea of you on his back and—"

Kheladin took form, obliterating Lachlan's next words. Wings sprouted, a tail grew. Haunches formed. Scales coated everything. In moments, an immense copper dragon stretched his wings and fanned the air. Spinning green eyes zeroed in on Maggie. *"Come astride me, lass. I would take you for a ride."*

"Lachlan?" Maggie's mind speech sounded shaky and hesitant. *"Are you inside somewhere?"*

*"Aye, my love. I'm part of Kheladin, and he is part of me. Doona fear, we shan't let you fall."*

# CHAPTER 14

*Me and my big mouth.*

Maggie stared at the dragon. She heard herself hyperventilating. Knowing Lachlan was bound to a dragon and actually seeing that dragon were two very different things. To buy herself time to think, she walked around Kheladin, reaching to touch his coppery scales with tentative fingers. The dragon stood at least eight feet from the ground to the top of his head. Leathery wings folded over his back. A sinuous tail wound around his back feet, much like a cat's might've done. Long, amber talons graced all four feet. They were curved and looked sharp as knives.

Smoke curled lazily from the dragon's mouth. His jaws split in what might've been a smile, displaying double rows of razor sharp teeth. *"What think ye, witch?"*

*"You're beautiful. I understand why Lachlan wanted to bond with you."*

Kheladin nodded his great head, as if he agreed with her assessment. Maggie tried to dredge everything she knew about dragons from her subconscious and came up dry. "So, my, uh, choices are to either stay here while you all go, or ride Kheladin and come with you?"

"Aye, lass," Arawn answered. "Ye must decide quickly. If we tarry, the plane will idle through its fuel and plummet to the bottom of the Atlantic."

*Of course I'll stay here.*

*It would be foolhardy to do anything else.*

Those were the same instincts, Maggie noted, that had kept her away from her magical heritage. "To hell with it," she snapped. "I'm going. Gran's in trouble. Lachlan is my husband, er, mate. I should be by his side if there's danger."

*Besides, I couldn't bear the waiting. It would tear my heart out.*

Jaw set in a tense line, she strode to Kheladin's folded rear leg. "How do I get on? It's a long way up there."

Ceridwen tossed an appraising glance her way. "Ye have mettle, lass. More than I would've guessed when ye cringed away from joining your body with Lachlan's in front of me."

"*Step on my knee,*" Kheladin instructed, tapping his bent back leg. "*Once ye are there, I shall lift you.*"

Within the space of three heartbeats, she sat astride the dragon. Maggie had done plenty of horseback riding, but horses didn't fly. No saddle here. No bridle. If she fell off a horse, she might break a leg. Falling off Kheladin, she'd break every bone in her body and then some. She wound her arms around Kheladin's neck, but it was so huge, she barely spanned a small part of it.

"*Nice, lass. Ye can hug me any time ye want.*"

Maggie laid her cheek against Kheladin's scaled neck. The coppery rounds were warm. *Maybe this won't be as impossible as I fear.* Her heart pounded so hard she was afraid she might pass out. A headache bloomed behind her right temple. "*Could we sort of do a quick practice flight before we leave?*"

"*I doona see why not. Draw magic to shield us from humans who might look to the skies,*" the dragon commanded.

"*Consider it done,*" Gwydion said.

Maggie forced herself to keep breathing as Kheladin furled his wings. They beat the air, once, twice. On the third downward stroke, they were airborne. She squeezed her eyes shut. Maybe if she didn't look down, it wouldn't be so bad. She thought about Lachlan —and Kheladin. It was curious Lachlan treated the Celts like the gods they were, and Kheladin didn't hesitate to order them about as if they were his lackeys.

*And they complied,* she realized with a start.

*"Of course they did. Dragons are special,"* Kheladin informed her smugly. *"Open your eyes, Maggie. See my world."*

Compulsion flowed beneath the dragon's suggestion, and Maggie's eyes snapped open. They were about fifty feet above the ground. Kheladin inscribed long, looping circles in the still air. She loosened her death grip around his neck, didn't feel she was in danger of plummeting to Earth, and folded her hands in front of her. There was something soothing about the air racing by them.

*"I think I'm good with this,"* Maggie sent, aware of time slipping past. *"We can leave anytime."*

*"No matter what,"* Kheladin cautioned, *"doona leave my back until we are back here, or I tell you 'tis safe."*

*"Why would I want to?"*

*"Rhukon can be most persuasive. He can conjure images of almost anything. If ye saw your kinswoman lying in a pool of blood, ye'd be sore tempted to go to her."*

*"There's so much I don't know."*

*"Good ye realize it."*

Maggie cursed herself again for being a short-sighted fool. She wondered why Mary Elma hadn't taken a harder tack with her—forced her to learn magic, whether she wished it or not.

*"It doesna work that way, lass. Ye must welcome your power, or your castings will backfire. They might even be the death of you."*

*"Oh."* While it didn't surprise her that the dragon could pluck thoughts from her mind as easily as Lachlan or the Celts, it was still unsettling to have everyone know exactly what she was thinking.

*"Convenient, though."* A whistling, snorting sound that might have been dragon laughter rustled through her. *"Like getting three wishes*

*and not even having to come up with one idea, because I already know what you want."*

An old Rolling Stones song about needing and wanting passed through her mind. Maggie snorted. Maybe Mick Jagger knew more than he let on about trips to fairyland. *"How long until we get where we're going?"*

*"Time is...different. 'Twill seem like hours, yet no time at all is passing in the world ye just left. One impression isna any more real than the other."*

*"I thought Gwydion—or maybe it was Arawn—said Rhukon couldn't move the plane away from Earth?"*

*"Poor choice of words. Earth is a big place."*

*"Ye willna understand with your modern mind,"* Lachlan cut in. *"Psychic layers circle the Earth. Rhukon took advantage of one. He wove his barrier into its weft."*

*"Aye,"* Kheladin added. *"We must be verra careful not to damage something critical when we attack his binding."*

Maggie didn't ask what might happen. She didn't really want to know. Lachlan was right about her twenty-first century brain being in full rebellion. People didn't ride dragons or go off to fight bad guys who'd shanghaied airplanes—and her grandmother. Look at the World Trade Center. Despite knowing what was about to happen once the planes diverted from their flight plans, the full power of the U.S. Government had been helpless to intervene.

Time, indeed, passed. Warmth rose through the dragon's scales. It was enough to countermand the wind-chill eddying about her. If her torso got cold, she leaned it against Kheladin's trunk of a neck. The first time she did it, the dragon made a lewd comment about the feel of her breasts, but Lachlan shut him up.

*"Where are Arawn, Gwydion, and Ceridwen?"*

*"Mayhap already there,"* Lachlan answered.

*"Child!"* Mary Elma's worried voice jangled discordantly in Maggie's mind. *"No! It's too dangerous. Go back."*

*"Gran? Is it really you?"* Tears threatened to overflow, and Maggie

knew she'd unconsciously prepared for the worst: Mary Elma's death.

*"Of course it's me. What the hell are you doing? Go back. I have things under control here."*

*"Whether ye will have us or no, we are coming to assist,"* Lachlan said.

*"Look, you young sprout."* Mary Elma sounded almost as overbearing and bitchy as Chloe. *"You're the dragon shifter linked to my granddaughter in the prophecies. Your job is to keep her safe. I breathed a sigh of relief when I knew she'd found you—finally. I can take care of myself. Take your dragon and go home. That's an order."*

*"Excuse me. Ye canna talk so to me."* Lachlan sounded furious.

*"Nay, to us,"* Kheladin seconded. Smoke streamed from his mouth.

*"This is the second reason I walked away from the coven."* Maggie broke in before a pitched verbal battle unfolded. *"Every single witch thinks she's hot shit. Gran, Lachlan's my husband. You have to be nice to him. Ditto on the other side of things. Gran is my closest kin."*

*"Child."* Mary Elma protested. *"You know nothing. You can't protect yourself."*

*"We'll talk about that later. How are the rest of the people on the airplane?"*

*"Asleep."*

Maggie's heart lurched. *"Did the oxygen system fail?"*

*"Christ! I put them to sleep. They were bellowing about like a bunch of stupid, angry sheep. I knew I'd never be able to figure a way out of things with them screaming and crying and carrying on."*

*"We are here, lass."* Kheladin's voice held a warning note. *"Keep quiet, I must concentrate."*

Maggie wanted to ask her grandmother if she'd seen Rhukon or the other wyvern or the Morrigan, but she bit back the words. This wasn't the time to assert herself. That Mary Elma was also quiet spoke volumes. Her grandmother was ancient and powerful in her own right. Maggie had never known her to bow to anyone— magical or not.

She looked about. A fine, white mist filled the air. If she focused hard and used her very rusty and almost untrained third eye, she could just barely perceive the outline of an airliner suspended in the murky ether. Kheladin flew back and forth. From time to time, he directed streams of smoke or fire at something in particular. Sometimes it flared back at him.

*"Hang on."*

She wasn't certain if Lachlan or Kheladin had barked the warning, but Maggie clasped her arms around the dragon's neck and not a moment too soon. Kheladin banked and veered. A huge jolt of power missed them by an angstrom. Maggie felt the backlash from it burn every inch of exposed skin. She could only imagine what it would've done if it actually hit them. The dragon dodged another strike. He flew half a figure eight and blasted something with fire. He rolled, surfaced, and did the same again.

Maggie swallowed her screams. If she clung with her arms and legs, she wouldn't fall off. *Yeah, right. Just keep telling myself that.* Where the fuck were Arawn, Gwydion, and Ceridwen? They were supposed to provide counter fire so Kheladin could do his work. The stench of something burning filled her nose. Terror paralyzed her. It took all her concentration to hold tight to Kheladin. She silenced a growing conviction she was going to die in this dark place.

Lachlan and the dragon might be immortal. She wasn't.

After another series of rolls and aerial acrobatics, where the bottom dropped out of her stomach, and her head spun crazily, Lachlan screamed at Kheladin that they had to leave, that it was too risky without help. Kheladin rolled again, spewing fire. Maggie's sweat-slick hands lost their grip. Limbs flailing, she fell for a long, heart-stopping moment before the dragon looped beneath and caught her.

*"We're leaving now,"* Lachlan screeched. *"Now. No arguments."*

*"But I almost had it, afore we were attacked,"* the dragon protested. *"I'm certain, with just a bit more—"*

*"Leave,"* Lachlan bellowed so loud Maggie's ears ached. *"Ye will kill the lass if ye continue."*

*"I-I'm all right. Really."*

*"Total horse shit. Ye are not."*

*"We can't leave. We're the only ones here. Gran will die."*

*"That may be true, but if we remain, I fear ye'll be killed…"*

Power zapped past them, focused on the barrier. Maggie cringed against Kheladin's scales and imagined herself invisible to boost her puny warding skills. "Shit," she muttered. "Now they're attacking from behind." More jolts crashed past them, so bright she squeezed her eyes shut.

*"Sorry to be late to the hanging,"* Ceridwen called merrily. *"They verra nearly trapped us. Damn that Morrigan, anyway. What a crafty old bitch she is."*

*"But we're here now."* Arawn zipped past Maggie's field of view, power blazing from his hands.

The dragon didn't wait for an invitation. He returned to his slow, methodical assault on the barrier. Power thundered around them, not quite so close as before, but near enough Maggie expected to be tossed from her perch at any moment.

If she hadn't been watching, she would've missed it. One nanosecond, the barrier was in place. The next, it was gone as if it had been nothing but illusion all along.

*"We did it,"* Mary Elma crowed. *"I'll wake the pilot. Get my granddaughter out of here. I swear, dragon shifter, if she's harmed, I'll hunt you through every circle of Hell and personally strangle you."*

*"'Twas a time I was looking forward to meeting your kinswoman,"* Lachlan muttered. *"Now I'm not so sure."*

Maggie considered making excuses, but witches were a bossy, overbearing lot, with limited tolerance for others with magic. No point in making up nice lies only to have Mary Elma blow them out of the water when they picked her up at the airport.

Kheladin wheeled. Arawn, Gwydion, and Ceridwen closed from three sides. *"Doona fight me,"* Gwydion cried. *"I'm using a different strategy to return us. I dinna care for what happened on the way here."*

Maggie steeled herself for, well, for just about anything. Projectiles, lights, a rocky ride. None of it happened. Before she had time to settle into her perch, where the dragon's neck joined his body, they were floating over the grove near her car.

Kheladin touched down so gently, she wasn't certain they were on the ground until he said, *"Let me help you down."*

Though he set her down easily, Maggie's legs buckled beneath her, and she landed on her butt, understanding how terrified she'd been. *Maybe not safe forever, but I'm safe for now.* Repeating the phrase in her head, she dragged herself upright and stood in place until her head stopped spinning, and her legs agreed to walk in a straight line. Part of her wanted Lachlan's arms around her, needed to hear him crooning soothing nothings. She looked around, hoping he was back in human form, and she'd just missed the transformation because she was so out of it.

Her gaze lit on Kheladin instead. Mouth open in a wide grin that displayed his double rows of teeth, he looked extraordinarily pleased with himself as he fanned the air with furled wings.

Maggie shook herself from head to foot, annoyed that all it took were a few rounds of sex to turn her into a helpless female who needed a man to tell her everything would be all right.

*I can do this. I did just fine before he walked into my life.*

*Of course I can. I rode Kheladin, didn't I?*

The Celts materialized out of nowhere and crowded around Kheladin, patting him and speaking in Gaelic. Maggie assumed they were telling him he'd done well. While she didn't want to interrupt his accolades, they had to get moving. As it was, they'd hit the early morning traffic around the Glasgow airport.

Maggie plucked her bag from the tall grass, amazed no one had stolen it. She stumbled to her car. Once there, she pulled the door open and made a grab for the bottle of tea wedged between the seats, drinking long and deep. She wished it were liquor. Any kind would do. Just something to steady her nerves. She thought about everything that had transpired since the dragon hoisted her onto his back and tried for perspective, but her mind recoiled.

*I'll think about it later, when I'm not so shaky.*

She sank into the driver's seat and drank more tea, grateful no one was paying the least bit of attention to her—or fussing over how rude Gran had been. Her eyes slid shut. She must've dozed sitting up, because Lachlan's voice dragged her from an uneasy half slumber.

"Lass, we must leave."

Her eyes flew open. Confused, she looked around them. "Where'd everyone go?"

"The Celts are convening their council. As far as they're concerned, the black and red wyverns and the Morrigan have declared open war on us. We will retaliate."

"Get in." She gestured to the far side of the car. "We still have to pick Gran up, since her plane will show up at the airport now."

He snorted. "Aye, I feared as much. She doesna care for me." He walked around the car, got in, and closed his door.

"That's not it." Maggie blew out a tired breath. Every bone in her body ached from tension, weariness, and holding on for dear life through Kheladin's aerobatic maneuvers. "She was worried about me and willing to lay waste to the world if it would keep me safe."

A slow smile spread over Lachlan's face. "Aye, then, mayhap we shall get on better than I thought, since protecting you is at the top of my list as well."

Maggie ferried the car out of the parking lot. "I'm going to look for a diner. I need coffee and something to eat." Lachlan fumbled with the radio's dials. "What are you trying to do?" she asked.

"I want to find that fellow again to see what he has to say about flight 427 being returned from the halls of the dead."

Maggie laughed, recognizing a fine edge of hysteria when she heard herself. *Guess I'm still pretty shaken-up.* "I'll get the station for you. Now that you mention it, I'd like to hear the news, too."

# CHAPTER 15

*L*achlan watched Maggie surreptitiously via a series of sidelong glances. It wouldn't do for her to see how frantic he'd been about her. He'd ordered the dragon to return just before she'd fallen from his back, but Kheladin—drunk on battle-fury—had ignored him. Granted, the dragon managed to fly beneath Maggie in time to catch her, but his staging was far too close for Lachlan's liking.

"Damn it," Maggie said. "Had a station dialed in, but I lost it. I don't have high def radio in this car, so we're stuck with the basic broadcasting networks."

"I have no idea what ye just said, but I'm thinking what occurred with the airplane was unusual enough, someone should be talking about it."

"You're not kidding." Maggie snorted. "Oh! Here's something. Let's see what kind of spin they're putting on it."

A woman's crackly voice continued. "…BBC News. I tell you, it's a bloody miracle. Air Blue Sky's Flight 427 disappeared off radar for one hour and fifty-nine minutes. Yes, you heard me. Nearly two hours. And then there it was again, as if it'd never left its trajectory. It reappeared in the same spot it disappeared and is en route for

Glasgow International Airport, where it will land in approximately one hour. Crews are clearing the airport and runways, just in case, but our latest report suggests the plane is undamaged. The Glasgow Constabulary has other ideas, and I have it on good authority that the British SIS are on their way…"

"Humph. No rush, then," Maggie muttered and reached to turn the sound down. "Hard to say when they'll let us into the terminal. In fact, think I'll call Gran once the plane is on the ground, and she's allowed to turn her phone on. She can take a shuttle to one of the nearby hotels. It will give us somewhere to wait for her."

"Hotel, as in a country house or inn?"

"Yes, you rent rooms. We can take showers, clean up, maybe even grab a nap."

"Mmph."

She reached across the car and patted his arm. "What's that supposed to mean?"

"Not that I wouldna welcome any excuse to lie down with you, lassie, but I told Gwydion I'd join them as soon as I could."

"Where are they having this council gathering?"

"Near Inverness."

"Do you suppose they'd let Gran be part of it? I'm sure she's steaming mad, and the coven could be a powerful ally."

"Ye should have been a tactician. I'm ashamed I dinna think of it first. How long do ye think—" Maggie's phone chimed. She reached for it, and the car swerved. Lachlan batted her hand away and dug the phone out of her bag. "Here. How do ye stand being summoned by that thing? Goddess's teeth, it's worse than a fretful bairn."

Maggie tapped the smooth display and mouthed *I'm putting it on speaker* at Lachlan. "Gran. You can't have landed yet."

"I haven't."

*So that's what she meant about speaker,* Lachlan thought. *Excellent. I can hear both sides of the conversation.*

"Then how are you calling me? It's against—"

"For godsakes, stop asking questions. I broke a lot of rules this trip. One more won't matter a whit. Is the dra—, er fellow still with you?"

"Yes."

Lachlan waved from his side of the car and opened his mouth, but Maggie shook her head.

Mary Elma blew out an exasperated-sounding breath. "Because of what happened, it's likely the plane—and all of us in it—will be detained for hours while officials question us."

"Yes. I'd planned to get a room near the airport."

"Don't bother. Turn the car around. Go back to the northlands. Certain things are…stronger there, and your new friend will be better able to protect you. Once they turn me loose, I'll come to you."

Maggie pursed her lips in annoyance. Lachlan didn't have any trouble reading her mind. Insofar as Maggie was concerned, she didn't need protection. After all, she'd managed Kheladin, hadn't she?

*Aye, lass, ye managed the dragon only because he allowed it.* Lachlan made a mental note to talk with Maggie about his link with Kheladin and dragons in general. It wouldn't do for her to underestimate them.

"Are you going to rent a car?" Maggie asked, still intent on her phone call.

"Maggie. Please."

"Um, sure, Gran. Sorry. It's been a hell of a night. I wasn't thinking clearly."

"You often don't."

Lachlan saw Maggie wince. Anger flared, turning the energy field surrounding her blood red. The lass had been through hell and back and shown an excess of courage in his book. "Now ye look here." He broadcast his voice toward the phone. "Your kinswoman is one of the bravest lasses I have ever met. I'll not have ye disparaging her."

Mary Elma brayed laughter. "Well, thanks for telling me we were on speaker, Mags. I assume you're Lachlan."

"Ye'd be correct. Furthermore, Maggie is now my mate. That means—"

"Stand down, man. I know exactly what it means. I'll look forward to meeting the man who actually coaxed my granddaughter into an emotional commitment." A few more snorts of laughter, then the faint hum of the phone faded.

"Fuck! She hung up," Maggie exclaimed and slammed the phone down on the console. "Not much point in wasting any more fuel. I'm pulling off at the next exit. We'll rustle up coffee and a snack, and then we'll head back north."

Maggie looked in a foul mood. Her eyebrows were drawn into a single line, and her jaw rippled with tension. He wanted to comfort her but wasn't certain just what she was so distressed about. Mary Elma had been a wee bit abrupt, but no more so than crones from his own time. Older women had a lot of latitude and clout.

Maggie pulled the car off the main road. It careened down a side street and came to a stop in a spray of gravel at an inn with one of the flashing signs that had rattled him back in Inverness hanging in a window. He infused a subtle calming spell.

"Whatever is wrong, lass? Your kinswoman is alive and well. She'll be by your side soon enough."

Maggie rolled her eyes. Her hands gripped the steering wheel so hard, her knuckles whitened. "Yes," she said through clenched teeth. "It's good she's alive. I do love her, but she annoys the living shit out of me. That last barb about emotional commitment rankles."

"Mayhap," Lachlan trod gently, "if ye could tell me what she meant by it, I'd understand—"

"—why I'm so upset?" she finished his sentence for him. When he nodded, she shut her eyes for a moment and captured her lower lip beneath her front teeth before turning to face him. "It's a long story. I'm exhausted and still not thinking terribly straight, so you'll get a synopsis."

"Aye, lass. Would ye like to get something to revive you in the inn afore telling me aught?"

"Probably a good idea, but let me at least kick the door open. Then if you have questions, you can hang onto them and ask me after we've eaten." She inhaled deeply. "Ever since I lost my parents, I've been pretty insular and self-sufficient. That was true even when I was a young child."

She hesitated, her brow creased in thought, and shook her head. "Uh-uh, those terms don't really cover it. I've prided myself on not needing anyone or anything. It's probably one of the reasons I walked away from the coven. Witches are quite interconnected with one another. I didn't want to depend on anyone else—for anything. It's one of the reasons I became a doctor. So I'd know how to take care of life-threatening situations by myself, without help."

Lachlan quirked a brow. "Well, at least it explains why ye werena married or even had an intended lurking about."

"This isn't funny." Fire flashed from her eyes.

He covered her hands on the steering wheel with one of his own. "I wasna poking fun at you, lass. Come inside. Ye'll not be so prickly with a full stomach."

"What I just told you doesn't bother you?"

He grinned. "Nay. Why should it? I like my women with spirit. Ye're a rare challenge, lass. One I look forward to."

"Christ! You make me sound like a prize horse you're about to break."

His mouth twitched. He tried not to laugh but failed utterly. After a dicey moment when she looked about to kill him, Maggie joined in. When he could talk again, he said, "Being together will take some getting used to. I suspect there may be a wee bit of *breakage* on both sides."

MAGGIE PULLED the car off the highway at Fort William. It would be good for both of them to get out and stretch their legs. Lachlan had been right. She felt much better after the smoked salmon, blood pudding, potatoes, and the mushrooms and tomatoes that were a staple of every Scottish breakfast. Three cups of strong coffee helped too. That had been over an hour ago, and her full stomach made her sleepy.

Lachlan dozed for part of the drive. Her eyes felt gritty. She wanted sleep too, but there was no way she could turn the wheel over to him. While it seemed unlikely Mary Elma would beat them to Inverness, Maggie didn't want to deal with her grandmother's ire if she wasn't there to greet her properly. Something else nagged at her, but she was too tired to process it.

She pulled the car into a spot across from Loch Linnhe and stroked Lachlan's arm. He started awake. "Where are we, lass?" He peered out the window. "'Tisn't Inverness."

"No, it's Fort William. I need to get out and walk around, or I'll fall asleep driving, and we'll get into an accident." She hesitated.

*Should I?*

"What is it?" He stared intently at her. "Your mind isna easy."

*I should've known better than to think I could hide anything from him.* "It might be foolish—maybe just nerves from not sleeping and everything that's happened—but I've felt something odd this past half hour or so."

Alarm radiated from him, and he shot to attention. "Odd, how?"

She felt stupid. "Like something's out to get us. The fine hairs on the back of my neck are prickling. I'm sure it's nothing, but—"

"Doona discount your instincts. They may not be honed, yet magic runs strong within you."

Her stomach clenched. "It's what I was afraid of. That what I sensed might be Rhukon on the loose again. I imagine he's pretty pissed at this point."

Lachlan grinned wryly. "That, lass, is the understatement of the century. Let's stroll by the loch. Doona be afeard. There are too many people about for him to try something. If it is, indeed, Rhukon, I'll know it quick enough."

"Then what do we do?" Her voice shook, and Maggie understood how rattled she was.

"It depends which form he shows up in. Come." He got out of the car and walked around to her side. She pushed her door open and got out. The air smelled like summer, ripe with growing things. The lake's clean scent was calming.

He placed a hand beneath her chin and brushed his mouth across hers. "Sweet. I could do with more kisses, lass."

She smiled. There was something about Lachlan that was so genuine, it was impossible not to care about him. Never mind the hotness factor. He was the most sensual male she'd ever laid eyes on. "I rather like the idea myself—after I've gotten a few hours' sleep."

"Mayhap we could find a gentlemen's shop here."

Maggie turned, got her purse, and locked the car. "That's right. We never did get you different pants at the airport." She jabbed her chin in the direction of town. "Let's go that way. Fort William has lots of shops. It's pushing nine, so they'll just be opening up."

Her feet scrunched over damp grass full of little, wild daisies. At the far end of the green, they crossed a footpath and moved onto old-fashioned cobblestone streets crowded with merchants. "Look!" Lachlan pointed at a kilt displayed in a shop window. "I'd much rather get another plaid—even though 'tisn't my house tartan, and 'tis skimpily cut."

Maggie glanced at the other people wandering the streets of Fort William. Every man wore trousers. "Look yourself," she countered. "Not a kilt in sight. You want to blend in, not stand out."

"I doona see why." He shrugged. "Rhukon already knows where I am. It doesna matter what the rest of these folk think of me."

Maggie leaned close. "Speaking of Rhukon…"

"I doona sense him."

She relaxed, but only fractionally, and kept her voice low. "Is it possible he's doing something to make himself undetectable now he knows you're awake again?" Maggie thought about the little she understood about magic. "If he were, um, keeping tabs on us, he'd have known you were asleep in the car. I'm a much more vulnerable target."

"I know ye're worried and edgy, lass. Try to believe naught can happen while I'm by your side."

"You were there when I fell off Kheladin..." Her throat thickened.

*Damn it. Got to get hold of myself. Nothing happened. I was just scared. It isn't like Kheladin didn't catch me, even with Lachlan distracting him by screaming we had to leave.*

"I'm verra sorry about that, lass. Most humbly sorry—"

"*I caught you, dinna I?*" Kheladin broke in sounding irritated.

"*Yes, and many thanks,*" Maggie replied.

"Let's try in here," she added brightly before Lachlan could apologize again—or he and Kheladin got into another argument about it—and tugged him toward a men's store. They were rooting through stacks of pants in the back of the establishment when a clerk approached them.

"Needin' help, are you?" The young woman had white-blonde shoulder-length hair and the bluest eyes Maggie had ever seen. Dressed in a micro-mini, tank top, and teetering on her high heels, she looked vaguely Goth with blackened lips and white eye shadow.

"I think we've about got it. Where are your fitting rooms?"

"Off to the left-hand side. May I hang those in a room for you?" The clerk held out a hand, but Lachlan just stared at her.

"Why are ye wearing so little, lass? And painting your mouth black?" Lachlan sounded outraged. "Surely your kinfolk—"

"Um, we'll manage. Thank you," Maggie said and poked Lachlan in the side. "Come on, let's try them on. That way you won't have the same problems as last time." As they found their way to the dressing room, she whispered, "Many young women dress like that. As I recall, I wasn't wearing much when you first saw me, either. It doesn't mean a thing. Just custom."

"Humph. At least your lips were flesh-colored." He went through the door she pushed open. Maggie followed him inside. "Och aye, and ye're going to watch?"

"No, I'm going to help, so we get out of here quickly. I'm still worried Gran might beat us back to Inverness."

"Why is that a problem?"

"She doesn't wait well."

He unbuttoned his trousers. "Somehow, that doesna surprise me."

Twenty minutes later, Maggie headed for the front counter with a pair of black sweat pants and two pairs of corduroy ones. She left Lachlan in the dressing room lacing his boots—quite the production number, but he'd had to take them off to get into the corduroy trousers. The pants hadn't been a perfect fit, but he agreed they were far better than what he'd worn into the shop.

The same clerk stood behind the register. She arched plucked brows and grinned with bleached teeth. "A bit of a Neanderthal you've got, eh?"

Maggie made a noncommittal gesture that she hoped conveyed something like, *Men! Can't live with 'em, can't live without 'em.* "I'd like to purchase these. Plus my, er, husband has another pair just like these corduroy ones that he'll be wearing out of the store." Maggie grinned at the clerk. "Maybe you could dispose of the jeans he wore in here. He's never liked them."

"Of course, ma'am." The clerk rolled her eyes in a show of solidarity at men's vagaries.

Maggie slipped her Visa card from her wallet and held it out to the clerk. Swiped, signed, and finished, she headed toward the door with her purchases wondering what the hell was keeping Lachlan.

*I'm just grumpy. Too much caffeine, not enough sleep.*

*What about too much excitement?*

*Yeah, that too.*

She stuck her head out the front of the shop and looked up and down the street. A bakery was two doors down. Maggie moved back inside the store and made a hand sign to get the clerk's attention.

"Aye?" The young woman hurried to her side.

"When the Neanderthal emerges from the dressing room, could you tell him I'll be in the bakery just down the street?"

"Sure." The clerk frowned and tugged at her short skirt. "He's been in there for quite a while. Do you suppose he's all right?"

"He's fine. His boots take time to lace, is all."

"Aye." The clerk's eyes gleamed with sudden interest. "I noticed them. Never seen the like. Would you know where he got them? I'd love a pair."

"Sorry." Maggie shrugged. "I'm afraid I don't. Normally, he does his own shopping." She pushed the shop's door open and walked briskly to the bakery.

By the time she carried a pot of tea and chocolate scones to a table, she'd begun to worry. Lachlan should've shown up by now. She set her things down and looked outside the bakery door, expecting to see him striding toward her, but he wasn't there.

She went back to the table, took a sip of tea and a bite of scone, but the food and drink tasted wrong somehow.

*Something's happened.*

*Calm down. Nothing's happened. He's all right. Just taking his time. Maybe he's talking to the clerk. She was a hot little number.*

Maggie pulled her phone out. She kept an eye on its clock. When five more minutes passed with no Lachlan, she couldn't stand it. She got up, gathered her bags, and hurried out the door. Something heavy pressed on her chest. She recognized the sensation as out-of-control anxiety, but that didn't make it any easier to breathe.

She hastened back to the men's shop and nearly ran headlong into the clerk on her way out the door. "Ma'am," the girl said breathlessly. "I was just about to close up shop and try to find you. Your friend…" Her voice shook. Bright color splotched both cheeks. "You see, it was seeming like it was too long, so I went to the changing room and knocked. He didn't answer. I knocked again."

Words rushed out of the young clerk in a torrent. "So I opened the door, and he wasn't there."

Maggie winced. It felt like she'd been kicked in the stomach. "Is there a back door?"

"No, ma'am. That's just it. There's no way he could have left the store without me seeing him."

# CHAPTER 16

Maggie scarcely remembered stumbling from the shop and the brief walk to her car. She tried to ward herself, but shook so badly, she couldn't concentrate. She'd wanted to calm the shop girl down, but she'd been so distraught, she hadn't had anything to offer. The young woman, who probably wasn't a minute past twenty, had snapped up her phone and said she was going to call a constable. Maggie told her not to bother, that it wouldn't make any difference.

"Och, and it's like that is it?" the girl had said, curving her fingers in a sign to ward off evil.

"Och, and that's how it is," Maggie repeated dully as she unlocked her car and got inside. She locked her door and felt like a fool. If Rhukon and his cronies could nab Lachlan, what hope did she have? A locked car door wouldn't even slow them down.

Maggie slid her iPhone from her bag and brought up its memory. She stared at her grandmother's number—and at Chloe's. It didn't take a genius to decide Chloe couldn't help, not from thousands of miles away. Shame swept through her, making her feel ill. Gran was right. She really was stubborn, and she'd done an incredibly thorough job of shutting herself off from everyone who'd ever cared about her.

Maggie closed her eyes for a moment, girding herself. She swallowed hard and tapped her grandmother's number.

"Yes?" Annoyance underscored that one word.

Maggie opened her mouth, but the only thing that came out was a croak.

"Margaret. Whatever is the matter? Say something. I'm still stuck in this goddamned airport. They've lined us up like terrorists and are interviewing us separately."

Maggie choked back a sob. She hadn't felt this helpless since her parents died. Around a tongue that felt thick and uncooperative, she managed, "It's okay, Gran. I'll—"

"From the catch in your voice, I'd say something is definitely not okay. What the fuck happened? Don't beat around the bush."

A tear rolled down her cheek, followed by another. Maggie wanted her grandmother's arms around her, needed her witch magic to set the world right again. "First," she said shakily, "if I get out of this, I'm going to beat a path to coven headquarters and sign that blasted pledge—with blood. This psychiatry fellowship in Scotland was a stupid idea."

"Hush! You have no idea who might be listening." A shock radiated through the cellular lines, stinging Maggie's fingers.

*Damn!*

She switched the phone to her other hand and flexed her reddened fingers. "That hurt. If I can't say anything, how can I tell you what happened?"

A sharp intake of breath. "Never mind, Maggie. I can pick it up in…other ways." A minute ticked by before Mary Elma spoke again. "So he disappeared about twenty minutes ago?"

Maggie nodded, and then remembered Gran couldn't see her. "Yes."

"I know you're not astute in certain, um, methods, but can you sense anything?"

"No. Earlier, when we were driving here—"

"Where's here? Are you home?"

"I'm in Fort William, not all that far from home. Maybe an hour. It's about sixty miles."

"Earlier, when you were driving there, what?"

Maggie leaned forward. She rubbed the bridge of her nose with her first two fingers. Conversations with her grandmother were often like this: odd and disjointed.

"Maggie?" Mary Elma's tone was so severe, it surprised her.

"I felt something dark and unsettling following us."

"Do you feel it now?"

*Well, do I?*

Maggie did her best to send her nascent power outward. "I don't think so."

"You have to do better than that. When you were getting all those worthless years of medical training, what would your professors have said if you told them you *weren't sure* about some deadly illness?"

*They would've chastised me just like you're doing now.*

"Point taken. Look, Gran. I'm scared. I'm running on almost no sleep. I'm not thinking very straight. I'm so far out of my depth I should pack up my things and go home, except that's not an option."

"What do you want to do?" A sly undercurrent underscored Mary Elma's question, but for the life of her, Maggie couldn't pin it down.

"I have to help him. He's in trouble."

"That was the right answer, child. By God, I think I finally found the key to getting you to accept your destiny."

"Fine." Maggie batted exasperation to a back burner. It was an indulgence she couldn't afford. "What do I do in the meantime?" *Crap! I sound like a ten-year-old.* "How do I keep myself safe until you get here, so you don't have two of us to hunt down?"

"Fort William, eh?" Mary Elma murmured. "Give me a moment. Stay put, and I'll call you back." The display flared *Call Ended.*

Maggie stared at the phone in her hand. And waited. Her eyelids felt ridiculously heavy. When she realized they'd drifted shut, she forced them open. It wouldn't do to fall asleep. Rhukon nearly made off with her in a dream. She'd have to be a bigger chump than she already was to make *that* mistake again.

Just when she'd decided to wait outside the car in hopes fresh air would keep her awake, the phone trilled. Maggie punched *Answer*. Before she could get the whole of *hello* out, her grandmother cut in, "I'm texting you an address. Go there and wait for me."

"But who is it and—?"

The screen flashed. Mary Elma had disconnected. The phone chimed its text tone. Maggie was so tired the letters and numbers blurred, so she made them larger. Clicking keys, she fed the address into the phone's navigation system. Ever obliging, it spit out a list of directions.

For a moment, she considered ignoring Mary Elma's edict. The least her grandmother could've done was talk with her, tell her where the hell she was sending her. "This feels like *Mission Impossible* where the tape self-destructs right after I hear the instructions," she muttered. Seized by sudden panic, Maggie stared at the phone, but the directions were still on its display.

*Guess that settles it.*

She turned the key in the ignition and headed north toward the far end of Loch Linnhe. As she drove, she forced herself to breathe deep, cracking a window for more healing air. It took a while to locate the indicated address. As frequently happened with the map system in the phone, it sent her on a wild goose chase, and she had to retrace her steps a couple times.

Finally, she found the place and got out of her car. A whitewashed cottage was set at the end of a long, brick walkway. Wild roses grew over a fence that was falling down in places. The flowers smelled wonderful, lush and heady. Who the hell had her grandmother sent her to? Would they simply accept her as blood kin of one of the most powerful witches on Earth?

*May as well find out.*

She got her bag and locked the car, then marched up the walkway. Maggie walked for a long time. Much longer than it should've taken. At one point, she turned around and stared at her car. Her eyes said it was only fifteen yards away. Her legs told a different story.

*Aha! This is another witch's house. That must be it.*

She thought about the tricks various relatives used to camouflage their dwellings and meeting places. Problem was she'd never developed her magic sufficiently to defeat another witch's casting. She walked for a few more minutes and turned to look at her car. It hadn't moved, so obviously neither had she.

Anger sparked. She was too tired to play games. She sat on the bricks and reached for her phone. In that moment, the darkness she'd sensed earlier rolled over her in a cloud and tightened, obscuring the brightness of the midday sun. Panic threw her heart into overdrive. She heard herself panting, her breath hoarse in a too-dry throat. Maggie pushed to her feet and ran toward her car. If nothing else, she could put distance between herself and what threatened her.

*"Enough. Stop where you stand,"* a woman's voice cracked like a whip in her head.

Maggie tried to keep going, but couldn't. It was as if her legs were stuck in deep mud. "Please," she moaned. "If you're going to help me, for Christ's sake do it now before I get swept off to wherever Rhukon's taken Lachlan."

*"Pull yourself together. Turn toward the house."* Maggie's body spun of its own volition. Fear turned her belly to water. She clapped a hand over her mouth and forced herself to take shallow breaths, afraid she'd heave her breakfast onto the tidy bricks.

*"Look at the house. Really see it."* Sounding less harsh now, the voice held an almost hypnotic quality.

Maggie focused on the house. The white cottage was gone. In its stead stood a three-story stone manse with ivy crawling up its sides. From the looks of it, it had been there for hundreds of years.

*"Now that you see it, walk toward it. The house will let you inside."*

She had no sense of propelling her limbs forward, but she moved inexorably closer to the house. The nearer she got, the more her sense of danger retreated. It wasn't dark anymore. The Scottish sun felt warm and welcoming once again. Somehow, never mind how, the good magic was strong enough to push Rhukon's aside. Maggie floated up a dozen steps and collapsed on the far side of a carved, wooden door that swung open to admit her and slammed shut in her wake. Sobs raked through her as she lay prostrate on a shiny, hardwood floor.

"For the love of Pete," a strident voice right next to her said, "if your kinswoman told me what a ninny you were, I wouldn't have been so quick to say I'd help. Get up and tell me what that mess in my yard was all about. Who in blazes is after you?"

"American?" Maggie pushed herself to a sit and stared at a buxom woman of about five-foot-eight. She was dressed in a floor-length denim skirt and a green T-shirt with a witch atop a broomstick. Beneath the picture were the words, *My Other Car is a Broom.* Bare feet with bright red toenail polish peeked from beneath the skirt. Red curls stuck out from her head in all directions before trailing down her shoulders and back. A pair of sharp, brown eyes radiated displeasure. The woman looked to be in her forties, but looks were often deceiving with witches. Power flowed around her like a gown. She fairly crackled with it.

"Once upon a time I lived in the States, but that's not important." The woman hunkered next to Maggie and laid a hand over hers. Maggie felt the spell, welcomed it because it cleared her head and settled her stomach.

"Thank you."

"I'm Mauvreen, and you're welcome. Come into the parlor and have some tea and biscuits. You can tell me what's got Mary Elma so fired up." She shook her head disapprovingly. "After that, you'll sleep for a spell. You need it. You're dead on your feet, woman."

∼

Lachlan flung magic about himself, but it didn't even slow his descent. One moment, he'd been kneeling and lacing a boot. The next, something slammed into his body out of nowhere and shoved him down into darkness. He hadn't had even a moment's warning it was coming. The sense of falling was absolute and disorienting.

*"Kheladin."*

*"I canna help. Something shackles my wings."*

His next thoughts were for Maggie, and he sent a mental entreaty to every Celtic god close enough to listen to keep his mate safe from harm. A bone-crackling thud sent pain ripping through him. For long moments, he was afraid he'd broken something and would need to cast magic to heal himself. He stretched his arms and legs experimentally and blew out a breath he didn't know he'd been holding.

*Thanks be to the gods, I only got the wind knocked out of me.*

Lachlan pushed to his feet and summoned his mage light. It took more effort than he thought it should, but it finally sputtered to life. He gazed at his surroundings. Stone walls stretched as far as he could see on both sides of him. A low stone ceiling dripped water. Red eyes stared at him in the reflected glow from his light. Rats.

What was this place? He bent closer to examine the stonework. Clearly manmade. Someone had carved this tunnel, or at least reinforced it so it wouldn't collapse. Corridors led in either direction.

*Where am I?*

Recognizing the stupidity of racing off half-cocked, he forced himself to catalog what he knew, which wasn't much. He felt for Maggie's energy but couldn't sense her at all. Maybe that was a good thing, unless the same magic that captured him had dropped her in a totally different location. Mage senses on full alert, he turned in a circle, emitting power like a dowsing rod. Though he took his time, Lachlan didn't know any more when he was done than when he began.

He turned his mind inward to the dragon. *"Do ye recognize aught?"*

*"Nay. Mayhap if we traded places…"*

*"There isna enough space. We're in some sort of underground tunnel system. I'll mark where we are and walk in one direction until either we're above ground or hit a dead end."*

*"Canna we use magic to leave here?"*

Lachlan considered it. The prospect was tempting, but the problem about using magic to travel was he needed a firm destination in mind and some sort of connection with it. He could try for Maggie's home but didn't want to rain disaster down on her. If he weren't careful, Rhukon, or whoever the author of the current disaster was, would snare her too.

If they hadn't already.

*"Do ye think the black wyvern is responsible for this?"* Lachlan asked sidestepping Kheladin's query about magic for now.

Snorting, whuffling dragon laughter filled his mind. *"Who else? He doesna like to lose, and we made him look like a fool in front of his cohorts."*

*"Can ye sense him—or the red—anywhere near to us?"*

Kheladin was silent so long, Lachlan started to ask again, when he heard. *"'Tis strange. I doona sense either Connor or Rhukon, yet I do detect other dragons. Many dragons. Just as it was afore Rhukon captured us in the sleeping spell."*

*"Ye must be mistaken. How could that be?"*

*"I doona know, yet I trust what my magic tells me. Pity ye canna let me look for myself."*

*"As soon as I get us above ground,"* Lachlan promised. Confusion jockeyed with uncertainty. He didn't know what had happened, but he had to act—and quickly before whatever attacked them struck again. He and the dragon were vulnerable in the relatively narrow

tunnel—open to strikes from both sides. It wasn't a defensible position. The warrior in him knew it.

Since one direction seemed as good as the other, he started walking. If the earth beneath his feet trended downward, he'd retrace his steps and go the other way. He walked for a long time. Lacking any other way to mark his progress, Lachlan counted steps. He'd reached six hundred thirty when the tunnel's floor developed a definite slope to it, an upward cant.

He dared to let himself hope he'd chosen wisely. Before Rhukon ensorcelled him, Lachlan always considered himself a lucky man and a blessed one. Now he wasn't so certain. With effort, he pushed his doubts and fears aside. They wouldn't help him, wouldn't return him to Maggie's side.

After fifteen hundred steps, the air began to smell cleaner, less dank. The rats, constant companions on his journey so far, thinned out, apparently preferring the darker, damper segments of the tunnel. Either his mage light was getting brighter, which meant his magic was strengthening, or…

He doused the light and shut his eyes to defuse the afterimage. When he opened them, his mouth split into a grim smile. Daylight. It was a way yet, but it spilled into the tunnel and provided pale illumination.

After close to three thousand steps, he marched from the tunnel into a thick forest. "Okay," he murmured, borrowing one of Maggie's words. "I'm out, but this forest could be anywhere."

He cast magic about himself, hunting for anything living and gasped. Kheladin had been right. There were dragons here, along with wolves, bears, coyotes, and a few, isolated pockets of people. He headed for the closest place he sensed men. They'd tell him what he wanted to know. In less than half an hour, he came upon a clearing with a small house. Not knowing whether he'd be seen as friend or foe, Lachlan cloaked himself with magic and approached carefully but stopped long before his presence might've alarmed the people he saw milling about. The dwelling's mud and stone walls and thatched roof answered his questions more poignantly than any person could have. If that weren't enough, a horse burdened with a plow yoke corroborated the unpleasant truth.

Lachlan faded back into the forest, the dragon clamoring in his mind. *"Kheladin. Be quiet. We're back in the sixteen hundreds. Or maybe it's the fifteen hundreds or fourteen hundreds."*

*"How—?"*

*"I doona know, and it doesna matter. Rhukon went to great lengths to separate me from Maggie, so he could sidestep the prophecy."* He pounded a fist into his thigh, cursing his own stupidity and inattention, and sank into the dirt at the base of a large tree. If he'd been at the top of his game in that blasted store, and not thinking about burying his cock in Maggie, he might not be in this predicament.

He thudded his fist into packed earth and then did it again and again until his hand ached. Lachlan marshaled his weary mind. Right now he was reacting, when what he needed to do was think.

*The Morrigan must be mixed up in this. The Celts mastered time travel eons ago.*

"Maggie." Her name leapt from his mouth in a breathy whisper, half entreaty, half prayer. "How will I ever get back to her?"

*"If we're really back in our own time, let me out. I can find our castle from the air."*

Lachlan recognized a good idea when he heard one. He'd barely stripped off his clothes when he felt himself shift.

# CHAPTER 17

Maggie woke to the soft murmur of voices. For the barest moment, she had no idea where she was and just enjoyed stretching out her limbs. Truth—cold and ugly—pushed the breath from her lungs, and she leapt from the bed. Jolted back to reality, she stared at the neat guest room Mauvreen had led her to and the double bed with its cheery patchwork quilt where she'd literally passed out.

*Bet my witchy host had something to do with that.*

Maggie hurried from the room. She had no memory of how the house was laid out, so she just followed the voices and hoped to hell the house wouldn't play any more tricks on her since she was inside. It took a number of twists, turns, and half flights of stairs before she found the main floor. Memory returned in filmy wisps. She dashed into the parlor where she'd had tea, but it was empty. A door on its far side stood open. Through it, she saw Mary Elma and Mauvreen sitting by an enormous stone fireplace drinking something out of heavy, ceramic mugs.

"Gran!" Maggie loped into the room.

"Child." Mary Elma shot to her feet.

Maggie didn't see her cross the large room, but somehow she

ended up in her arms. Maggie clung to her as if she were drowning, embarrassed by tears she couldn't control. They splashed from her eyes as if someone turned on a spigot.

"There, there. Pull yourself together." Mary Elma stroked her back. "I was about to waken you, anyway. There's not a minute to waste."

Something in her grandmother's tone got through. Maggie remembered that tone from her childhood. It didn't leave any room for argument—or self-pity. She disentangled herself from her grandmother and straightened her shoulders. Mauvreen thrust a mug into her hands. "Drink this."

"What is it?" Maggie sniffed the fragrant liquid.

"Booze."

Maggie turned her gaze on her grandmother's friend. "A bit early, isn't it?"

Mauvreen shrugged. "As they say, it's always five o'clock somewhere."

Maggie remembered telling Lachlan that, and it brought a fresh spate of tears.

"Drink it." Mary Elma's words were more command than suggestion. She drew herself up to her full height of six-foot-two and frowned at her granddaughter. "You have to learn to pick your battles, child. This isn't one of them."

Maggie's lips twitched into half a smile. "For once I agree with you." She moved the mug to her mouth and sipped. Yes, there was definitely alcohol in the mix, but it contained herbs and other things too.

"Better." Her grandmother's mouth curved into a wry grin. "We only poison our enemies."

*Enemies!*

"I've got to find Lachlan. Do you know where he is, Gran?"

Mary Elma's grin flattened into lips pursed in a hard, flat line. "Yes."

"That doesn't sound good." Maggie's hands shook enough, she worried she'd drop the mug.

"It's not," Mauvreen seconded. "Grab a seat. We need to strategize." She flicked fingers at the cold hearth, and it blazed to life. "Fires are good for many things, not the least of which is dispelling chill shadows from fell deeds."

Maggie sank into a deeply padded, needlepoint chair. The two other witches dragged their matching chairs close. "How long did I sleep?"

"A few hours," Mauvreen said. "You needed rest, so I saw you got some."

"I suppose that's why I have absolutely no memory of getting from the parlor to that bedroom I woke up in."

Mauvreen quirked a brow but didn't say anything. She exchanged glances with Mary Elma who said, "We can give it to her straight. My granddaughter's a doctor. While she may have been foolish about her magic, she's far from squeamish."

Maggie took a large swallow from her mug. The drink had something in it that strengthened her, made her less shaky. "Give what to me straight?"

Mary Elma skewered her with bottomless, dark eyes. "Did you consummate your bond with Lachlan?"

To her dismay, Maggie felt herself blush. "Yes. More than once, if it matters."

"Did you meet the dragon?" Mauvreen asked.

"I not only met him. I rode him."

Mary Elma clapped her hands together. "Better and better. This won't be as difficult as I feared."

Maggie twisted her head from side to side to ease the iron bar of tension sitting between her shoulder blades. "Stop talking in riddles. Just tell me where Lachlan is and how I can get him back. Are we all going to go fight Rhukon or something?"

"Tell me what you know about Lachlan and Rhukon." Mary Elma

sat straighter in her chair. "In fact, start at the beginning, and tell us everything."

Maggie raised her cup again, drank, and was surprised she'd drained it. Mauvreen plucked it from her hand, refilled it from a kettle Maggie hadn't noticed sitting atop the hearth, and gave it back. "All right." Maggie nodded. "A few days ago, I'd taken off some time in the middle of the day. I was walking near the intersection of…"

Her story took much longer to tell than she expected, since one witch or the other interrupted with requests for either more information, or clarification, over and over again. "…Anyway, that's about it," she finished.

"Fascinating." Mauvreen's brown eyes glowed.

"Yes, isn't it?" Mary Elma agreed.

The circular conversation sucked her dry but didn't tell her anything she wanted to know. It grated on Maggie. She waited while the witches stared at one another, presumably communicating telepathically. She tried to listen in but couldn't. After about five minutes, Maggie cleared her throat, but the other women ignored her. Finally, she'd had enough. "Hey! I need to know where Lachlan is. At least an hour ago Gran said there wasn't a moment to lose. I want to get moving."

"Oh you do, do you?" Mary Elma focused intently on her. Maggie forced herself to stare right back. "Alrighty, child. Lachlan is back in the middle of the sixteenth century. He'll be right at home there, since he lived through those times. I imagine his castle is intact. Dragons still fly free, which should please Kheladin."

Maggie's eyes widened until the room lost focus. "What? You must be mistaken. How could he possibly have traveled hundreds of years into the past?"

"It isn't as if he did it on his own," Mauvreen cut in. "We're certain he had help. An assist from the dark side, as it were."

Because sitting felt far too confining, Maggie set the cup down and bolted to her feet. After pacing the length of the room twice, she ended up in front of her grandmother and put her hands on her hips. "Can you do that?" she demanded.

"Do what, child?"

"Time travel. It's what we're talking about."

Mary Elma shook her head. "No. It's not one of my skills. There hasn't been a witch who could bend the strands of time for centuries."

Maggie digested the words. "What I just heard was it's not on the current menu of magical skills, but it's something we could do in the past." Her grandmother nodded. "Is it something I could learn?"

*I can't believe I said that. I'm not equipped. It's too dangerous. I could die somewhere, lost in time...*

Mary Elma got to her feet. She moved to Maggie's side and draped an arm around her waist. "All those things in your head are true. Even if you'd taken to magic when your moon blood first flowed, you'd have a hell of a road mastering time travel."

Her thoughts jumbled into eerie, kaleidoscopic images. "Someone understands the mechanics of time travel," she said slowly, "because their casting moved Lachlan."

"The Celts," Mauvreen muttered with a bitter edge. "They don't often use it, but they figured it out millennia ago. At least I think they did. Scuttlebutt for the years I've been around was they at least know how."

"Idle rumor," Mary Elma broke in. She rolled her eyes. "But probably with more truth in it than not. The Celts aren't big on sharing their secrets with witches. Dragons command that particular magic too. They need it to visit Fire Mountain."

Even if she wasn't a witch but a far more powerful magic wielder, Maggie wasn't at all certain Ceridwen, Gwydion, or Arawn would help her. "Lachlan mentioned some sort of Celtic Council gathering to plan a war strategy."

"Humph. You didn't mention that when you told us what you knew," Mary Elma snapped. "What else did you leave out?"

"Never mind." Mauvreen flapped her hands at the other witch

and returned her attention to Maggie. "Do you know *where* they're meeting?"

"Somewhere outside Inverness."

"Close enough," Mauvreen muttered. "Has to be Inverlochy Castle, where the Celtic Council always hangs out. Let's go. The local witches will likely know about the meeting, even if they're not included."

"We can take my car," Maggie offered.

Her grandmother snorted. "We'll get there our own way. It's faster—and more unobtrusive."

"Yes," Mauvreen said. "Come here. Mary Elma and I talked about this while you were asleep. We're going to share blood with you. It will hasten the development of your magic, particularly in light of your carnal connection with Lachlan."

Fear and indecision pounded through her. "Once I do this, it's like signing the coven's pledge, isn't it?" Her ambivalence about her witch heritage throttled her like an out of control tsunami, narrowing her airway. Never mind what she'd told her grandmother about racing to coven headquarters to sign on.

The two witches closed on her, one from either side. "That darkness that nearly had you in my yard," Mauvreen hissed. "It hasn't left. It's still here. The other side needs you here and Lachlan right where they chucked him."

"You don't have enough power to do this on your own," her grandmother said sternly. "Not even close. Even if you studied twenty hours a day, you're years away from marshaling enough power to be more than a hedge witch."

*"By that time, the damage Rhukon, the Morrigan, and the red wyvern have done to Earth will be so extensive, it will be impossible to reverse."* Mauvreen spoke into her mind.

Picking up the telepathic thread, her grandmother continued. *"You feel torn because darkness sits just outside these doors. It's bending your mind with subtle suggestions. Mauvreen and I have ways of dealing with it, but you're vulnerable. You need our blood. It's a shortcut and cheating—"*

"*And breaking every coven's rules,*" Mauvreen cut in.

"*But we deem it necessary. And so we are willing to risk censure and punishment at the hands of our peers,*" Mary Elma finished.

Maybe it was the drink, maybe the power oozing from her grandmother and Mauvreen, but Maggie heard raw truth in their words. In that moment, she kissed her old life, the one where she wore neat, tidy lab coats and enjoyed being called doctor, goodbye. Her crusty, judgmental grandmother was bending the rules for her. The least she could do was cooperate wholeheartedly.

Maggie looked from one woman to the other. When she said, "I'm ready," her voice was amazingly steady.

Mauvreen pulled an ivory-bladed knife from her skirt. She cut deep into the ball of her thumb and then into Mary Elma's. A small part in the back of Maggie's mind rebelled at the blade that couldn't be sterile and at the prospect of opening herself to blood borne illness, but she stifled it.

*I did it when Ceridwen joined Lachlan and me. When I'm done with this, I'll have magic to heal myself.*

The blade stung when it cut her. Mauvreen pressed Maggie's bleeding flesh against her grandmother's, and then the witches traded places, and she shared Mauvreen's blood. Power flowed into her, heady in its strength and scope. Bits and pieces of castings ran into her mind and formed cunning patterns, deceptive in their seeming simplicity. Senses thrown wide open, Maggie felt like a child of the universe when the witches finally withdrew their hands.

*It's like I plugged into a motherboard, and it's filling my circuits with knowledge.* A wild, untamed intensity raced along her chakras. When she realized she could identify all her body's psychic power points, laughter bubbled from her and filled the room.

Her grandmother laughed along with her, but it held a grim edge. "Yes, it's a bit like that. We're giving you everything we can because before this is over, I fear you'll need every scrap of it and more."

"Thank you." Maggie wrapped her arms around herself, feeling like she might explode into a million motes of psychic energy.

"It is done," Mary Elma intoned.

"Yes, it is done," Mauvreen echoed.

Maggie glanced at her hand, expecting to see an open, oozing wound. Smooth, pink skin met her questioning gaze. The women had used witch magic to heal her. There wouldn't even be any kind of scar. "How—?"

The corners of her grandmother's mouth twitched. "We mingled healthy cells with the cut ones until they all looked the same."

"I finally understand why you weren't thrilled about me going to medical school. What you do is a whole lot more sophisticated than modern medicine. I suppose I always knew that at some level, but I never let myself appreciate what it meant." Maggie took stock. "I feel...more alive than I've ever been. Like I could do anything."

"Well, don't get too cocky until you sort out all that magic we shared," Mauvreen murmured.

"Yes, you wouldn't want to paint yourself into a corner," Mary Elma said. "If you're ready, we need to leave."

Maggie walked back to the parlor and picked up her bag. "Sure." She called over her shoulder, still marveling at the miraculous transformation realigning her body and its abilities.

"Get back in here and watch carefully." Her grandmother sounded like her old, grumpy, imperious self. "You'll lend your new power to our traveling spell, so you can understand how it works and how we come out where we want to."

IT DIDN'T TAKE LONG, perhaps only moments, before Maggie found herself back on the outskirts of Inverness in front of a crumbling medieval cottage. This time she wasn't fooled, and she focused her third eye on it. Its lines wavered, straightened, and formed a tidy, stone lodge with a broad front porch and the low lintels that gave away its origins as seventeen or eighteen hundreds.

With a flash of skirts, Mauvreen disappeared inside.

"Why do all of you hide your houses?"

Mary Elma eyed her with more than a touch of asperity. "Last time I checked, you're now one of us. So the operative question would be why do *we*—?"

Maggie flapped her hands at her grandmother. "Yes. Fine. I'd like it a whole lot better if you just answered my questions and skipped the lectures."

"The beginnings of wisdom are knowing which questions you truly need the answers to. We hide our homes for the most obvious of reasons. So people will leave us alone."

Maggie thought about it. Though she hadn't been privy to any but the most perfunctory ceremonies, she'd always suspected blood sacrifices were involved in the ones she'd been barred from.

*Blood. Chanting. Robes. Nudity. Group sex. No wonder they, er we, wouldn't want witnesses...*

Mauvreen emerged from the house with a broad grin and told them the Inverness coven knew exactly where the Celts were meeting because they'd been invited. Mary Elma wiped a triumphant smirk off her face, and for the first time, Maggie picked up her grandmother's thoughts which ran along the lines of, *It's about fucking time they appreciated us.*

*Celts and witches hold different kinds of magic. Who knows, maybe there's untapped synergy here.*

Drunk on borrowed power that made her feel she could conquer the world, she rolled her mental eyes at her automatic foray into scientific inquiry.

*It's going to take time,* she lectured herself, *to integrate who I am now with who I was.*

"Well?" Mary Elma snapped her fingers, and Maggie's head popped up. "Don't you want to come to the meeting?"

"Of course." She trotted to her grandmother's side. An image filled her mind, and she pushed on it just like she'd done when they used magic to leave Mauvreen's. Once her mind view cleared, she was in a large, richly appointed room with candle chandeliers. People, presumably Celts, milled about in small groups. The scarred, wooden floor was scattered with large, colorful cushions and thick woven rugs. Ceridwen sat near one end of the room stirring her cauldron and muttering, her brows drawn into a single, frowning line.

"Where are we?" Maggie whispered to her grandmother.

"The Celts maintain several old castles scattered through the Highlands. This one is Inverlochy."

Maggie remembered a trip she'd taken to visit the older Scottish castles. "But it's in ruins," she protested.

Mary Elma smiled. "Not today, it's not. Welcome to the power of magic."

Maggie felt someone's energy focused on her. She glanced up, not surprised to meet Ceridwen's speculative gaze. Glad to see the goddess, Maggie darted forward. She'd only made it a couple feet before Mauvreen grabbed her arm. *"Not so fast. We are guests here, which means we don't move about freely until they give us leave."*

*Lots of new rules.* She gazed about, hunting for Arawn's dark, swirling hair or Gwydion's blond braids.

Something pushed against her psychic edges so hard, Maggie instinctively raised her hands and then looked at them in surprise. What was she doing? She had no idea how to draw power to defend herself. Not yet, anyway. She dropped them to her sides, hunted for the source of the power buffeting her, and found it. Ceridwen was still staring at her.

The goddess's inscrutable gaze locked on hers. "Ye've come," she crowed. "I told the others Lachlan's mate wouldna desert him. Come forward. We shall send you to rejoin your beloved."

Mary Elma stepped between her granddaughter and the

goddess. Legs spread, hands on her hips, she tipped her chin up and said, "I think not, goddess."

Ceridwen flowed to her feet. Maggie thought she could see sparks arc across the room. "Ye dare to speak against my will?"

"She's my kinswoman. It is my right."

Maggie stared in disbelief. She wanted to help Lachlan. If Ceridwen was willing to send her, why the hell was Gran standing in the way? "I'm sure it will be fine—" she began.

"Silence. You know nothing," Mary Elma hissed, looking nothing like the woman who'd raised her. Power crackled around her until the air grew blue-white with electrical charge.

"You heard her." Ceridwen raised her voice and threw her arms wide to encompass the whole room. All conversation ceased. "The lass is willing to go. Dinna she say that?"

"Not exactly." Maggie cut in, too annoyed at feeling like a pawn to care she was probably violating some sort of protocol. "What I said was I was certain things would be fine."

"Oh, they'll be just peachy," Mary Elma muttered. "Once they send you tumbling through time, you won't have any way to get back. Not under your own power, anyway. If you can't find Lachlan or raise the Celts—or sweet-talk a dragon—you'll be stuck there."

# CHAPTER 18

Kheladin soared high above the Scottish forests. From time to time, a dragon he knew trumpeted, and he greeted them in return. If it weren't for the lass, their mate, he'd be just as happy remaining in a familiar world. One where he wasn't almost the only dragon outside Fire Mountain. Maggie complicated everything, yet he didn't begrudge Lachlan for including her in their bond. In his own way, he felt her absence fiercely.

He needed to talk with other dragons, older kin who'd been alive for millennia. They might know a way to find the lass. She'd ridden him. It cemented his commitment to her, plus she bore his mating bite. Kheladin focused his gaze at the thick canopy below. They'd actually come out leagues from Clan Moncrieffe's castle, but his powerful wing beats shaved the remaining distance quickly.

*"At least the castle will still be standing,"* Lachlan commented.

*"Unless 'tis afore thirteen hundred, and it wasna yet built."*

*"Ever the optimist, aren't you?"*

LACHLAN SANK into thoughts of how to get back to Maggie. About the only avenue was to throw himself on the Celtic gods' mercy. He shook his head. The gods weren't known for clemency. Far from it. He could imagine Gwydion arguing that now Lachlan knew his part in world events to come, he could work things from this end to make certain he wasn't snared by Rhukon.

The logic was indisputable. If Lachlan didn't end up asleep in his cave, Rhukon wouldn't be able to work his behind-the-scenes treachery. No, the only help he was likely to get from the Celts was they might corral the Morrigan to limit damage from that quarter. Even that wasn't likely, though. Celts shielded their own, no matter what they'd done.

Lachlan gazed out at the world through Kheladin's eyes. If he'd been in human form, he would've ground his teeth together in frustration. What good was immortality if the one woman he'd ever had feelings for was lost to him—forever?

Familiar Highland mountains rose around them. If he were any judge, they'd be home very soon. Home. Except it didn't feel that way anymore. Not without Maggie by his side. Kheladin circled, losing elevation. The dragon banked his wings and brought them down in the central courtyard of Clan Moncrieffe's castle.

Twenty or so people backed away, their eyes round with fear. Two of the men picked up cudgels and watched them warily.

*"What is the problem?"* Kheladin asked.

*"We must have returned afore ye and I bonded. Let me shift into myself."* He felt the dragon's resistance, even understood it. If Kheladin had his way, he'd be off hobnobbing with dragon friends he hadn't seen in over three hundred years. Dragons he'd been afraid were lost to him forever. An unpleasant understanding horned its way in. *"Ye'll get to choose again—or not. Once I'm back in my human body, we'll have to redo the magic that bound us, since it hasna happened yet."*

A long pause. *"Not that I doona wish to link our life paths, but would ye mind if I had a brief respite?"*

It was a risk, but if he didn't agree, he might have a rebellion on his hands. *"Not at all. Ye were young when ye chose me. Frolic all ye wish, but 'twould make my heart sad if ye werena to return."*

*"Mine as well...bondmate."*

Lachlan felt the dragon's hot breath embrace him as he found his body. For the first time in hundreds of years, he stood in human form, buck naked, and watched his dragon spread its leathery wings and take to the skies without him. Tears pricked behind his lids. He blinked them away. It would never do for his people to see their Laird cry.

"Laird." Shock made the stableman's voice sharp. "I last saw ye within." He bowed low. Lachlan made a non-committal gesture. He existed in one place. Either here, in the future, or in the past. He held no concerns about running into a duplicate of himself inside his castle, but blundering through an explanation would be awkward.

Another man saved him the trouble by asking, "And where did ye get the handsome dragon?" The few maids passing through the courtyard whispered and giggled, reminding Lachlan he was naked.

"Could one of you find me a cloak?" With a flurry, the stableman, John, unclipped his and draped it around Lachlan. "Thanks be to you." Lachlan nodded curtly. "I shall return it verra soon."

"But where were ye, Laird?" John persisted.

Lachlan leveled his gaze at the crowd, managing to catch the ones staring at him and the ones pretending not to look. "Mage business. Ye doona wish to inquire too deeply." With that, he turned and strode into the castle. His castle. When he'd first wakened in the year 2012, he would've given every gold coin in Kheladin's hoard if his castle were still standing. To find it gone had been a horrible shock. Despite that, he took no joy in this homecoming.

He worked his way up passageways and stairs to his rooms on the third floor. Someone had changed the rushes. The room smelled sweet, and a fire burned in its hearth. Despite it being summer, the stone castle was always cold. He opened a clothing chest, removed a plaid, and wound it about himself. Next, he picked up his familiar brush that still had his hairs twisted amid its bristles and worked the snarls from his hair. He was lacing up a pair of soft, deerskin boots when a knock sounded on the door.

"Come."

"Laird." Vanessa, the lead housekeeper and someone who occasionally shared his bed, inclined her head. Her long, red hair was drawn back from her face and hung in a braid draped over one shoulder. Black skirts topped by an embroidered, rust-colored tunic set off her creamy complexion. "I was told ye'd returned, Laird. Is there aught ye desire?" Though she kept her hazel eyes downcast, he had no doubt what she desired. Even without Kheladin's enhanced senses he smelled her heat.

"Nay. Thank you for asking."

"Will ye be wantin' supper at six?"

"Bring a tray to my rooms."

She glanced up at him through dusky lashes. "Would my Laird wish company with his meal?"

"Not tonight."

"As my Laird wishes."

"Vanessa."

"My Laird?"

"Ye will think the question strange, but what year might it be?"

She shot him an odd look before dropping her gaze again. "Why the year of Our Lord, fifteen hundred and sixty-seven, Laird."

"Thank ye kindly. Ye may leave me now."

Lachlan paced the length of his rooms over and over. His heart ached for Maggie, and his mage's soul ached for the dragon who'd become first a part of him and now a part of them—him and Maggie. Because the turmoil in his mind was making him crazy, he left his quarters and loped down the stairs, intent on taking a horse and riding to the Celts' sacred grove. Mayhap he'd find one or more of them, so he could lay out his problem and ask for help. He considered using his magic instead of a horse but was reluctant to test it quite yet. He'd lost Maggie and Kheladin—perhaps not permanently, but they were gone nonetheless. Lachlan didn't think he could stand any more unpleasant revelations today.

*Doona hope for too much,* he cautioned himself and threw a leg over Brandywine, a favorite stallion that he remembered well. The horse tossed its head and whinnied before taking off at a near gallop. Lachlan didn't mind. The wind in his face and hair cooled the fire raging inside. Fear for Maggie ate at him. What had happened to her? Was she still in the future? Had she found her kinswoman, the grandmother with magic strong enough to protect her?

The grove was empty, but he'd expected as much. Beech, ash, and hawthorn trees grew tall and straight, interspersed with standing stones. He gathered simple magic and commanded the horse to stay within the grove. That done, Lachlan knelt to pray. He opened his mind and his heart. The tears he'd held back in his own courtyard streamed down his face. He clawed great handfuls of dirt and let agony pour through him. Maybe it was better Kheladin was gone. If the dragon saw him like this, mad with grief, he'd never respect him again.

"Lachlan." A gentle hand settled on his shoulder. He started and scrambled to his feet, gazing into Ceridwen's ageless face. "Doona speak," she crooned. "I will read what is in your mind."

While she stood, one hand on his shoulder, another atop his head, Gwydion and Arawn materialized. Time slipped away. The sky passed from day into night before the goddess released her hold and exchanged glances with the other two gods.

"Ye wish our help," Gwydion intoned.

Not trusting himself to speak because if they refused him he had nowhere else to turn, Lachlan nodded.

"We must confer," Ceridwen said. "At present, Rhukon is nothing but a mischief-maker, and the Morrigan is useful on the field of battle, though nowhere else. The only red wyvern I know about presides over the red dragon clan across the great land mass in the Far East."

"Ye might scry the future, now ye know where to look." Lachlan shook his head. "'Tis sorry I am. Ye will find your own way without my paltry suggestions."

"Apology accepted." Arawn favored him with a rare smile. It transformed the severe lines of his face into something quite striking. "Ye love this woman."

"He must," Ceridwen said. "I wouldna have officiated at their mating if I dinna sense their commitment, one to the other."

"I cherish her, love her more than life itself." The words cut like sharp glass as they tore out of him. "Rhukon is strong enough to rip me from the future and strand me here. I fear what he may have done with Maggie."

"She has magic of her own," Gwydion pointed out. "Witch powers."

"Aye, but she is untrained."

"Why would a woman fully-grown not have taken her magic to hand?" Arawn frowned.

"Things are different in the twenty-first century. Everything seemed magical to me there. Invisible waves travel through the air and make small things ye can talk on ring…"

Ceridwen held up a hand. "Enough. I will scry what is to be seen in my cauldron. We will come to you with our decision."

"Please." Lachlan heard pleading in his voice, knew he was groveling, and didn't give a damn what they thought of him. "Please. I doona fully understand this, but I canna live without her by my side. She is part of me. Part of a prophecy that links us through time."

"Aye." Gwydion nodded. "We saw that in your mind."

Arawn added, "I must speak with Bran. As our god of prophecy, he'll know of it if 'tis truly of import."

Lachlan fought despair. If the prophecy was so obscure Arawn didn't know about it, perhaps it didn't hold the power he hoped.

"Shield your mind. It bleeds like an open wound." A corner of Arawn's mouth turned down still farther. "Prophecies havena been of much use to me. The dead who walk my halls often cite failed divinations." He shrugged. "They are just as dead. I doona pay much heed to foretellings."

"When I spoke with you in the future," Lachlan said slowly, "ye knew of the prophecy then."

Arawn's eyes narrowed, but he didn't reply.

"Waiting is hard." Ceridwen met his gaze. "I suggest ye make things up with Kheladin. He, too, is part of this. I doona know if ye can find the woman without him."

Arawn nodded. "Twisting the strands of time is a skill we possess. 'Tisn't a matter of simply thinking ye wish to land in a certain year, though. Ye must lead with your heart."

Understanding blossomed. "My heart must be the same. When I met the lass, it was linked to Kheladin."

"Not only that," Gwydion said. "The lass rode the dragon and bears his mating bite. She is joined to the two of you."

"Furthermore." Arawn winked broadly. "I shouldna tell you this, but dragons were the first to master time travel. How do ye think they get back and forth to Fire Mountain, a world outside of time? 'Tis as easy for them as it is for us."

"Enough." Ceridwen's voice rang, loud and grating. She shot Arawn a withering look. The air in the grove shimmered. When it cleared, Lachlan was alone.

~

"WHAT DO you mean I wouldn't be able to get back under my own power?" Maggie heard the shrill note in her voice and didn't care for it.

"Which part of it wasn't clear?" Mauvreen asked, quirking both brows. "Time travel hasn't been a witch's gift for centuries."

"We doona know that. Not for a fact." Ceridwen focused her energy on Maggie. Warmth, persuasion, confidence she'd make the right decision rolled over her in waves.

"The hell we don't," Mauvreen muttered.

Maggie shook her head. "Stop that. I can't think when you bombard me with magic."

"Good for you," Mary Elma muttered and turned so she faced both Maggie and Ceridwen. "This gathering…" she made an encompassing gesture with both arms, "…was a war council, was it not?" At Ceridwen's terse nod, Mary Elma continued. "Is it also not true that if you send my granddaughter back in time, back before Lachlan slept ensorcelled like Sleeping Beauty, it kills two birds with one stone? Presumably, the dragon shifter wouldn't be so stupid as to be caught twice. With Lachlan wide awake and vigilant, Rhukon could never tap into the amount of power he now controls." She slapped her hands together. "Voila! No more problem. No need for a war council. No need to corral the Morrigan." She glared at Ceridwen. "One of your own, I might add."

Maggie bit hard on her lower lip to force thought before she opened her mouth and something untoward slipped out. As usual, her grandmother got an A+ for being astute and cutting to the chase. "I don't get it," she said at length. "The Celts don't need to include me in anything. Lachlan's already back in the middle of the fifteen hundreds, over a hundred years before Rhukon became a threat."

"Smart lass," Ceridwen said, with a smile reminiscent of a scimitar. "Doona be so certain about Rhukon being less of a threat four hundred years ago, though. Once a mage has developed certain skills, they often retain them, no matter where they land in time." She shrugged. "Returning to the topic of you and your beloved, we were just being kind."

"Hogwash!" Mary Elma sniped. "You Celts are never kind. You have some sort of ulterior motive. I just haven't totally figured it out yet."

"Well, I have," Mauvreen said. "Regardless of what they know— or don't—about the extent of Rhukon's powers, they want to make certain Lachlan stays put long enough to at least try to short-circuit all the damage Rhukon, the Morrigan, and the red wyvern have done."

She took a measured breath and blew it out slowly. "The best way to accomplish that is to ferry Lachlan's lady love to his side. Otherwise, he'll move Heaven and Earth to find her. Even now, he's probably half mad with worry and fear that something's happened to her."

"Sort of how I'm feeling about him," Maggie said softly. "If I weren't so stubborn, I'd have told him I loved him. Now I'm afraid I'll never see him again. Never have the opportunity." Her heart constricted. Maggie always prided herself on cool rationality, but when she reached for it, it flitted away. In its place, pain and loss loomed. A lifetime without Lachlan might be fitting punishment for her years of emotional detachment, but she didn't want to go there.

"What do you want?" Ceridwen asked. Compulsion ran beneath her words.

"Be careful," her grandmother cautioned. "Best to say nothing, than be snared in their magic."

"Is this like the genie in the bottle and three wishes?"

"I don't know," Mary Elma said with a little sniff. "Until we do, prudence is your best path."

"Okay." Maggie spread her hands in front of her. "Why couldn't Lachlan get back to modern times? If he could go one way, why not the other?"

Ceridwen didn't answer, which told Maggie that Mauvreen was onto something. The Celts were willing to help her move back in time because it helped them avoid out and out war against the Morrigan. Once she was back there, they didn't need her anymore, and Lachlan was better placed there than he'd been in 2012.

*Well, how do I feel about living in the late middle ages? What do I even know about life then, except on the most cursory level? Short life spans, rampant disease. Zip in the way of any conveniences but lots of servants. So my choices are living in comfort in familiar surroundings without him or trading everything I've ever valued for love.*

"Holy crap!" she muttered. "I really don't like my options here." She rolled her eyes. "Knowing what you all do, why can't some earlier version of yourselves kill off Rhukon, hobble the Morrigan somehow, and as an act of kindness, return Lachlan to 2012? It's not as if he didn't live through the years after he was ensorcelled. He doesn't deserve to have to live them again."

Gwydion stepped to Ceridwen's side. "What ye ask, lass, is far more work than simply moving you back in time."

"Fine." She crossed her arms over her chest. "How about if I pay you for whatever extra effort it takes? I can show you where Kheladin's hoard is located. There's a fortune in gold and gemstones."

"Stealing a dragon's hoard means lifetimes of bad luck." Gwydion waggled a finger at her.

"What then?" Maggie blew out a tense breath. "Surely there has to be another way. One that meets all our needs, not just yours."

"I'd applaud," her grandmother hissed into Maggie's ear, "but it would just piss them off."

"I heard that, witch," Ceridwen said and cracked a wry grin. "And ye're right. 'Tis damned easy to piss us off these days."

"Why are you haggling?" A tall woman, built like one of the ancient Valkyries and dressed in battle leathers, stepped forward. "I'm Andraste, goddess of victory. I like my battles clean, not full of *sub rosa* bargainings. We clearly have an enemy lurking in the past. I say we pluck him off afore he causes us angst—and deal with the Morrigan while we're about things." She gathered her heavy, blonde hair and pushed it over one shoulder. Aquamarine eyes glittered with bloodlust.

The Celts fell into a spirited discussion, mostly in Gaelic. Maggie blew out another harsh breath. *Good.* It would give her time to think. Her grandmother, Mauvreen, and several other women, who had to be the Inverness witches, gathered around her.

"I'm proud you stood up to them," Mary Elma murmured.

*Is that what I did?*

Maggie shrugged. "Maybe it's all those years of dealing with mentally ill people. They're not the easiest to reason with sometimes, but there's usually a way to find common ground."

Mary Elma pulled her off to one side while the other witches spoke low to one another. "I know Ceridwen asked this, but what do you want to do?" Mary Elma caught Maggie's gaze and held it. "I love you, child. I'll support whichever way you want to go, even if it means I never get to lay eyes on you again in this life."

Maggie's thoughts ran in circles, but they always returned to the same place. She nodded to herself and let the words loose. "I love him. I can't imagine my life without him, Gran. No matter what the Celts decide, I'll do whatever it takes. If I have to live my life in a drafty castle with rats and moldy bread, I guess I'm up for it." She'd no sooner spoken than her head cleared. Doubt fell away like yesterday's news.

"That means you made the right decision." Mary Elma kissed Maggie's cheek, having obviously read her mind.

"Thanks."

"Don't take this wrong, but I'm so grateful something finally touched your heart. I worried about you for years. You were just so…removed from everything." Her grandmother patted her cheek. "Before we consign you to that drafty castle, let's see how this plays out. You may have found an unlikely ally in Andraste." Mary Elma made a sound between a snort and a grunt. "The last time I saw her, blood was dripping from her chin, and she held her enemy's heart in her hand."

# CHAPTER 19

*L*achlan clucked to Brandywine. The bay stallion trotted over and nuzzled his hand. He started to mount and then changed his mind. He needed Kheladin back, but was that even a possibility? *Is my magic gone, right along with the dragon?* He'd done a few small things since Rhukon chucked him hundreds of years back in time, but even the rawest acolyte could summon a mage light or corral a horse. Lachlan remembered his long years of training to make himself worthy of the dragon bond and grimaced.

He slapped the horse on its rump and sent it home. People might worry about him when the horse returned riderless, but he planned to be back before daybreak. Once the horse was safely out of the way, he cast one spell after another, pulling so much magic, his body thrummed with effort. Time passed. Hours. When the sky was just beginning to lighten in the east, he was shaky and drenched in sweat but satisfied his magic was unaffected. He had every bit as much as he'd ever had, no matter what year he found himself in.

*Thanks be to the gods.*

Lachlan bowed his head in a moment of silent prayer.

"Finally, something went right," he murmured as he summoned one last spell to return him to the castle without the ignominy of having to walk. He planned to sleep for a few hours and then work on re-bonding with Kheladin.

Something Arawn said was intriguing. If dragons could travel through time, maybe he didn't need the Celts to return to Maggie and 2012 after all. So long as Kheladin had mastered that particular skill. Lachlan frowned. If the dragon could manipulate time, it was odd he hadn't mentioned it when they found themselves stranded hundreds of years in the future.

"Och aye," Lachlan muttered, his earlier elation fading. He wasn't truly any closer to Maggie than he'd been before. "Just because my magic hasna eroded doesna mean my dragon will return at all. Even if he does, he may not know aught about time travel."

Lachlan set his jaw in a hard line. He fluffed up his half-constructed spell and returned to the castle. His hopes of sneaking inside shattered when he ran into one person after the next, beginning with cooks he surprised in the side yard, where he materialized just inside the postern gate. Though the many people who worked for him—both as servants and indentured labor—were used to his unusual comings and goings, nonetheless it had to be damned unsettling when he emerged from thin air.

After half a dozen conversations, Lachlan finally let himself inside through the castle's main door and strode through the great room, hoping to make it to the far end without further interruptions.

"A moment, if ye please, Laird." His steward walked out of the small parlor. "If ye could take a quick look at planned assessments for the farmers..."

"Aye, and when ye've finished with him, I've a wee bit of a problem," his chamberlain murmured. "Early flooding and all. We must plan carefully, or there shan't be enough food through next winter."

"Of course." Lachlan followed the steward. Irritation ate at his stomach, making it burn, but these were his people, his lands. It wouldn't be right to tell them he was too busy to help. "What would you do if I wasna here?" he asked his steward.

The man, actually one of Lachlan's younger cousins, tossed a mischievous grin his way. "Ye can scarce be angry for decisions made by others when ye're not available." He shrugged slightly and waited for Lachlan to sit at his work desk. "When I canna find you, I do as I think best."

Lachlan considered that as he reviewed long columns of numbers. The estate was well-run. His steward and chamberlain would do just fine without him. If he was gone long enough, the next male in line would become Laird of Clan Moncrieffe. Given his lengthy sleep, that had probably happened within months of his disappearance a hundred years hence.

He dipped the quill pen into a clay ink pot and made a few notations in the margins of a parchment scroll. "That should do it." He rose and faced his chamberlain, hovering off to one side. "How bad was the flooding? What percentage of our crops were lost?" After listening to the answer, he said, "'Tis still early enough to plant more. Use the back acreage we cleared two years ago and never cultivated."

The chamberlain's round face lit with hope. "Thank ye, Laird. I hadna considered that." The man bolted from the room.

The steward glanced up from the scroll and nodded at Lachlan. "I thank ye as well. I manage when ye're gone, but I appreciate your experience when ye're here."

Feeling less guilty about his half-formed plans to fight his way back to Maggie any way he could, Lachlan stumbled to his rooms past midmorning. His sleepless night and all the magic he'd run through caught up to him, and he fell face down on his bed and slept.

A fist pounding on his door vied with dragon trumpeting to wake him. Still drunk with sleep and groggy, it took Lachlan several moments to orient himself.

"Laird." The fist thudded on his door again.

"Come." Lachlan pushed to a sitting position and rubbed his eyes. He was still tired. Without the current interruption, he was certain he would've slept at least a few more hours.

The door opened. Vanessa bounded inside. "Sorry to disturb your rest, my Laird." She bowed low. "But a dragon is askin' for you. A talkin' dragon," she clarified and then clasped her hands together in front of her. "Of course, he'd have to be able to talk since he is askin' for you. And I'm supposin' they all talk, but one has never actually talked to me afore…" She shook her head in irritation. A few wisps of red curls escaped to frame her face. "Doona be mindin' me. I'm blatherin'. 'Tisn't like creatures such as he—or mayhap 'tis a she—stop by the castle every day." With a half-bob of her head, she backed out of his rooms.

Lachlan bolted from the bed and ducked beneath the heavy window coverings. Even through the wavy, uneven glass he could see that this side of the castle yard didn't have a dragon in it.

*Let's be smart about this.*

*"Kheladin."*

*"How did ye know 'twas me?"* Dry humor underscored the question.

Lachlan snorted. *"What other talking dragon would be asking for me? Give me a moment, and I will join you."*

*"Doona rush. Women with their breasts half bared are fawning over me."*

Lachlan laughed. *"Ogle a few for me. Just so ye doona think me unappreciative. Thank you."*

*"For what?"*

*"Coming back. What else?"*

The dragon paused for the space of several heartbeats. *"We are part of one another. Even if 'tis a hundred years afore our bonding, 'twas still a vow we took, one to the other. Ye know it, and so do I. We shall speak further when ye join me."*

Lachlan's throat thickened with emotion. The dragon could've chosen to remain with his own kind, yet he hadn't.

*I was a fool for ever doubting him, for not trusting in the magic twined betwixt us.*

He rewound his plaid. Hunting for his boots, he realized he hadn't taken them off. He had one hand on the door latch when he turned back and strode to the wall behind his bed. Chanting low, he cast a spell to open a well-hidden panel. Lachlan thrust his hand into the hole and withdrew a substantial packet wrapped in soft hides and tied with heavy ribbon. He didn't waste time sorting through the jewelry he knew lay within. Maggie might not want most of it, but he would use the yellow diamond ring, with its large central stone set in gold, to plight his troth to her. He grabbed up a sporran. Securing it about his waist, he dropped the jewels inside and reversed his spell to close the secret cubby. After a final glance about his bedchamber, he hurried out of the room and down the castle's stairs.

*If she doesna want the pearls and other gemstones, I'm certain Kheladin will.*

He burst into the main courtyard outside the castle's enormous front doors and stopped dead. Kheladin hadn't been joking. He was in the middle of at least twenty maids patting him and fawning over him. Some of them were, indeed, showing more skin than modesty dictated.

*"Quite the ladies' man, eh?"*

"Not too many lassies when one is asleep. I'm making up for lost time." Kheladin's out loud voice had a deep, rumbly quality. Lachlan tried to recall if he'd ever heard the dragon speak, other than through his own vocal chords. *Aye, when he and I first met...* He hurried down the castle steps, and the maids scattered with murmurs and blushes.

"Och," Kheladin chortled, and steam puffed from his mouth. "Ye've gone and scared them all away." He twisted his neck and looked meaningfully at the empty spot between his shoulders.

Lachlan understood, gauged the distance, and drew just enough magic to land in the same spot where Maggie had sat. Excitement thrummed through him. He felt like a young lad, unable to rein in his eagerness. He'd never actually ridden a dragon, and the prospect was intoxicating.

*"Ye've flown with me afore."*

*"Only when we were joined. Never like this."*

Dragon laughter floated upward, sounding like fluted chimes. Kheladin's wings beat the air and carried them above the castle. The dragon turned north.

"Where are we going?" Lachlan asked.

"Where we can talk without fear of being overheard."

It was good enough. Lachlan trusted the dragon, something he'd rarely gifted anyone. He gazed over lochs, trees, and stately manor houses as they flashed by beneath them. Scotland. Nowhere else could ever be as beautiful. Not in his eyes. The view from Kheladin's back was remarkable, ever so much better than when he'd shared the dragon's whirling vision. Hope flared, painful in its intensity. If he had Kheladin by his side, maybe there'd be a way to forge a path through time and back to his beloved Maggie.

He shut his eyes, and a vision of her formed against the darkness, blonde hair swirling around high, firm breasts. A jolt of pure lust shot through him, and his cock sprang to attention.

"Best watch it." Kheladin's voice was partially ripped away by the wind. "'Twould be a shame if ye plummeted to your death afore we could resurrect our bond—and your immortality."

Lachlan laughed and wrapped a hand around one of the dragon's horns, growing from the base of his neck. "Appreciate the warning."

"Anytime, bondmate."

They floated downward, landing within a ring of standing stones on the Isle of Skye, an ancient Celtic meeting place. Lachlan jumped down, using a bit of magic to soften his landing. He settled on the sandy ground with his back against one of the stones. The smell of the ocean was strong in his nose, the sky so brilliant a blue it almost hurt his eyes to look at it.

Kheladin wound his sinuous neck low, so his head was nearly

level with Lachlan's. "I have been busy," he announced. Lachlan waited. Kheladin's story would unfold as the dragon wished. Steam washed over him. "Are ye not going to ask aught?"

"Nay. 'Tis good to have you by my side again, though. We werena apart for long, yet I missed you."

The dragon's jaws parted, revealing hundreds of teeth set in double rows. "I missed you as well—and the lass." More steam. Kheladin's scales clanked as the dragon shook himself from head to toe. "I conferred with one of the dragon elders. There was much of our lore I missed, because I was less than five centuries old when we bonded. At the time, the elders told me I was too young to bond with you, but like all younglings, I dinna listen."

Lachlan sucked in a breath. He wanted to be patient, but he also wanted to dive right into talking about how they could get back to Maggie. "What exactly did ye not listen to?" he prodded.

"Dragons were the first time travelers." Kheladin was so excited, fire flashed from his mouth. He turned his head to avoid crisping Lachlan's hair. "Fire Mountain exists in a place outside time. I dinna ken that as a youngling, mostly because I dinna pay attention to aught but the joy of flight, the allure of battle, and the dragon maids." His green eyes whirled so fast, Lachlan felt their hypnotic pull. "Ye must travel through all known eras, and those yet to come, to reach the dragons' ancestral home."

Lachlan bit back an exultant whoop. It came out as a whistle. "Can we stop anywhere we wish along the way?" He shook his head. "First, I should probably ask if ye can travel there, to Fire Mountain."

"Aye to the second question. I know, because I went there last night, just to make certain I could. Mother moved her brood to Earth soon after we were born, so I'd never traveled betwixt there and Earth on my own. Locating the 2012 time may take a bit of experimentation, but I doona see why we couldna manage it." The dragon's whirling gaze danced with excitement. "The lass rode me. I know her essence. 'Twill help me find her."

"Do we need to resurrect our bond first?" Lachlan jumped to his feet, too agitated to sit still. As far as he was concerned, his love for Maggie shone so brightly, it would act like a homing beacon and draw him to her. Between that and Kheladin's magic, success was within reach, so close he could taste the sweetness of Maggie's mouth and inhale the wildflower scent that clung to her.

"Aye. I found out more about the bonding magic too. Ye were so anxious to find a dragon—and I a mage—we picked the shortest path. There is another that would allow us more...latitude."

"Explain."

"More air and less fire in the casting will mean we can exist as individuals yet still be bonded. If the need arises, ye can still move within me, or I within you."

Wonder filled Lachlan. "Marvelous! How did ye puzzle that out? 'Twould be far better, especially for fighting, since there'd be two of us. With all my studies I dinna find such a spell."

"There isna time to tell you everything. In short, to be bound as we were gave humans the upper hand. 'Twas fine for the mage, many of whom harbored a secret fear of dragon energy." Smoke curled from Kheladin's mouth, and his words dripped scorn. "Of course, the arrangement was less advantageous for the dragon. That may have been why it took you so long to find one to bond with. The older ones were wiser than me."

"Ye are wise beyond measure—" Lachlan began, but Kheladin blew steam in his face.

"Human mages hid the other casting, and because 'tis so old, many of the younger dragons like me dinna know of it—"

Heartily sick of magicians and their endless posturing as they jockeyed for power, Lachlan's patience evaporated. "Did ye write it down?"

"Better. I memorized it. If ye trust me, I will cast it now."

Lachlan wound his arms around the dragon's neck. "Hurry. The sooner ye're done, the sooner we can get back to Maggie."

"Aye. I have worried much about her. Do ye suppose Rhukon abducted her too?"

Apprehension raced in like an unwelcome army flanking his hopes with dread. "I doona know. One thing at a time, Kheladin. We canna go after her until ye're done with the bond. I have missed the connection. I canna wait to be well and truly joined with you again."

Steam bathed him, and the dragon began a sing-songy chant that warmed Lachlan's soul.

MAGGIE HUGGED HER GRANDMOTHER. "Guess I'm more like you than I realized."

Mary Elma's mouth twitched. "Yes, dear. I've known that for a long time. Blamed myself, actually, for your chilly disposition."

"Grandpa didn't think you were all that chilly."

"Well, he didn't stick around, either."

"That was because you were always so busy with coven business…" Maggie's words ran down. She'd always kept herself more than busy as a hedge against emotional commitments too. "Is there, um, anything you would've done differently?"

Her grandmother eyed her speculatively. "And you're asking because?"

"Maybe so I can avoid the same mistakes with Lachlan. I love him, ache for him." She tapped her breastbone. "But I'm old enough to understand it takes more than love to keep two people together."

A soft smile curved Mary Elma's full lips. "No matter what I tell you, you'll find new mistakes. Life's a bitch that way."

Maggie shrugged. "At least it will narrow the playing field. Right now our physical attraction is so electric, I'm sure we'll forgive one another anything, but that intensity can't last."

"Oh yes, it can. Sex is like any other flame. It just needs tending." Her grandmother got a wistful look on her face. "Listen to him. Ask what he needs and wants. Put him first. If you go into this believing your love is more important than anything else in your life, you'll find ways to get through the rough spots."

"Gran, that's probably the first time you've ever told me anything personal."

"Maybe it's because this is the first time you were open to hear it."

"Touché!"

Mauvreen sidled over to them. "I think they've come to a decision."

Maggie looked up. Ceridwen met her gaze and gestured her toward the front of the room. Maggie started forward, but her grandmother caught her up on one side and Mauvreen on the other. Both witches hooked a hand under one of her arms. *The power of three,* Maggie thought, warmed by their support. They stopped ten paces from Ceridwen.

"Whatever you have to say," Mary Elma said sternly, "is still open for discussion."

"Yes," Mauvreen seconded, sounding fierce.

"In your dreams, witches." Andraste stepped forward.

"What we have decided is this," Ceridwen cut in smoothly. "It will require a certain amount of…faith on your part."

The hands still holding Maggie's arms tightened. Neither witch was impressed so far. "Let's hear what they have to say," she murmured, "before we react."

"Wise lass." Ceridwen winked at her. "What we propose has several stages. The first will reunite you with Lachlan in the fifteen hundreds. Once ye are there, ye must find the earlier iterations of us." Maggie opened her mouth, but Ceridwen shook her head. "Hear me out afore ye ask questions. Lachlan will know how to raise the Celtic gods. Any mage of his time could do so. In fact," she quirked a brow, "I'm certain he has already petitioned us for assistance returning to your side."

"Fine." Maggie drew in a measured breath. "I'll wait for him to return to me, then."

"Ye could be waiting for a verra long time." Ceridwen tossed both hands skyward. "We are not in the habit of assisting mortals unless it benefits us directly."

"Okay." Maggie met the goddess' unsettling gaze. "Back to plan A. Assuming you send me back in time to Lachlan, once we find you, then what?"

"It gets a wee bit stickier after that," Andraste said. "After you've done away with Rhukon, we'll see the two of you returned to modern time—if you're of a mind to do so."

"How do you even know they can kill Rhukon?" Mauvreen asked.

"We don't," Andraste replied.

"Humph. Interesting." Mary Elma's eyes narrowed. "If they do manage to kill him, what are you going to do about the Morrigan?"

"That," Ceridwen rose to her full height, "is none of your affair."

*Kill. Holy fuck, she said kill.*

"Hold up." Maggie jerked away from her grandmother and Mauvreen and marched forward until she was nose-to-nose with Andraste. "You expect Lachlan and me to kill Rhukon? Lachlan told me he and that dragon of his were immortal."

"Well, there's apparently nothing wrong with your hearing," Andraste sniped. "There are ways around immortality. Lachlan should know since he fell into one of them. You could also rustle up one of us to sever the bond betwixt dragon and mage. Once they're no longer bonded, killing the mage becomes trivial." She shrugged. "Dragons pose a somewhat more challenging problem. Your best bet would be having Kheladin escort Malik back to Fire Mountain to face justice afore the Dragon Council."

"What if I don't want to be part of killing anyone?" Maggie closed her teeth together with a *clack.*

The goddess shrugged. "Then all bets are off, and ye're on your own getting back to your heart's desire."

"Seems it leaves you in a bit of a pickle too," Maggie sneered.

"Lachlan won't stop trying to return to me, which means he won't be doing what you want him to back in the fifteen hundreds."

"Ye doona know that." Aquamarine eyes grazed over her, sharp as razor blades.

"Yes," Maggie said. "I do. I've never been more certain of anything in my life."

The air in the room took on a numinous quality. Maggie sent her fledgling magic spinning outward. Were more Celts arriving? It didn't feel like their brand of energy, though. Not quite. Mary Elma and Mauvreen raised their hands to call power. Both witches' wore grim expressions. The Inverness witches raced to them. They formed a rough circle and dragged Maggie into its heart.

"What's happening?" Maggie cried. "Are we under attack?"

# CHAPTER 20

Lachlan wandered deep within Kheladin's magic. The first bonding had been different because he'd been the one casting the spell and controlling it. This time, he caught glimpses of the dragon's mind and heart that he'd never seen before. "To think I missed so much," he murmured.

"We both did," Kheladin replied. "The mage version of the bonding was fast, but it cheated both of us out of the richness we could've shared. There." The dragon, who'd kept a taloned foreleg on Lachlan's shoulder throughout the casting, moved back. His whirling eyes speared Lachlan's gaze and held it. "I believe 'tis complete."

"Ye doona know?"

Smoke streamed from Kheladin's open mouth. "How could I? 'Tis my first attempt. We must test it afore we depart."

Lachlan nodded. "Aye, sound plan. See if ye can merge yourself within me."

Kheladin shook his head. "Nay. Ye must join with me. If it works, we shall separate and tackle the tunnels that link time."

Lachlan opened his mouth to protest but thought better of it. The dragon had risked goddess-only-knew-what to bring them a priceless gift. It wasn't a time to argue about who would control their partnership. A thought intruded, and Lachlan recognized it as truth.

*In the future, we shall truly be equals, the dragon and me. 'Tis better this way, and I doona wish to get us off to a rocky beginning.*

Resolve firmly in hand, Lachlan summoned the magic to merge with Kheladin. Surprise nearly undid his casting. Rather than it taking any effort at all, he flowed effortlessly into his bondmate. Before, such a spell took a fair jolt of power and an ongoing infusion of magic to hold himself within the dragon.

"Is this easier, or is it my imagination?"

Kheladin's rumbling laughter sounded in Lachlan's mind. *"'Tis the original spell meant for this purpose. It shouldna come as a surprise for it to feel natural."*

"Of course. I should've known."

Lachlan had bent many spells to other than their unique purpose—always at great cost to himself. Magic had a price. It took time to recover from expending great gobs of it. That the new dragon bond wouldn't take away from their mutual power came as a pleasant surprise. The thought racing in on its heels was, *Perhaps this will give us the edge we need to defeat Rhukon.*

Lachlan shimmered back into his human form. "Unless there is aught else we need to do here, 'tis long past time to be gone."

"Agreed." Kheladin looked at the spot where his neck and body joined.

Lachlan gathered air into a cushion and rode it to the dragon's back. "Ready. What exactly will we be doing when we time travel?"

"I'll tell you as we go. Hold tight. I must summon the tunnel, and then we shall fly into it." Kheladin chanted a few words.

A whooshing filled Lachlan's ears. The day's brightness shaded to pearlescent gray as they took to the air and entered a portal that formed before them. The sensation of being snared in powerful magic surrounded him. Everything from his scalp to his fingertips tingled, but the feeling wasn't unpleasant.

*I've been bonded to this creature for a verra long time. How could I have underestimated his power so badly?*

"Because you never took the time to truly explore it."

"Forgive me. I willna make the same mistake twice. Tell me more."

"Dragons were forged in the heat of Fire Mountain. For long years, they stayed on that world outside time. 'Tis hard to explain precisely, but Fire Mountain exists in its own universe, separated from Earth by time veils. We would've stayed there forever, separated from humankind, but one day long years ago, a group of Celtic goddesses paid us a visit."

"Brighid and Andraste?"

Kheladin snorted flames. "Aye, and Arianrhod. If I recall correctly, Ceridwen wasna in favor of inviting dragons to Earth, but she was outvoted. The Celts convinced our elders that dragons were needed if Earth was to survive. The Trojan War had just ended, and things were in disarray. The Cyclops and the Minotaur were running wild...

"Anyway, ye know history. No need for me to repeat it."

"They induced you to help." Lachlan mentally rolled his eyes.

"In a manner of speaking. They can be quite persuasive when they want something. Keep in mind all this happened long afore we considered bonding with strong mages."

Lachlan nodded his understanding. *Persuasive* was an understatement. Pushy, abrasive, and insistent described them far better. "Help me understand. Arawn told me dragons were the first time travelers. If you never left Fire Mountain afore the goddesses' visit—"

"Our seers figured it out eons before, in case we needed to leave. We'd just never used the skill." Kheladin blew out smoke and fire. "There are tunnels, for want of a better word, that circle Earth. Passageways that go both forward and backward in time. They're not particularly easy to access, but once within them, ye can move through time. In addition to them, dragonkind have our own method of traveling back and forth to Fire Mountain, but it wouldna help us return to Maggie since they're a direct link betwixt Fire Mountain and many other worlds."

Something plucked at the edges of Lachlan's consciousness. "Hold. Do ye sense aught in here but us?"

The dragon stiffened. Lachlan felt a shift in the rolling bands of muscle beneath his legs. He joined his magic to the dragon's and threw his senses wide open. *Yes!* He hadn't been mistaken. Alien energy, edged with darkness, lurked behind them. Someone was trying their damnedest to shield it. Lachlan's stomach tightened.

Kheladin loosed a string of Gaelic curses. *"I doona know how, but someone followed us into the tunnel. They're keeping their distance, but 'tis only a matter of time afore they make a move."*

Lachlan gazed about them, taking in their surroundings with a practiced eye. Not a good place to defend themselves. There wasn't much room for the dragon to maneuver. *"What happens to the tunnel if we loose defensive strikes?"*

*"I doona know, but we mustna injure it. If we do, I fear we shall render it unusable. We'll be trapped wherever it leaves us."*

Lachlan considered that piece of information but not for very long. Much as he wanted to race to Maggie's side, needed to feel her body pressed against him, and know she was safe in his arms, continuing their present course would be foolhardy. He wound strong magic around his next words to shield them. *"It doesna matter where we are. Exit the tunnel. We will stand and fight."*

The dragon hesitated so long, Lachlan wondered what was wrong. Waiting was excruciating, but he bit back a frantic flow of words.

*"Thank ye for giving me time to think,"* Kheladin said at length. *"What follows us is closer. I canna abort the spell midstream, but I believe I can return us to the fifteen hundreds with your help."*

Lachlan groaned inwardly. They'd already lost more time than he was comfortable with. What if Maggie had been captured too? Yet he recognized the dragon's wisdom. *"How can I help?"*

Magic buffeted him from all sides, pressure growing until he was afraid they'd be crushed. He clung to consciousness by digging his hands into Kheladin's scales. Pain from their sharp edges kept him awake. As his blood mingled with the dragon's hide, he felt slightly better.

*Aye.* He laughed grimly. *Never underestimate the power of blood.*

The pearl-toned gray brightened, and Lachlan looked out at the standing stones on the Isle of Skye. Kheladin landed, wheeling on his haunches to face the still-visible swirling vortex of the tunnel. He drew himself tall and trumpeted a ringing challenge.

Lachlan readied himself to jump down, but the dragon said, "Stay atop me until we see what we face. Doona lower your guard. Something comes."

"It must be Rhukon."

Fire streamed from Kheladin's mouth. "My thoughts exactly. Who else would chivy us so? What I wish to know is how he got hold of the magic to enter the tunnel."

"I know ye would wish it otherwise," Lachlan picked his words cautiously in an attempt at diplomacy, "but he is still a dragon."

"Barely." Contempt filled Kheladin's tone. "I've always been sorry I dinna kill that one after he offered me a bond. 'Twould've been my right. Had I known any dragon would be stupid enough to link themselves to his perverted energy, I wouldna have hesitated." The vortex pulsed, turning an angry crimson. "See." He angled a wingtip. "Even the tunnel knows it hosts unnatural energy."

"I'll thank you to keep a civil tongue in your head, youngling." The black wyvern shot from the tunnel in a halo of sparks. As Lachlan watched, the dragon's form shimmered into Rhukon. *Aha! So he must hold one form or the other.* Lachlan was just congratulating himself on an easy victory, when the red wyvern burst from the vortex just before it snapped shut with an earsplitting clang.

"What have ye done with Maggie?" Lachlan gritted the words out.

"What makes ye believe we've done aught with the lass?" Rhukon simpered. "Not that I wouldna love to sample the goods. Did she tell you I kissed her—?"

"Shut the fuck up," Lachlan screeched. "Ye besmirch her name when it passes your lips. She is my wife and mate."

Rhukon shrugged. "It willna do you much good if ye canna return to her."

Lachlan's gaze flickered to the red wyvern. Apparently, Connor planned to remain within Preki, his dragon bondmate. Well-versed in warfare, Lachlan understood they were evenly matched that way. Mage and dragon against mage and dragon. Unfortunately, it could mean a lengthy contest—something he could ill afford without knowing for certain if Maggie was safe.

"How did ye enter the tunnel?" Kheladin's voice vibrated with barely suppressed fury at what he obviously considered a violation of sacred ground.

"Sloppy work on your part, youngling." Connor's dragon form smirked. "Ye dinna close off your casting soon enough. But even if ye dinna leave the door open for us, all dragons know how to manipulate the time travel portals. 'Tis far less work to locate you, though, when we're hard on your heels."

"Quiet," Rhukon roared. "We dinna come here to chat."

Lachlan recalled that Connor had never been known for his brilliance. Surely there'd be some way to make use of that information. He opted for flattery first.

"Rhukon." Lachlan inclined his head from his perch atop Kheladin. "My compliments. Ye were sly. Ye bested us about a hundred years hence."

"Aye." Rhukon's mouth split in a satisfied grin. "That I did. It willna take much to do so again."

Fire roared from Kheladin. Rhukon sidestepped the blast handily. The red wyvern opened its mouth, but Rhukon aimed a dismissive hand gesture his way. "I propose a bargain."

"We doona bargain with those like you," Kheladin snarled.

"Let's at least hear what he has in mind," Lachlan murmured. "It might be...instructive."

Rhukon brayed laughter. "Humph. Your lengthy nap seems to have sowed the seeds of wisdom. What I propose is really quite simple. Ye remain here—or any other place in time away from the lass—and I will let ye live."

"If I refuse?" Lachlan tried to keep his tone neutral but failed. Danger ran beneath his words, its barbed edges rough against his tongue.

"We shall engage you in battle here and now—"

"What are we waiting for?" Kheladin cut in. "I stand more than ready." He roared a challenge. Fire spewed from his mouth. The metallic stench of magic filled the air. Electricity crackled, and the fine hairs on the back of Lachlan's neck stood on end. The dragon was probably right. Nothing could be accomplished with talk, yet he would've prolonged the conversation to give himself time to craft a strategy.

Lachlan clamped his jaws together. Time, if there'd ever been any, had just been snatched away.

Kheladin's bloodlust trumped everything. It raced through Lachlan like a heady stimulant. He didn't remember jumping to the ground in front of Rhukon or raising his hands, but power blazed from them. When the first rush of finally trading blows with his archenemy faded, Lachlan wasn't certain he could best Rhukon, but it didn't dampen his enthusiasm. He jumped and spun to avoid direct hits. Off to one side, the dragons clashed together in a shower of fire, sparks, and scales, but Lachlan couldn't divert his attention to see how Kheladin fared.

Futility crept into the corners of his mind. His shirtsleeve smoldered and caught fire. *Mayhap I canna do this...* Lachlan sidestepped another blast from Rhukon. In a moment of clarity, he understood the other mage was manipulating him by sending hopelessness mingled with compulsion. He closed his mind to all but Kheladin.

*"'Tis about time,"* the dragon cried. *"I was about to intervene. Damn it!"* Kheladin rose into the sky with a flurry of wings, roaring his displeasure at the red wyvern who'd just scored his flank with magic.

Lachlan whirled in time to see Connor—in the form of his dragon, Preki—follow Kheladin upward. He was surprised it took the dragons so long to move their battle aloft.

"Aye, now 'tis just the two of us," Rhukon growled. "Ye canna kill me."

"Nor can ye deal me a mortal blow," Lachlan countered, dancing back and forth on the balls of his feet.

"I verra nearly did. Asleep is as good as dead." A sly expression crossed Rhukon's features. "I placed you in a time afore ye and Kheladin were bound. That you're in separate bodies argues against ye being immortal."

Lachlan decided to play along. He tried to gin up a sheepish expression. "Guess I canna slide aught past you."

Rhukon snorted derisively. "Surprised ye'd even try."

An idea hit with such ferocity, Lachlan nearly missed his footing. He didn't have time to fence with Rhukon for hours, tossing barbs and magic back and forth. Rhukon was devious. There must be a reason he was working hard to keep them occupied. Sending a silent prayer upward, Lachlan pulled magic as fast and hard as he could.

Rhukon stated the obvious when he said *asleep is as good as dead.* Lachlan chided himself for not recognizing it before. He couldn't kill Rhukon, but if he could immobilize him, for even as little as a few minutes, it would give him and Kheladin an opportunity to escape into the time tunnel. Connor was such a craven, he'd never go after them on his own.

Once Lachlan was certain Maggie was safe, maybe he could get the Celts to imprison Rhukon somewhere he couldn't escape. Or better yet, break the dragon shifter bond so he wasn't immortal anymore.

"Doona forget I'm stronger than you," Rhukon snarled through gritted teeth.

"Correction," Lachlan snarled back. "Ye used to be, afore I joined my life with Maggie." He pushed every shred of magic he could summon at his adversary. Rhukon swayed on his feet. Lachlan ratcheted up his casting. The other mage blocked him.

*I canna give up. I must make this work.*

Desperation jangled his nerves and soured his stomach. Lachlan dug deep, deeper than he ever had. His body became nothing more than a conduit for magic so strong and so ancient, he'd been afraid to tap into it before. Power rolled through him in violent waves.

*"Ye can stop. He is down."* Kheladin's voice came as a shock. Lachlan had been so consumed by his spell, he'd lost all sense of anything beyond the magic devouring him. *"Send your power skyward,"* the dragon instructed. *"Now."*

Legs shaking, breath harsh in his throat, Lachlan merged his power with the dragon's. Kheladin's magic felt almost friendly compared with the vein of arcane wizardry he'd stumbled onto. He glanced at Rhukon's prostrate form and wondered just how much time he'd bought them.

"Nay!" Kheladin's outraged cry shook the earth. "Cowardly bastard." The skies lit with dragon fire.

Lachlan snapped his gaze upward, scanning through flames. The other dragon was gone. "What?" he blurted, still so weary he couldn't think. "Where?"

"Slimy, craven, worthless bastard left. Guess he dinna like the odds." Kheladin fanned his wings. "To my back. We should leave while we can."

Grateful at least one of them was still thinking clearly, Lachlan didn't wait for a second invitation. Once astride Kheladin, he slumped against his neck.

*"Ye did well,"* Kheladin murmured, *"but we are far from done."*

*"Och aye, and thank ye for that reminder."* Lachlan laid his palms flat against the dragon's neck and shamelessly let power flow into him. The pearl-toned time travel tunnel formed. Kheladin moved within its folds and stopped on the far side of the entrance, fanning his wings to hover. Lachlan tried adding magic to the casting to seal

the access point. He wasn't surprised when most of the power he managed to raise already belonged to the dragon.

Kheladin chortled. "Thank ye for trying. 'Tis the thought I appreciate. There. The gateway is shut. Connor was correct. 'Twas sloppy of me last time, but it never occurred to me they'd be fast on our heels."

"Doona apologize. At least that bastard is out of the way for now. Connor isna a threat without Rhukon to back him up."

"Do ye have any idea how long Rhukon will sleep?"

"Nay. Probably only a few hours. Mayhap only a few minutes. I must ask the Celts about the vein of magic I tapped into. 'Tisn't one I've found afore today, and I doona understand how it works." Lachlan heaved a sigh and laid his head against Kheladin's neck. "I tell you, it took every scrap of mage strength I had to control it once I found it. Without you, I fear it might've swept me away."

"To where?"

"I doona know."

The rocking that meant they were underway and moving forward through time began. Lachlan welcomed the power flowing through the tunnel and its kinetic charge. He hoped some of it would sink in and replenish his badly depleted magic. They still had to find Maggie. If Rhukon had caught her in one of his nefarious webs, maybe she'd manage to escape while the dark mage lay unconscious.

Comforted by the thought, Lachlan did everything he could to prepare himself for whatever they'd have to do to free his love.

# CHAPTER 21

"**I** don't know what's going on," Mary Elma snapped. "Keep quiet and shield yourself. We'll do the rest. Don't even think of moving outside this circle."

Being ordered about rankled. Maggie swallowed back her instinctive reaction to protest and adopted a defensive posture. She was plenty scared. The coppery taste of it flooded her mouth. Her heart hammered wildly. The air in the room darkened. When she peered through the murk, it was obvious the Celts were just as uncomfortable as the witches. The gods and goddesses bunched in groups of twos and threes, hands raised to rain destruction down on whatever threatened them.

*Maybe it's Rhukon, and we can at least wipe his sorry ass off the face of the Earth. Andraste said there were ways around immortality.*

Fire erupted out of nowhere. Small flames flickered in a corner of the room, and smoke filled the air. Maggie coughed and instinctively hunkered closer to the floor where the air would be clearer.

"Enough," a voice rang out. "Ye'll suffocate the lot of them, and us, too, if ye burn up all the air feeding your fire."

"Lachlan!" Maggie sprang upright and stared through the murky air.

"It could be a trick," Mary Elma warned. Sparks flew from her outstretched hands.

"Aye," Ceridwen said. "Doona relax your guard."

The air was so thick with fire and magic it felt like a live thing. The unmistakable sound of wing beats filled her ears.

*Kheladin. It's Lachlan and the dragon, but why can't they get through?*

"Drop the shielding around this room," Maggie shouted.

"Now why would we want to do that?" Andraste raised a graceful hand to her mouth and coughed into it.

"Because I know I'm right. It's Lachlan. He's found us. He and Kheladin, but they can't get in."

"Don't make me laugh, girl." Andraste smirked. "Ye forget yourself. Ye havena enough magic to keep a toy ship afloat, yet ye're issuing orders."

The fire roared into life. A hole formed around it like a ragged doorway that got bigger and bigger. Maggie broke through the witches' circle and raced forward. She sent her magic ahead of her. Working blind, she urged it to rip whatever was keeping Lachlan apart from her to shreds. A copper wing punched through, followed by the rest of the dragon with Lachlan on his back.

She didn't understand how she did it, but Maggie launched herself through the air and landed right behind Lachlan. She wrapped her arms around him and held on for dear life. Tears streamed down her face. Coughing, choking, crying, she gasped his name over and over again and showered kisses on his neck, his hair, any part she could reach.

"I know ye're happy to see him," Kheladin rumbled. "What about me?"

"Oh my God, I didn't mean to leave you out. I love you too. How could I love one and not the other? I've thought of you both constantly, ever since I realized Lachlan wasn't in the dressing room in Fort William." She unwound a hand from Lachlan and patted Kheladin's scaled hide.

"Lass, oh, Maggie. Maggie, my love," Lachlan twisted, tried to hug her, kiss her, but their position was so awkward, body parts just bumped into one another.

The smoky air was clearing. Someone must've opened windows, or worked magic, or done something. Maggie didn't care. All she wanted was Lachlan's arms around her, his body pressed close, his lips on hers. "We have to get down, so I can hold you."

"Aye, lass. Hold tight, and I'll move us."

"Before you do that," she buried her hands in his hair, "I love you. One of the worst parts of thinking I'd never see you again was knowing I'd never told you how much you mean to me."

He leaned back against her and turned his head. "I love you, too, lassie. Take a deep breath, and we'll be on the ground in a trice."

Her legs almost wouldn't hold her upright when her feet met the ground.

"Focus your magic to steady yourself." Mary Elma's voice was stern. She hurried forward and inserted herself between Maggie and Lachlan, just bullied her way right between their bodies. "I've wanted to meet you for years," she exclaimed. "Ever since I saw you connected to my granddaughter in a vision."

"Never mind that." Ceridwen pressed forward. "Did ye at least kill Rhukon afore ye came back here?"

"Ye must be joking." Kheladin showered the goddess with steam. "When in the nine hells would we have had time for that? Besides, he's immortal so long as he's bonded to Malik."

"Show a wee bit of respect." Ceridwen waved her hands to clear the steam.

"Mayhap ye can take care of Rhukon yourself, after ye take a bite out of the Morrigan's colossal ego," Lachlan suggested snidely. After a beat, he added, "I put Rhukon to sleep, but he's likely thrown off my spell by now. When we have a spot of time, I need to talk with you about the magic I used. I doona fully understand it."

Maggie stared at Lachlan and Kheladin as they traded jibes with Ceridwen. Reality sank in. "You're separate. What happened?"

"Doona fear, we're still bonded." Lachlan favored her with a rakish grin. "If 'tis all the same to everyone here," he waved an expansive hand, "I'd like to take my mate to a less crowded location. How far are we from your home, lass?"

"Not so fast." Mauvreen closed on them. "First, you'll come by my place, share a meal, and tell us everything."

"Yes." Mary Elma beamed at Lachlan. "I want to get to know my grandson-in-law before the two of you retire to a bedroom and don't surface for a month."

Maggie couldn't stop grinning. "Guess we'd better do what they want. It's the only way we'll get out of here." She tapped her grandmother's arm. "The dragon's coming too."

"Cozy." Mauvreen tugged her top a little lower. Kheladin leered at her.

"What about us?" Ceridwen asked. Gwydion and Arawn rushed forward. "Aye," Gwydion said. "We deserve to hear all the juicy details as much as the witches—particularly since ye're still asking for our help."

Lachlan blew out a breath. "How about this? We can gather for midsummer at the stones on the Isle of Skye. That shouldna be more than a few days hence. Kheladin and I will tell you what we know, and then we must strategize. Rhukon is still on the loose, powered by Celtic magic from the Morrigan. 'Twill take stealth and cunning to defeat them."

Andraste clumped forward. "I still think 'twould be best to return Lachlan to the past, so he can kill Rhukon and be done with it. I can teach him how to sever the dragon shifter bond, and then—"

"I doona think so." Lachlan favored the goddess with a stern glance. "I dinna return only to have ye banish me. 'Twould be far better if ye found a spot to imprison him until the end of time. Or ye could sever the bonding and kill him yourself."

Smoke streamed from Kheladin's mouth. "We're not leaving the year 2012—unless and until we choose," the dragon huffed.

Arawn laid his hands on Andraste's shoulders. "Consider this, sister. Such a strategy might've worked, had Lachlan not found his way back, but we canna ask him to return to the past again. Another problem is it appears Rhukon's newfound strength extends into whatever time he inhabits."

"I wasna planning on *asking* Lachlan to return," Andraste snapped. "I'm used to being obeyed—and without question, mind you."

Other Celts jumped into the fray, each with a divergent opinion.

"Looks like a good opportunity to leave." Mary Elma poked Maggie. "You know where Mauvreen's is. We'll meet you back there." She and the other witches shimmered. Power crackled and flared. In seconds they were gone.

Maggie laid a hand on Kheladin and held out the other to Lachlan, who took it. "I'm not very good at this yet, but look into my mind and go where I lead."

It was neither neat, nor elegant. Maggie tried three times before the Celts' hall disappeared for good, and the walls of Mauvreen's home wavered about them. "Crap," she muttered, looking at the witch's front room. "Kheladin's too big. I wasn't thinking."

"He's within me for the moment," Lachlan said. "Both of us guessed he'd never fit in a normal-sized room. We've much to tell you, but there will be time for everything now we've found each other again."

She liked the sound of that—it made her heart feel all fluttery. Maggie wrapped her arms around his neck. He closed his around her body and bent his head. When the kiss came, it was long, deep, heartfelt. Lost in kissing Lachlan, her body alight with desire, Maggie started when someone poked her shoulder.

*Gran.*

"Yes, dear. It's me. Come into the parlor. Mauvreen's putting out tea, supper, and an assortment of booze that would lay an army on its back."

"Before we do that." Lachlan dug into his sporran. "I brought something special back. 'Tis been in the Moncrieffe clan since Roman times, and it has always graced the hand of the Laird's beloved." He fumbled with a soft, tanned hide and withdrew the biggest diamond Maggie had ever seen.

Her eyes widened, and a hand flew to her mouth. "Oh my God. It's exquisite. You can't mean to give that to me."

"Why ever not?" Lachlan slipped it onto her ring finger. "Och, and 'tis a perfect fit." He brushed his lips over hers in the tenderest of kisses and smiled at her.

"But I couldn't possibly—" she sputtered, her heart so full the love spilled over, painting the room in a luminescent glow that shimmered through her tears.

"Of course you can," Mary Elma said pointedly. "Come along now. We shall toast your nuptials."

❧

"THANK YE, KINDLY FOR EVERYTHING." Lachlan exchanged a meaningful glance with Maggie. "But 'tis truly time for us to take our leave." He patted his midsection. "I doona know when I've been quite so well-fed."

"You never starve in a witch's house." Mauvreen's dark eyes danced with glee. "It's a long tradition that started when we lured Hansel and Gretel astray."

Mary Elma rolled her eyes at Mauvreen, then turned to Lachlan and grinned. "I expect to see a lot of both of you. After all, Maggie needs training to control all that magic we stuffed into her."

"How long are you staying?" Maggie asked.

Her grandmother shrugged. "A couple weeks, maybe longer. I always meant to link up with the covens here in Scotland. This is as good an opportunity as any."

"Excellent." Lachlan beamed. "Then we shall be getting to know one another better. Wait, Kheladin wants—"

"Several things." The dragon spoke through Lachlan, but it felt easier than it had with their earlier bonding. "First. Witches should come to the Isle of Skye for midsummer. 'Tis long past time for magic-wielders to begin working together. The Celts will be there. So will we."

"That's easily enough arranged." Mary Elma picked up her cell phone and tapped through menus. "It's only a few days away. What else?"

Steam boiled from Lachlan's mouth. *"Stop that,"* he told the dragon.

"I will return to my cave and my hoard to bide a bit."

Lachlan's mouth dropped open. He'd just assumed the dragon would remain with him and Maggie. *"Ye dinna say aught about this afore."*

"Nay." Kheladin spoke through him again. "I wasna certain until just now. But ye and our mate deserve privacy, without me playing voyeur. I could use a spot of help clearing my cave. Rhukon made quite a mess of things."

"I volunteer." Mauvreen winked at him. "Two magics are always stronger together."

"I thought ye'd never offer."

Sensing Kheladin was done, Lachlan puzzled over how to finesse their separation into mage and dragon. "Is there a space large enough nearby where—?"

Mauvreen anticipated his question. "My yard is circled by strong wards. Come out front. No one will see the dragon. He and I can leave from there." She got to her feet and headed for the door. Lachlan grabbed Maggie's hand, and they followed Mauvreen down the hall and out the front door.

To say he was anxious to drag her off alone somewhere was an understatement. Maggie had been sitting side-by-side with him for the past two hours eating, drinking, and chatting. The heat of her, intermingled with her irresistible scent, made him half-crazy with wanting her, yet he'd done his damnedest to be polite to her kinswoman and the other witch. They were all kin now, but beyond that, he liked Maggie's grandmother and Mauvreen. Two no-nonsense crones, they'd helped demystify modern times as they asked questions and answered his.

Once in the yard, he breathed deep. At least the scent of Scotland hadn't changed much. It had a metallic overlay, but the smells of green, growing things overshadowed it. He felt Kheladin flow out of him. The dragon took form a few feet away, copper scales glittering in the sun.

Mauvreen hurried to him and ran her hands over his side. "You're just the most beautiful thing," she murmured. "I've always loved dragons."

"And we've always thrived on humans who adore us. 'Tis a verra old tradition. Why, there used to be festivals devoted to just that purpose." He lowered his voice conspiratorially. "'Tis why many dragons retreated to Fire Mountain. They dinna leave on account of Rhukon, but because their hearts were broken that no one loved them anymore."

"I'm all for getting dragon-love back online. Sounds like a match made in Heaven." Mauvreen laughed. "Send me an image of where we're going. We'll get that cave of yours set to rights in a jiffy. I'll bet I can rustle up a few witches who'd love to get to know you."

"Truly?" Kheladin's eyes spun faster. The dragon's obvious joy was contagious. Lachlan mind-linked with him and sent good wishes.

The air took on a luminescent quality. Lachlan felt the sting of a backlash when Mauvreen's magic collided with Kheladin's far more ancient skills.

*Who knows? Mayhap the two of them will learn something from one another.*

"I'll stay here," Mary Elma said from the porch. "Run along now."

Maggie tugged her hand from his. She loped to her

grandmother's side and hugged her. "Thanks, Gran. We'll talk really soon. You'll have to come to Inverness—"

"We'll do it all, dear." Mary Elma kissed her granddaughter's forehead. "For now, I'm not your priority. Remember our little chat?"

Lachlan made a note to ask Maggie just what the "little chat" had been about. He opened his arms. Maggie ran to him. "I'm ready."

He held her tight against him and laid his cheek against her forehead. "I've been ready since I first laid eyes on you. Ye did a sloppy job getting us here. Let's see if ye can do a wee bit better taking us home."

"Here I thought you loved me for me womanly assets. My charms. Not my magic."

"I love all of you, lass. But your kinswoman was right, ye do need practice, and here's a golden opportunity."

Maggie laughed up at him, her dark blue eyes ablaze with joy. "Great! Now I've got two of you to lecture me. Alrighty. You asked for this. Here we go."

# CHAPTER 22

Maybe because she was as anxious as he for them to be alone, Maggie's spell went off without a hitch. One moment they were in Mauvreen's yard, and the next, the familiar walls of her flat outside Inverness rose around them.

"Much smoother, lass."

"I was motivated." She tugged at his plaid. "Let's get you out of these clothes."

"What? No undying words of love and devotion?"

"Later." Now that the prospect of having him next to her skin-to-skin was a possibility, Maggie couldn't wait. Her nipples pressed against her top, hard as polished stones. Her breasts felt heavy with need, and her clit throbbed mercilessly. She yanked again at his plaid. "How do you get this damned thing off?"

"All ye need do is lift it out of the way." He captured one of her hands and slid it beneath his kilt, where it closed on warm, ridged flesh. Lachlan groaned and pressed himself into her hand. "'Twill be a small miracle if I doona spend afore we even divest you of your clothing."

His cock twitched in her fingers. Lachlan bent toward her and slashed his mouth down on hers. His lips bruised hers with the intensity of their kiss. She opened her mouth and welcomed the thrust of his tongue. Her free arm closed around him. His scent, heady and exotic, rose around them. Like the heather on the moors, he smelled of the very heart of Scotland. The scent lured her, sucked her in, made her think of couples cavorting beneath a Beltane moon as they blessed the earth with the juices of their passion.

She wrapped a leg around one of his and pressed her overheated core against his thigh. He wasn't the only one with a climax so close it threatened to overwhelm him. Legs tangled together, they toppled to the floor. From a great distance, she heard her phone, but she ignored it. Maggie let go of him long enough to push her pants out of the way. They snagged on her shoes, which was a problem. She had to free at least one leg.

"Lass, let me." He slithered down her body, leaving a trail of kisses that seared her skin. When he snaked his tongue into her streaming pussy, she moaned and buried her hands in his hair. The shoe would have to wait. Maggie spread her legs as much as she could. He licked and sucked her clit. It didn't take much before a climax roared out of her, shattering her with its intensity. He didn't stop after she came, and she felt a second orgasm spool on the heels of the first.

"Hey!" She wriggled from beneath his talented tongue. "That was amazing, incredible, you could do that all day—"

"Aye, lass. Then why did ye move away?"

"You know why." She rounded into a sit and unlaced a shoe. "Finally," she murmured and slipped her pant leg out of the way. The other shoe was looser. She managed to toe it off, laces and all. Lachlan gripped her top and pulled it over her head. He unclasped her bra and lunged forward to capture a nipple in his mouth, pushing her back onto the floor.

Longing turned her nerves into a bundle of untrammeled lust. She wrapped her arms around his head and rained kisses on it. "I want you inside me. We can catch up on all the other stuff later."

He raised his head from her breasts. "How would ye like us to be?"

"Me on top. Then you on top. Then you can take me from behind. And then—"

Lachlan laughed. The sound filled her with a joy so pure and sweet, she could hardly contain it.

"Hold up, lassie. My brain's a wee bit addled just now. I doona know if I can remember such a long list." He grabbed a cushion from a chair and stuffed it beneath his head.

Lachlan opened his arms wide. "I do recall the ye on top part." He moved his kilt aside. She gazed at his cock, mesmerized.

"Is something amiss?" Green eyes held a glint of humor. "I thought the moment ye laid eyes on me, ye'd not be able to restrain yourself."

Maggie tried to talk, but her throat thickened with love and need. "You are so beautiful," she finally managed. "The most stunning man, ever. I could get drunk staring at you."

"We're both drunk with love. 'Tis as it should be." He settled his hands on her hips and helped her straddle him. When she sank onto his shaft, Maggie couldn't believe the exquisite sensations. They started in her pussy and spread to every cell, every neuron. He showed her the motion he wanted and rocked against her, using small muscle movements to make his cock twitch inside her.

Her next climax rolled through her, catching her by surprise. One moment, she was close, the next she tumbled over the edge, pussy muscles clenching him tight, holding on, never wanting to let go.

He pulled her body down and angled his mouth to suckle her nipples. Between kisses, he murmured in Gaelic.

"Guess I'll have to learn to speak it."

"'Twould be an honor to teach you. Turn over, lass. Up on your knees."

She rolled to hands and knees and waited. Lachlan knelt behind her, but he wasn't entering her. "What?" She wiggled her butt. "Back inside. We're not done."

"I was admiring the view. Do ye know your cunnie looks like an exotic flower, all damp and glowing, framed by blonde curls?"

Ever so slowly, he sank inside her. Maggie reveled in the sensation of him stretching her, filling her, touching places she was certain no other man had ever reached. He started with long, easy strokes, but after a few, his control took flight. He gripped her hips and pounded into her. She met him with every stroke. Though she didn't see how it was possible, another climax spooled in her belly.

Lachlan moved a hand between her legs and rubbed her clit. "Lass." His voice was ragged with lust. "I canna wait much longer."

"You don't have to." Trapped between his hand and his cock, she gave in to the heat swirling through her. His cock juddered hard, again and again. She came right along with him, shrieking her delight and hoping to hell none of her neighbors were home.

They collapsed in a sweaty heap on the carpeted floor of her living room. Once their panting subsided to almost-normal breathing, Lachlan made a rich, purring, satisfied-male sound. "Now that was worth waiting for, lassie."

She wriggled out from under him and grinned. "That was just the beginning. We're going to take a shower, and then I'm going to make you come with my mouth, and then maybe we'll take a food break—"

Lachlan rolled to a sit and laughed. "Lassie. And are ye going to plan out all the moments of our lives?"

"Yes. That would be me. I plan almost everything. Gran used to complain about it. Said I lacked...spontaneity. Do you have a problem with that?"

"Not so long as I get to alter the plans from time to time." He leveled his green gaze at her. "What did your kinswoman mean about a *little chat*?"

Maggie felt heat rise from her chest to her face. *He's my lover, my husband, my friend. No secrets.* "I asked her what to do to make sure we stayed in love."

He leaned toward her, curiosity lighting his strong-boned features. "What did she say?"

"To put you first. She said a whole bunch of other things too, but at the moment I'll be damned if I can remember a one of them."

He got to his feet and pulled her upright, clasping her close, so her body leaned against him. "So long as we love and cherish one another, we'll be just fine." Lachlan kissed her forehead. "I love you, lass. Ye've made me a verra happy man."

Her heart swelled, spilled over, and broke open. "I love you too. I'm so glad I ignored all the reasons I should've walked by you that first day we met."

"Were there really that many?" He smoothed her hair back and gazed at her.

"Oh my, yes. There's lots you don't know about the twenty-first century. We've become a cautious lot. By the way, what's the deal with Mauvreen and Kheladin? They can't do anything, um, kinky can they?"

He grinned. "If by *kinky*, ye mean sexual, aye, there are ways of working things out. More importantly, Kheladin had things right when he spoke of humans revering dragons. Long ago, there used to be cults of dragon worshippers…"

～

THE DAY EDGED into evening and then into night. Lachlan couldn't remember ever being so happy. He and Maggie made love, bathed, ate, and made love some more.

*Hold onto the good times,* an inner voice cautioned. *There are battles to be fought afore I can truly relax.*

She snuggled closer into his arms. They lay in her bed with the curtains pinned back so they could see the stars and the moon.

"Remember what you said about seeing me in dreams?" she asked sleepily.

"Aye, lass. I told you I was born loving you, and that I would die loving you. But I told you that in your dream. I had no idea ye'd recall it."

"How could I forget? It's just so beautiful. One of the most beautiful things I've ever heard." She turned and kissed the hollow at the base of his neck. "Maybe it's the magic, courtesy of Gran and Mauvreen, but I've been catching glimpses of visions. Familiar ones. Now that I've slowed down enough to pay attention, you were in my dreams too. From the time I was young."

"'Tisn't surprising. We were made for one another. Probably loved each other in other lives along the way."

"Let's hang onto this one as long as we can. As much trouble as it took us to be reunited, maybe we don't want to have to do it all again."

"I will be by your side till ye die."

"And then what? You're immortal. I'm not."

"I'll wait until ye're reborn, and we shall find each other again."

"I know I asked, but this isn't a time to talk about dying." A small shiver moved down her body.

"Nay, lass. 'Tisn't. Yet, doona delude yourself. Rhukon hasna gone away. We've defeated him thrice running now, so he'll be cautious, lick his wounds, but he remains a problem."

"Maybe the Celts will…fix it somehow."

"Not if they can get someone else to do it for them." Lachlan spread magic more thickly around them. He didn't wish to be overheard. "Kheladin and I glossed over how we managed to return from the past."

"I noticed." She changed position and propped her head on an upraised hand so she could watch him in the moonlight. "I was surprised Gran didn't press for more details."

"I spelled my words so no one would ask me to elaborate.

Dragons were the first time travelers. 'Twas Kheladin's magic that returned us to you."

Maggie sat upright in bed and smiled. "The Celts told me about dragons and time travel. It means we could go back to when your castle was still standing. I'd love to see what life was like back then. The Celts were ready to send me back to you, but Gran told me if I went, it'd be impossible to return if I couldn't find you, or a Celt or a dragon..." She shook her head. "Sorry. I'm so tired I'm babbling." She tossed her body atop his and kissed him on the mouth.

"I love your enthusiasm," he said after surfacing from their kiss, "but if we go back, 'twill be hard to find an excuse to not do the Celts' bidding and corral Rhukon—if I can."

"Let them do their own *corralling*."

*Would that it were so simple.*

"It doesna work like that, lass. If I tell them nay, the next boon I ask, they'll spit in my face."

The chime of her phone sounded. "Who the hell could that be?" she muttered. "It's closing on ten at night."

"Leave it," he suggested.

"I can't. Not yet. Not until I extricate myself from my commitments here. It might be the hospital." She felt around on a table, picked up the phone, and said, "Dr. Hibbins."

Because he wanted to understand the life she'd be walking away from, Lachlan extended his magic to listen. If it were the grandmother, or one of the witches, he wouldn't be able to hear anything, but somehow he didn't think Mary Elma would bother them.

"Maggie. I've been trying to reach you for hours. Glad you're back in Inverness."

"It's a bit on the late side, Dr. MacDuff," she murmured. "I was just going to sleep. Is there some emergency at the hospital?"

"Oh no, my dear. I wanted to firm up a dinner invitation for you and your grandmother. Say around sixish tomorrow?"

Maggie sat up in bed. "That's terribly kind of you, Dr. MacDuff—"

"Frank."

"All right, Frank. I'd planned to get hold of you tomorrow. Something's come up. I won't be able to finish my fellowship here. I'm terribly sorry, and I'll work the next two weeks, or even a month if necessary, to make certain you can get coverage, but—"

"What's happened, Maggie? Let me help." MacDuff's voice dripped concern, and Lachlan wanted to punch him.

"Just family matters. Nothing to be done about it, really. I'll go by work tomorrow and sign a letter of resignation. I'll also work on continuity plans for my patients."

"I'm coming over there. You need someone to talk with."

Lachlan reached for the phone. Maggie batted his hand away. "No." She infused compliance into her words with cunningly woven magic, no doubt a byproduct of the infusion from her kinswomen. "You are not coming over here. It's late. You have no need to speak with me outside the hospital."

"Certainly. Goodnight, Dr. Hibbins."

Maggie blew out an exasperated breath. She scrolled through something on the phone's display before laying it down. "Well, that explains why the phone kept ringing," she said. "It was—"

"I know who it was. I listened."

"You're shameless." She met his gaze.

"Not shameless. Ye're my woman. Mine." The dragon's fierceness surged, running hot. "All Frank wants is—"

"Sssh." She laid fingers over his mouth. "What he wants doesn't matter. All I want is you. Now and forever. I love you. Never forget that. Never doubt me. I'm yours, Lachlan, heart, body, and soul. I'm quitting my job because I want to, not because you're making me."

Lachlan's anger evaporated in an instant. Maggie's words were like a balm. "And I love you, lass. Forever, my love."

She twined her fingers with his. "Yes, forever."

You've reached the end of *To Love a Highland Dragon*. Please leave a review. They're so important.

This series began with *Highland Secrets*, a Dragon Lore prequel. It continues in *Dragon Maid*, Dragon Lore, Book Three and is completed in *Dragon's Dare*, Dragon Lore, Book Four.

Read on for a sample of *Dragon Maid*.

# ABOUT THE AUTHOR

Ann Gimpel is a USAT Today bestselling author. A lifelong aficionado of the unusual, she began writing speculative fiction a few years ago. Since then her short fiction has appeared in a number of webzines and anthologies. Her longer books run the gamut from urban fantasy to paranormal romance. Once upon a time, she nurtured clients, now she nurtures dark, gritty fantasy stories that push hard against reality. When she's not writing, she's in the backcountry getting down and dirty with her camera. She's published over 70 books to date, with several more planned for 2019 and beyond. A husband, grown children, grandchildren and wolf hybrids round out her family.

Keep up with her at www.anngimpel.com or http://anngimpel.blogspot.com

If you enjoyed what you read, get in line for special offers and pre-release special reads. Sign up for Ann's newsletter on her website or her blog.

# DRAGON MAID

## DRAGON LORE, BOOK THREE

### Prologue

Lachlan bent his head and kissed Maggie. She arched against him and opened her mouth. He tightened his hold on her. Maybe leaving her with her grandmother, even for the short time it would take him to do what he needed, wasn't the best idea. He tangled his hands in the blonde hair streaming down her back.

Someone tapped his shoulder. Mary Elma, Maggie's grandmother—and the most powerful witch alive—cleared her throat. She didn't say anything. She didn't have to. They had a plan, and a damned good one, but he needed to do his part. He broke away from Maggie and gazed fondly at her. "Lassie. Open your eyes."

She did, her brilliant blue gaze twinkling with amusement. "If you're going to let Gran push you around from the get-go, there'll be no hope for us. I heard her too." She shot a sidelong glance at Mary Elma. "I chose to ignore her."

"*Tsk*. No respect." But Mary Elma was smiling. It was obvious she loved her granddaughter dearly and was willing to overlook a lot.

Lachlan laid a hand on Maggie's cheek. "I willna be gone long. And ye really do need to work on your magic."

Maggie rolled her eyes. "I suppose a crash course is long overdue, especially given I had zero interest in anything witchy until I met you."

"What a gross understatement!" Mary Elma pursed her lips. "The enormous infusion of magic Mauvreen and I force fed you needs to be shaped and honed. You could actually do damage without more knowledge."

"Your gran speaks true." Lachlan arranged a stray strand of hair behind Maggie's ear. "I felt great power within you, even afore your gran and her witch associate, Mauvreen, added to it. Ye're truly a force to be reckoned with now." Lachlan brushed a knuckle over Maggie's full lips and stepped away from her. He'd never leave if he couldn't put some distance between himself and her body still pressed against him.

Maggie looked from him to Mary Elma. "What if the *force to be reckoned with* wants her brand new husband to stay a while longer?"

"Och, mo croi, I do love you. We've had such a wee bit of time together, 'tisn't easy to leave you, even for a span of a few hours."

Mary Elma made shooing motions with her hands. "Never fear, dragon shifter, I'll take good care of your bride."

"I know ye will. Kheladin and I will be back verra soon. I suppose he's still in the yard with Mauvreen."

"That would be a solid deduction," Mary Elma said wryly. "I'd never have guessed a dragon would be such a sucker for attention."

Lachlan bristled. "Kheladin is far from a pushover. He recognizes Mauvreen's adulation as genuine. 'Twas a time when humans worshipped dragons and he misses it."

It was amazingly difficult to leave Maggie's presence, but Lachlan forced himself to turn and walk out the door of Mauvreen's house. Swathed in spells, it appeared to be a charming, whitewashed cottage to passersby, but it was actually an old, multi-story stone manse, sitting just north of Fort William deep in the Scottish Highlands.

Lachlan located his dragon and Mauvreen chatting up a storm. Steam billowed from the copper-colored dragon's nostrils, and he gestured with his forelegs when he talked. Mauvreen nodded enthusiastically, apparently agreeing with whatever pearls of wisdom Kheladin dispensed.

She waved eagerly when she noticed Lachlan. He strode down her front steps and across the yard, which was shrouded in wardings and *don't look here* spells. Kheladin blew steam at him. "I was wondering if we were ever going to leave," the dragon said.

"Yes," Mauvreen seconded. "Here we were thinking maybe you changed your mind about visiting the Celts."

Lachlan shrugged. Truth be told, he was of two minds because he saw their trip as a fool's errand. Nevertheless, he had to try to secure the Celtic gods' assistance. The Morrigan, also known as the Battle Crow, was one of their own. By rights, they needed to be the ones to control her. Like all the Celts, she was immortal, which further complicated matters.

Kheladin eyed him shrewdly. He and Lachlan were bondmates. Over the hundreds of years they'd been a pair, they'd gotten to know one another eerily well. "We must do this thing," he rumbled and belched a gout of fire.

"I ken as much, but it doesna mean I believe it a wise course of action."

Kheladin hunkered until he could lay a taloned forefoot on Lachlan's shoulder. "Rhukon and his dragon, Malik, nearly bested us—again. Connor and his dragon, Preki, aren't as big a problem, but the Morrigan controls them too. If it werena enough that they ensorcelled us for over three hundred years, they just dragged us back to the fifteen hundreds to try to keep you away from Maggie."

Lachlan nodded tiredly. "I havena forgotten. If it wasna for you and your quick thinking, we'd still be stuck hundreds of years in the past."

*Leaving the Morrigan free to spread chaos and poison throughout time.*

Kheladin twisted his long stalk of a neck and looked pointedly at the spot between his wings. Lachlan drew magic and vaulted into place.

"Is the invitation to bring my coven to your cave still open?" Mauvreen asked, hope shining from her amber eyes.

"Of course. I'll join you there once Lachlan and I return from the Isle of Skye." The dragon spread his wings.

"Thanks. See you soon." Mauvreen winked. "We can finish our conversation then."

"Ye'll have to remind me where we left off," the dragon called.

"Glad to." Mauvreen turned and walked toward the house.

"I'd love to fly with you," Lachlan told the dragon, "but doona ye think we should use magic to travel?"

"I miss the time we came from," Kheladin grumbled.

"Aye, I understand, yet we willna accomplish anything if some modern do-gooder sees us and tries to shoot us out of the sky."

Kheladin folded his wings. "I would kill them."

"And then we would be in even deeper trouble. We havena spent long in this era. 'Twould be wise for us to blend in as best we can." Lachlan summoned a traveling spell. He visualized the standing stone circle on the Isle of Skye and took them there. He wasn't certain he'd find any of the Celts, but the stones held a great deal of ancient power. If the Celts were elsewhere, perhaps one would notice him waiting and deign to come.

He cast invisibility about himself and his dragon. No point in scaring the hell out of tourists who might be visiting the standing stones. He had ways of getting rid of them, but he had to be closer to accomplish them. He smelled the salt air before he saw the sacred circle.

Deserted.

Lady luck was with him. He glanced at a clear blue sky and

imagined a thundercloud or two. A few drops pattered down, settling into a steady downpour. Nothing like a little rain to discourage stray visitors. Kheladin dug into the sand, his jaws parted in his approximation of a grin. Lachlan jumped down, using magic to soften his landing. The dragon was large enough, falling from his back would be like tumbling off a six foot precipice.

Lachlan settled in to wait, creating a minor spell to divert rain from the top of his head.

"'Tis good to see you happy." Kheladin nudged him with his snout.

"Aye. Maggie is everything my dreams were made of." Lachlan twisted so he looked Kheladin in the eye. "She makes up for having to live in the midst of concrete, asphalt, toxic water, and poisoned air."

The dragon snorted steam. "She said she'd be willing to come back to the fifteen or sixteen hundreds with us, for at least part of the time."

"Aye, that she did." Lachlan leaned against Kheladin's warm scales and lapsed into thought. Maggie was his destiny. Their pairing was foretold eons ago and held enough magic to save the world from the Morrigan and her henchmen, which was why Rhukon tried so hard to corral both him and Maggie, and keep them apart.

Rhukon had even gone so far as to separate Maggie from the dream world, intent on capturing her. Thank the goddess, her magic was potent enough to stymie him. She'd been frantic, and her efforts fueled by fear, but it was hard to argue with success.

In spite of Rhukon, the Morrigan, and the red wyvern, the pull of destiny was impossible to deny. Lachlan found Maggie despite all of it. Or she found him. That they were together infuriated the Morrigan. She upped the ante and escalated from an annoyance to an outright menace. Even though Mary Elma cautioned him the Celtic gods were unlikely to help—something Lachlan already knew —both of them saw today's journey as necessary.

Light leached from the long, summer's day. Lachlan was getting ready to tell Kheladin it was high time they left. If the Celts knew he stood in their sacred circle, they apparently weren't going to acknowledge him. He could force the issue by calling for them directly, but didn't wish to anger them. The air shimmered off to one side. Lachlan blinked. When his vision cleared, Ceridwen, Gwydion, and Arawn stood in a semicircle, glowering.

Ceridwen, goddess of the world, crossed her arms over her chest. Long black hair, shot with silver, cascaded down her robed body. "We know what ye want," she said without preamble, and certainly without so much as a greeting to preface her stark words.

"Aye." Gwydion, master enchanter and warrior magician, blew out a tired sounding sigh. Blond hair wafted about him, dampening quickly from the rain. He jabbed a richly carved wooden staff into the ground for emphasis. "'Tisn't as if ye havena asked afore."

Lachlan focused his gaze on Arawn, god of the dead. Today his midnight-dark hair was plaited and his dark eyes solemn. "Ye must figure this problem out on your own," the god of the underworld said.

Ceridwen shook her head. Lightning flashed next to her, so Lachlan understood she was furious. "We almost dinna come."

"Aye," Arawn added. "The reason ye waited for hours is because we argued about it."

"'Twas only my fondness for you that prevailed," Gwydion muttered. "Doona push me, dragon shifter. I wouldna like to think ye'd take advantage of my good nature."

"But I havena even opened my mouth yet," Lachlan protested.

"Ye doona have to," Ceridwen snapped. "We see what is within your mind."

Kheladin got to his feet and turned to face the gods. "The Morrigan is one of you," he said flatly. "When a dragon misbehaves, we address it among ourselves. We doona foist the task off onto another race."

Lachlan winced. Kheladin's words were true, but he was afraid they'd make things worse.

"Humph." Gwydion pounded his staff into the ground again. "'Tisn't as if the Morrigan has done anything worse than her usual."

Arawn nodded agreement. "If anything, she may have been a wee bit better here of late."

"Only because there are no wars to feed her blood lust," Ceridwen growled. "Not big ones, anyway." She walked to Lachlan and thumped him in the chest with an index finger. "Rhukon and Connor are dragon shifter mages—just like you. Malik and Preki are dragons—just like Kheladin. We," she spread her arms to encompass Arawn and Gwydion, "have discussed this thoroughly. We see them as *your* problem."

Lachlan opened his mouth to protest, to tell them the Morrigan made Rhukon, Connor, and their dragons a much bigger problem than they'd be without her magic powering theirs.

Kheladin spoke deep within his mind. *"Doona argue."*

Ceridwen waited. She glanced from Lachlan to Kheladin and back. "Much better," she said and shoved sodden hair behind her shoulders. "Now, we'll hear no more of this."

Gwydion trotted to Lachlan's side and clapped him on the back. "There's a good lad. Come visit when ye doona want something." His broad-shouldered form took on an insubstantial air. Moments later, the Celtic gods were gone.

*"There's a good lad?"* Lachlan snarled. He pounded a fist into the nearest stone and yelped.

Kheladin blasted fire toward the skies, a sure sign he was seriously displeased. "The only way this could've gone worse," he growled, "would've been if they'd challenged us to a battle."

Lachlan knew better. He walked to the dragon's side. "Nay," he said. "Had they been truly bent on harming us, they'd have dissolved our bond."